The Christmas Cafe

A Holiday Romance

Seth Sjostrom

 **wolfprint**Media

wolfprint, LLC
Hernando Beach, FL 34607

Trade Paperback
ISBN-13: 978-1-960501 00 4

First wolfprintMedia edition 2023. wolfprintMedia is a trademark of wolfprintMedia, LLC.

For information regarding bulk purchases, please contact wolfprintMedia, LLC, at wolfprint@hotmail.com.

United States of America

To Kathi, my inspiration and angelic guide
for so many aspects of my life.
To Hayden, the light in my heart.
To Linda who has always been my biggest supporter.

To the Downtown Camas Association for supporting
independent small businesses.
To Caffe Piccolo for fuel, a place to launch books and visit with
readers and kindness that embodies the season.
To my neighbors, friends and small business owners in
Hernando Beach.

Thank you, Jen Boles editor extraordinaire, a friendly voice who whispers
sage corrections into many of my titles, including
The Christmas Café.

The Christmas Cafe

A Holiday Romance

One

Jake glanced out of his office window. Light drifting of snowflakes danced through the air. As he followed them down from the clouds and scattering over the office building parking lot, he frowned.

"Something wrong, Jake?" a voice called from his office doorway.

Turning away from the window he saw his assistant, looking in, concerned washed across her face.

Jake shook his head, "No, Carol. Nothing's wrong. I was just thinking while this building is nice, I kind of miss being downtown."

Carol scowled, "Downtown Wintergreen? Not much of a downtown and that old drafty building with all of us crammed in there. No, I can't say as though I miss it."

"Hmm," Jake silently nodded as he returned his glance to the snow drifting softly to the ground.

"Besides, this is where all the new businesses are popping up. We are in the thick of Wintergreen's future," Carol said.

"Yeah, I suppose. These office buildings just don't have any character," Jake said.

Carol laughed, "If we were an architectural firm, I might agree. But for marketing, I think our clients prefer a new building with actual parking spaces. And we're right off the highway. My commute is ten minutes less than it used to be. No complaints here."

Jake glanced at his watch, "Oh, I need to get going."

"Coffee meeting?" Carol asked.

"Yep."

"Don't forget the video call with corporate at three," Carol said.

Jake grabbed his coat off the rack, "Thanks. Do we have the numbers from the Wallace campaign?"

"We do, and they're pretty good. I don't know how you do it. Getting people to even consider remodeling their homes before the holidays… I couldn't imagine," Carol said.

Jake grinned, "Families preparing for guests, tons of time in the kitchen, fretting about shared bathrooms…"

"Wow, tapping into people's fears before the holidays, that's shrewd," Carol scowled.

"Not fears, possibilities…" Jake said.

Carol gave Jake a gentle push toward the door, "Fair enough. Now don't be late for your… meeting."

"I won't," Jake said, moving toward the foyer and the awaiting bank of elevators.

Climbing into his car, Jake pulled out of the parking lot and onto the freeway on ramp.

Passing the new shopping mall Jake eyed the grand opening signs scattered throughout the massive complex. One of the early arrivals, the first to open a few months ago, was in full operation.

"Java Universe," Jake muttered.

A long line of cars awaited their turn while even more parked and streamed inside. Just in case the shop didn't attract enough attention, cheerleaders in flashy, Santa inspired outfits danced out front, waving at cars as they passed.

"They must be chilly," Jake muttered, noticing their outfits left them quite exposed to the blustery December air.

Ignoring the next two signs, Jake turned toward the downtown exit, "This used to be so much busier."

Driving down Wintergreen's Main Street, he admired the classic decorations and wreaths attached to every streetlamp. Pulling to the curb, Jake hopped out. Giving Main Street a scan, he smiled. The light dusting of snow only made the scene more quaint.

He pulled up his collar to ward off the chilly breeze. After a quick wave at a shop owner next door, he pushed his way into the coffee shop, holding the door open for a couple coming out with their hands wrapped around to-go cups. Wishing them a Merry Christmas, Jake walked into the shop himself.

The whir of the grinder, the scent of the beans and the crooning of Christmas carols filled the room giving Jake a great sense of warmth.

As Jake walked through the shop, he stopped at a table and smiled, "Karen and Lou, it's so good to see you!"

"Jake Myers, it's good to see you. We don't get to see you as often," Karen said.

Jake nodded, "Yeah, since the move it is a little harder to get down here. Can't just walk down the sidewalk anymore."

"Well, that building is lovely. I bet your staff is thrilled in their new space," Lou added.

Jake shrugged, "They seem happy. I miss seeing all the regulars down here."

Karen and Lou smiled.

Jake nodded and moved toward the counter to place his order.

"Jake!" a voice rang from across the barista counter. "Look who's home!"

Jake studied the young woman across from him. She rolled her eyes at her grandmother's announcement but flashed a smile at Jake.

"Sara Bailey. Welcome home," Jake said.

"It is good to be here. Even better to be done with school," Sara said.

"Congratulations," Jake said. Hands in his pockets, he surveyed the coffee shop, "A little quieter than I would have expected."

"Well with Java Universe and their constant radio ads and discount coupons pasted around town, they've attracted some attention," the barista said.

"Well, Bea, there's nothing quite like a cup from the Coffee Corner. You're a Wintergreen icon," Jake said.

"Thank you, Jake. If you're up for some marketing, you're hired," Bea teased.

"That's right, the big marketing executive. I heard you got the job at the Wintergreen branch. What brings you in?" Sara asked.

Before he could answer a woman in expensive clothes stormed in. Seeing Jake, she beelined in a huff, "Jake, we could have met at Java Universe. I could have had a Soy Mocha Mint Frappuccino!"

Jake stepped back, "Tracy, meet Bea Bailey and her granddaughter, Sara. Bea owns the Coffee Corner and I assure you, whatever Java Universe's machines churn out, these ladies can make it by hand way better."

Tracy looked squarely at the ladies behind the coffee bar and feigned a smile, "No offense, I have some Christmas shopping to do and the other place is closer to the shops."

"You should check out the shops downtown. You have a much better chance of finding something unique, something special," Bea suggested.

Tracy was blank for a moment before responding, "Right, unique."

"Here is your coffee. Merry Christmas. It was good to see you, Jake," Sara said, placing two drinks on the end of the bar.

Grabbing their coffees, Jake offered an apologetic smile, "Good to see you, Sara. Bea."

"See you tomorrow, Jake. I'm serious about the marketing," Bea called.

Jake nodded and ushered Tracy out of the shop and onto the sidewalks of Main Street.

Tracy scoffed at the classic holiday décor on the lightly traveled streets of Wintergreen. "It is time Daddy gives you that promotion and you can finally get out of here," she said.

"Hmm," Jake merely grunted as he took in the quaint décor of Main St. He found the town's effort rather subdued this season.

"They do make a good cup of coffee, though," Tracy offered.

Jake walked past their cars and past the storefronts of the downtown markets.

Tracy's eyes scanned for brands that she recognized. She paused briefly at the jewelry shop where the gems in the window display defied labels and stood out for their intrinsic quality. A little further, she took in the antique shop. The classic Christmas vignette seemed to spark something in her for just a moment. To Jake's disappointment, Tracy spun and pulled her collar up before lacing her arm into his, "Let's go. It's cold out here."

Jake nodded and gave Main Street a final glance before escorting Tracy to her car.

Two

Pulling a wreath from the back of his truck, Jake took a moment to enjoy the rich pine scent. "*That* smells like Christmas," he said.

With a knock on the door, he opened it and called, "Mom!"

"I'm in the kitchen. Just getting started with some Christmas baking," Jake's mother said.

Jake made his way into the kitchen, "Cardamom, cinnamon, peppermint…"

"And now pine," Jake's mother kissed him on the cheek as she kept her floury hands far from his suit.

"A little frankincense and myrrh and we've nailed it," Jake said.

Returning to her work on a ball of dough, Jake's mother said, "I think we'll do."

"Need help?" Jake tentatively asked as he surveyed the busy kitchen.

"As soon as I get the bread set to rise, there's not much left to do."

Jake set his jacket on the back of a chair and rolled up his sleeves, "Except clean."

"You don't have to do that," his mother protested.

"I know. I might also be angling for a loaf of cardamom bread when it's all said and done," Jake said as he turned on the water.

"Are you going to bring Tracy around this holiday?"

"We're trying to get our schedules synched," Jake replied.

"I hear that Sara is back in town. Such a cutie," his mother said.

Jake nodded as he scrubbed a bowl, "Yeah, I saw her at the coffee shop."

"You still go there? Isn't that new place closer to the office?"

"It is. I like downtown. The stuff at the mall is all so cookie cutter," Jake shrugged.

His mother frowned, "Doesn't your firm represent a lot of those companies?"

"They do," Jake nodded. "I like to support the local businesses. Bea built that coffee shop long before the others became popular. It isn't just a place to get coffee. It connects the community. I like that."

"Always the romantic. Speaking of which, what are you getting Tracy for Christmas?"

"I don't know. Her family doesn't exactly do Christmas like we do," Jake said.

"What do you mean?" his mother asked as she set a warm towel over several bowls of bread dough.

Jake shrugged, "They usually meet up at a ski resort for the day, have dinner together at the lodge and go back to work the next day."

"Where's the fun in that? No Christmas Eve carols? Waking up in pajamas and gathering by the tree?"

"Everyone's different, Mom. That's why I'm not sure if I'll get her over here. Maybe we'll try and sneak in dinner one night this week," Jake said.

"And the present?" his mother pressed.

"She's not exactly the easiest to buy for. She's, uh, very particular," Jake replied.

Jake's mother set her towel down, "The best gifts have meaning. Something that conjures a feeling like a memory or establishes a new one. Not just adding to an already full closet or jewelry cabinet."

"Yeah," Jake nodded absently.

"What wonderful memory from the time you two spent together would you like to memorialize? Or what meaningful moment in time in your near future would you like to set in motion?"

"If you are meaning… I don't think I'm ready for that," Jake said. "As far as this past year… I mean, this has been kind of a focus on growth at the job kind of year."

"What about that trip you two took to the coast?"

"You mean the one on the way to her dad's party? It was filled with clients and ad brokers. We didn't really get a lot of time on our own," Jake said.

His mother bit her lip, "Well, there must be something in those memory banks. You two have been together for over a year now."

"Yeah," Jake nodded thoughtfully as he stared out the window into his parent's snowy back yard.

Jake's mother changed gears, "How is work?"

"Good, I guess. I am taking on more and more accounts. The return on investment numbers for our clients are running above average," Jake said.

"But..."

"But they are a bit boiler plate. We like to "keep things safe". Messaging is all about trusting in the power of the national brand, consistency of product," Jake said.

"That sounds all right," his mother shrugged.

"It is. It's just... it's like wine. Some large wineries work really hard to produce wines with consistency. And they are okay. But I prefer the boutique wineries where each vintage is a little different. They're those really special ones that really stick in your memory," Jake said.

"Doesn't that put them at risk for bad ones?"

Jake winced, "Yeah, I suppose. I mean I'm not sure I would call them bad or they wouldn't bottle that year. I would say good with the potential for that magical vintage."

Giving her son a squeeze, she smiled, "You're searching for a great vintage in marketing?"

"Something like that," Jake sighed.

Three

The tires of Jake's truck crunched over the layer of frozen snow covering the parking space in front of the Coffee Corner. Hopping out, Jake blew on his hands to ward off the instant chill.

Glancing down the quiet Main Street of Wintergreen, the only signs of life were the wave from the insurance agent next door and the soft lights streaming out of the coffee shop.

Jake pushed his way in.

"Good morning, Karen. Lou," he nodded as he passed by. Each smiled and hoisted their coffee mugs in the air.

The only other occupied table was Sara who was working on a tablet.

Bea called from behind the coffee bar, "Usual this morning, Jake?"

"For me, yes. I have a few orders for the office too," Jake said, handing Bea a list of drinks. "Chilly out there."

"Well, this will warm you up. I'll have your drinks ready in a jiffy."

"Thanks, Bea," Jake said.

As the coffee shop owner went to work, Jake paced around the shop enjoying the Christmas carols softly playing over the speakers. Hovering his hand over the giving tree, he snatched a tag. Flipping it over, he read under his breath, "Markie. 5. She wants a doll. I think I can handle that, Markie."

Bea handed over his drink while she worked on his office order.

With a nod of appreciation, Jake brought the cup to his lips, and the warmth quickly began working to erase the chill.

Absently, he meandered around the shop. He didn't consciously mean to spy, but he was drawn to peek over Sara's shoulder.

Startled, Sara shook herself from her work and looked up at him. Her scowl was erased with a look of curiosity.

"I'm sorry. I didn't mean to invade your creative space. It's just… It's beautiful," Jake said.

Reluctantly, Sara turned the screen so Jake could have a better view of the winter scene she was creating.

"I remember you were good," Jake said.

"You do?" Sara gasped.

Jake nodded, "Yeah. You won the top prize in the school art competition as a freshman. You painted a scene of people singing around the flagpole. It was great."

Sara blushed, "I can't believe you remember that."

"Well, amazing art shouldn't be forgotten. I'm glad you're still at it," Jake said.

"Oh, this is just for fun. After the New Year, I start work at my parent's accounting firm," Sara said.

Jake looked out toward Main Street, "Isn't their office right here in downtown?"

"It was. They moved into your building, actually. In January," Sara said.

"Seems like all the businesses are moving. Even the insurance agency next door is leaving," Bea said as she set the coffees for Jake's office on the counter in a tray. "It's even worse when the mayor and the city council give tax breaks for new businesses like Java Universe to come to the new sites by the highway. Makes it tougher for us little guys to keep going."

Jake nodded, "I have noted it is pretty quiet down here."

"All things have a season," Bea said, a note of sadness in her voice.

Jake looked thoughtful. Before he could speak a man walked into the shop. All heads turned as he strode between Jake and Sara.

"You look lovely as usual, Sara," the man said. "As do you, Bea. It's your radiance that keeps me loyal to the Coffee Corner!"

"I'll have you know I am no longer on the market, Shawn," Bea gushed.

"Hmm, if only you had a younger version of yourself equally beautiful but a bit more available," he teased.

Jake felt awkward standing in the direct center of the conversation. In the corner of his eyes, he watched as Sara hid her screen. "Thanks, Bea. I should get these to the office while they are hot."

"Nice of you to take care of your people, Jake," Shawn said.

"Thanks, Shawn. Grabbing some coffee for your office too?" Jake asked.

"Not today, I have a council meeting. Just wanted my morning pick me up," Shawn said, flashing a smile toward Sara.

Grabbing the tray of coffees, Jake began to make his way out of the shop, offering a friendly nod to Karen and Lou.

"Nothing gets me in the spirit more than you two ladies and a splash of pumpkin spice in my cappuccino," Shawn said.

"Coming right up!" Bea sang.

As Jake reached the door, he turned abruptly, "I'll help!"

All eyes fell on Jake.

"With your marketing. I'll help," Jake blurted.

Bea shook her head at the news, "Jake, that would be wonderful."

"Yeah," Jake nodded. "I'll put something together and stop by tomorrow."

Pushing through the door and out into the cool air, he frowned. He wasn't sure what came over him. With Main Street still glistening in the morning frost, he climbed into his truck and drove away.

Four

A knock on Jake's office door broke his attention from his screen. Carol stood in his doorway with an armload of packages and baskets, "More Christmas stuff! Your clients love you."

"They love *us*. I couldn't begin to do what I do without you," Jake said.

Carol flushed, "Well, you are a terrific boss."

Jake glanced through the items, smiling as he read the notes on the cards, "Could your family use any of this? Don't you have a party coming up?"

"Well, yeah, but these were sent for you," Carol protested.

"Us. They sent all of this to us. Your kids will love this," Jake pulled out a large box of peppermint bark. "And if I recall, Jeff will be making his famous nog. I think there is something in these packages to help with that."

"Are you sure?" Carol asked with her hands on her hips.

Jake laughed, "I'm sure."

Carol nodded towards his computer and a half completed storyboard, "Working on the Tire King account? If anyone can get people interested in tires right before the holidays, it is you."

"Yeah. Not sure how people feel about a set of radials under the tree, but I think I have an angle. 'Give the gift of safety this Christmas. Winter tires ensure everyone makes it home safely for the holidays.' Needs some work, but I'll get there," Jake said.

"I like it. I never would have thought of tires as a gift. But if someone really needs them and puts them off in order to focus on other Christmas shopping, I can see where that would be helpful. I get the gift of safety but…" Carol started.

"Sounds a bit commercial, I know," Jake nodded.

"Maybe focus on the home safely for the holidays bit and allow a different part of the ad to drop the Christmas gift hint," Carol suggested.

"I like it. See? Couldn't do this without you," Jake said.

"You could. You just wouldn't *want* to," Carol said.

"Very true," Jake nodded.

Carol began to walk out of the office when she spun on her heel and asked, "Are you spending time with Tracy this Christmas?"

"Yeah, I think so. We don't have the details worked out but I think Henry is flying her home on Christmas Eve. I was invited but… I think I'll stay with my family this year. My nieces and nephews are still at that fun age," Jake said.

"Well, there's still time to finalize details, right?" Carol asked.

"Sure," Jake nodded.

As Carol walked away, his eyes fell back to his work. Making a few notes inspired by their conversation, Jake gave a satisfied nod as he reviewed the campaign.

His mind drifted. Images of Main Street at Christmas filled his thoughts. Wintergreen's downtown was so charming and quaint. He hated to see so many businesses leave for the new commercial developments by the highway.

Jake tapped his pencil against his forehead as if to help him think. He thought of the feeling he got when he was downtown. Bits of nostalgia mixed with a charming small-town feel made Main Street a pleasant place to visit.

He put himself in the Coffee Corner. He tried to think of how the atmosphere and friendliness made him feel. Each barista knew every regular client's name and drink preferences. It was a natural gathering place for locals to connect, if just for a moment, out of their busy lives. Somehow, Wintergreen's downtown felt like traveling at a slower pace. Jake thought of how to wrap all of that into an ad campaign.

Another knock on the door stole his attention, "Sorry to rush you, Jake, but we'd like to get that Tire King project moved out ASAP. They'd like to capture some pre-holiday sales."

"Yeah," Jake nodded.

The office's president stood impatiently in front of Jake's desk.

"I had Jeff in sales tell the client it would be ready to present first thing tomorrow morning," the president said.

Jake breathed, "I told Jeff end of day tomorrow, Frank."

"I know. But I also know how fast you work. I didn't think it would be a big deal. Besides, Henry is coming to town. It would be a great way to finish the year strong with one more solid campaign. If we can get some early numbers in, we'd be in line for office location of the year," Frank said.

"Henry's coming to town?" Jake asked. "No one told me that."

"Sounds like a last-minute kind of deal. Supposed to have some big news of some sort. Might be that we have already won, but why not stack the deck, right?" Frank grinned.

"Absolutely," Jake shrugged.

"So… what do we have so far for the campaign?"

Jake shared his updated storyboard.

Frank crossed his arms and considered the proposal, "Hmm. I like it, the whole home safely for the holidays thing, but I think really hitting home with tires make a great present, especially with their voucher program, would seal the deal."

"I had something like that, but the quick market test suggested that we lead with the home safe for the holidays and allow the final declaration to be the sales closing piece," Jake said.

"It's good work. Put the Christmas present bit in upfront. We want a sense of urgency. That will move the dial faster while the safe holiday stuff is the icing on the cake," Frank said.

"I'll write it up both ways and let Jeff work it out with the client," Jake sighed.

"That's not too much on your plate to get it done today?"

"It'll be done," Jake promised.

Frank smiled and pointed at Jake, "You're the star of ad copy, Jake. You've got a bright future here, and not just because you are dating Henry's daughter."

Jake frowned as he watched Frank leave the office after that piercing comment.

Pulling his Tire King storyboard out, his eyes glazed over it. The contrast between Java Universe's focus on speed and moving the line versus Coffee Corner's stay and relax warmth plagued him. There was a message there that he wanted to tap into.

Pulling out a blank storyboard template, he got to work.

Five

The world outside Jake's office window had gone dark and cold by the time he looked up from his work. The marketing firm had become ghostly quiet as he walked through the halls to deliver the two versions of the Tire King ad campaign.

Leaving a packet on his boss' desk and one for the account agent Jeff, he grunted when he found their offices vacated and dark. With a shrug, he plopped the files on the representative desk.

Through the halls, he heard a low Christmas carol ring out. With a curious brow, he followed the sound until he found himself in his own office. Glancing at his desk, he found his phone ringing wildly with a picture of Tracy on the screen. Her number appeared four times in the recent call log.

Lifting his wrist, he saw the time, "Oh, no."

Snatching the phone, he answered, "Hello."

"Where have you been? I've been calling you," Tracy's voice snarled through the phone.

"I'm sorry, I just finished up at the office. I guess your dad offered my services for an advanced deadline," Jake confessed.

"Well, your hard work will pay off soon," Tracy said. "Meet me at the restaurant?"

"That sounds great. I'm on my way," Jake said, hanging up the call.

Grabbing his bag and the portfolio he had put together, Jake shut off his light and began making his way through the building.

Tracy waved her hand wildly as Jake arrived at the hostess stand. With a nod, he made his way through the crowded restaurant.

Giving her a quick kiss on the cheek, Jake shed his coat and took his seat.

"This place isn't great, but it is the best place I could find in Wintergreen," Tracy said.

Jake pulled his napkin from the table and sat in his lap.

"At least they have cloth napkins," Tracy scoffed.

"Yeah," Jake nodded numbly. "We should really try the Tavern on the River. They also use cloth napkins and have this great view of the water. Even at night, they light it up. It's beautiful."

"Hmm. Sounds okay. What kind of food do they have?" Tracy asked.

Jake shrugged, "Just Americana fare. Locally sourced steak and potatoes kind of place. They have this great burger with a homemade tomato sauce…"

"You mean ketchup?" Tracy asked.

"Well, kind of, but not like any I've had," Jake said.

"You should like this place. The marketing firm billed it as a taste of France in your hometown," Tracy said.

"Yeah, that was my ad copy," Jake said.

Tracy smiled, "I think it sounds great."

"Well, I came up with that because, as a national chain, it can feel a bit out of touch with the community. I mean this one looks the same as the one in New Jersey or the ones in California. And they are placed near the shopping mall instead of the heart of town," Jake said.

"You are such a romantic if not very realistic," Tracy said. "It is one of the things I like about you. Though…"

"Though?" Jake frowned.

"Daddy says it can hold you back at times. You run against the grain of the corporate marketing team," Tracy said.

"Speaking of Henry, I heard he is coming to town. I didn't know about that," Jake said.

Tracy shifted in her seat, "He kind of wanted to surprise you and the rest of the team. He also wants to take you and me out to dinner while he's here."

"I see," Jake said slowly. "What evening? I told you my family has a lot of holiday events leading up to Christmas."

"I know, but I figured you would prioritize for me and Daddy," Tracy said. "I mean, it's important."

"My family is important, too," Jake defended.

"I didn't mean to imply they aren't. It's just, Daddy has your future in mind," Tracy said.

"Yeah," Jake said softly, allowing his eyes to drift to his menu, grateful for the waitress coming to their table and taking their orders.

Jake drove his truck through downtown. Glancing over at Tracy through the soft glow of the dashboard lights, he asked, "You want to go for a walk?"

Tracy's face screwed into a horrified expression, "It's cold out."

"Yeah, but its Christmas. See the lights, peek into the storefront windows…" Jake pressed.

"Thank you, no. I think I'll just turn in for the night. I will say, the new hotel near the office is quite nice," Tracy said.

"It's not bad. You should check out the Wintergreen Bed and Breakfast. It is right down the road from the tavern on the river I mentioned. Evening wine tastings, fire pit at night on the weekends. It's like a Christmas movie house during the holiday season," Jake said.

"Yeah, but with the big hotels, I know what I am going to get and I get traveler points," Tracy said.

"Right. Very practical," Jake nodded as he pulled into the covered entrance to Tracy's hotel.

Getting out, he opened Tracy's door. Walking her into the lobby, he stopped. Giving her a quick hug and a kiss, he turned and walked out. As he reached the driver's side door, he paused. Looking through the hotel windows, he watched as Tracy paused at the bank of elevators and walked off towards the hotel bar.

Climbing in, he started the truck. Instead of heading home, he took the downtown exit. Pulling to a stop in front of the location his firm used to have on Main Street, he got out.

Hands in his pocket, he strolled down Main Street on his own. Tracy was right. It was cold out, but he liked it. The wool coat and scarf did their best to keep the chilly air at bay, but the wintry night air made itself known. Jake didn't mind. It added to the ambiance of Christmas time. It matched the snowflakes, wreaths and angels adorning the storefronts. The lightest dusting of snow sprinkled the landscape. It was Christmas and Wintergreen was a wonderful place to experience it.

Jake enjoyed making his way down the sidewalk, appreciating how each location decorated their storefronts. Scenes of Santa at the North Pole, depictions of the Nativity, and decorated Christmas trees adorned many store windows. Others would have Chanukah or simple snowy scenes in their windows.

Nearly every business participated sharing their vision of the season. Regardless of their choice of décor, the effort was an inviting, beautiful place to visit, no more so than at Christmas.

At the end of Main Street, where the road edged close to the river, was a large park. A small, paved trail with old fashioned light posts wound through evergreen trees. Picnic tables and a large gazebo were the centerpiece with the river flowing in the background. Near the gazebo was a large tree, towering above the others.

Jake stood in front of the tree. Allowing his eyes to rise to the top where a star twinkled in the sky. He realized, the tree wasn't decorated like it used to be. There was once an event held each year at that site. Carolers, cocoa stations, and gingerbread decorating would culminate in a town sing-a-long. The event finale was the lighting of the tree. It was a beacon of Downtown Wintergreen.

Standing, hands in his pockets pulling his jacket tighter, he realized the town stopped hosting the event when the new shopping center opened. Instead of the community coming together in the park with local vendors selling handmade items and baked goods, it became sales and coupons for the stores at the shopping center.

With a sigh, Jake turned on his heel and started the walk back to his truck. He felt blessed to be part of a small town where anyone could feel safe and comfortable. He wasn't sure Wintergreen was headed in the right direction.

On his return walk, Jake counted the number of store fronts and businesses that had closed. He appreciated that the neighbors included them in their decorations to make the festive nature of Main Street fluid and continuous.

Glancing at the empty office where the branch of the marketing firm used to call home, a wreath, and strand of lighted garland draped across the door and windows. That was what he loved about downtown. It was a community of businesses. They worked together, and they supported each other. That was what he had been missing once the branch moved into the business park.

Arriving first at the firm, Jake flipped the lights on. Walking through the cubicles to his office, he settled in behind his desk.

Opening his laptop, he sighed as he sorted through his overnight emails. "Two more rush projects for the new year. To be completed for presentation *before* Christmas. Of course," he muttered to himself.

Pulling the portfolio for the Coffee Corner, he quickly went to work.

Buried in his project, Jake didn't hear the first knocks on his office door. "Ahem… Jake!" Carol hissed.

Looking up, Jake's eyes adjusted from his screen to his assistant, "Yeah? I'm sorry, Carol. I was just focused."

"Clearly," Carol said. "Your Tire King proposals seem to have made Frank and Jeff happy."

"Enough that they gave me two more rush jobs to complete by Christmas," Jake said.

Carol nodded, "Yeah, I saw that. Good to feel wanted, right?"

"I suppose," Jake replied.

"On top of all that, Henry is here," Carol said.

"He is? Do I have a meeting scheduled?" Jake asked.

"Not on the calendar, but he asked for you to meet him in the conference room," Carol said.

Jake glanced at his work on the Coffee Corner before nodding. Closing the laptop, he grabbed his leather notebook and followed Carol out of the room.

After a quick peek in the conference room, Jake saw a small group reviewing his Tire King proposals side by side.

Seeing Jake standing in the door way, he was waved in.

"We were just reviewing your campaign with Henry," Frank said.

"It's good work, particularly given the timeframe you had to work under," Henry said.

"The client will be pleased," Jeff said, holding up the print out of the ad proposal.

Henry pointed at the screens displaying the projects, "Clean, clear, concise. While the safe for the holidays is a great attention getter, the action-oriented give the gift of safety is more actionable. You were given two more ad copies to create prior to the twenty-fourth. To save some time, keep that concept in mind. Warm and fuzzies are great, but what is the end result we are after for our clients? Sales."

Jake crossed his arms and nodded slowly, "I get the end goal. I was thinking the best way to drive action is to get the consumer to think about the why. Appeal to their wanting to ensure their loved ones are safe for the holidays and that they can play a part in that."

"And that's good," Henry said. "But by focusing on the action, you can appeal to the more pragmatic in the audience as well. They might tune out the mushy stuff."

"Mushy stuff?" Jake frowned.

"Yeah, you know, the Christmas movie-style family gatherings. I mean, who does that anymore? Our firm helps companies move the needle into the future, not the past," Henry said.

Jake pursed his lips slightly, "I see."

"You have a great mind for appealing to the customer base and painting a picture… telling a story. You just need to be on point with the Banks Marketing brand," Henry said.

"The future…" Jake said in nearly a whisper.

"Yes!" Henry exclaimed. "Progress. Growth. Leaving the past and their competition in the dust."

"You are one of the best we have. You just need a little nudge into the fast lane," Frank added.

"A little nudge," Jake repeated absently.

Jeff stood up with the proposal in his hands, "Well, I'm glad we are all on the same page. I look forward to the new campaigns, Jake. I hope the timeline doesn't give you any issues. I need to get this to Mack at the Tire King."

The sales executive left the office in a rush.

"There's something else we wanted to talk to you about," Frank said. Both he and Henry focused their attention square on Jake.

"Have a seat," Henry offered, waving his hand at an empty chair across the table from them.

Jake complied, settling into the chair.

Henry leaned forward planting his elbows on the table and lacing his hands together. "We have been watching you for a long time. This probably doesn't come as much of a surprise, but we see a great future for you in Banks Marketing. As the Tire King conversation illustrates, you need to move from the small-town mindset to the big stage. We want to make sure you are ready for that. The proposals that were emailed to you for fast track - think of them as your final exam. If you pass, there are very big things in store for you, Jake."

Jake's eyes moved from Henry to Frank and back to Henry again.

"I understand," Jake nodded.

"Great!" Henry and Frank exclaimed together.

"I should get to work," Jake said. "Unless there is something else?"

"We love your enthusiasm," Frank said.

As Jake rose, Henry said, "I would like to take you and Tracy to dinner. I'll send you a time."

"I, uh, I look forward to it," Jake said and walked out of the conference room.

Sliding back into the chair behind his desk, Jake pulled up the specifications on the urgent proposal requests. Sorting through the requested strategy, Jake felt uninspired. Both accounts wanted to focus on the strength of their size and national reach.

Tapping his pencil, Jake tried to find the consumer hook, the appeal that would stop someone from scrolling or fast forwarding through a commercial to hear and see the message. "Dependability…" he mused. "Sure. Dependably average food shipped across the country and served according to a mechanized kitchen. Dependably uninspired, over-extended staff to offer rooms full of furniture that will help you keep up with Joneses because, well, you'll have the same furniture as the Joneses."

"Sorry to interrupt, I mean, it sounds like you have established some gold star ad copies there…" Carol teased from the doorway.

"Not to pile on, but you have been handpicked to launch an exciting bathtub resurfacing ad campaign, and you guessed it, they want a January 1 start date."

"Wow, as if a color-in-the-lines burger franchise and a vanilla furniture store chain weren't satisfying enough to work on," Jake quipped.

"I am a fan of vanilla," Carol smiled as she placed the new request on the desk.

"With the flecks?" Jake asked hopefully.

"You think these bites of vanilla have the flecks in it?" Carol asked.

Jake winced, "I fear these are those odd hues of beige vanillas."

"That is why you get paid the reasonably appropriate bucks," Carol smiled. "Good luck. I know you'll come up with something amazing."

Jake slumped back in his chair as he read through all three requested portfolios and let out a large sigh.

Staring at the screen, hands hovering over the keyboard with nothing to type, Jake decided a change of scenery was needed. Grabbing his jacket, his laptop and pile of campaign requests, he headed out of the office.

"Jake!"

He froze as he passed by the conference room. Turning to see Frank and Henry staring out of the open meeting room door, he took a step in their direction.

"Thanks for taking on that latest request. Figured you'd be holed up in your office hammering those out," Henry said.

"Working on them. Just stepping out a bit to get a fresh perspective," Jake said.

Henry chuckled, "Creatives."

"Whatever it takes for them to churn out winning ideas," Frank shrugged.

"I'll get them done," Jake assured.

"Be sure you do. Clock is ticking," Henry said.

Jake offered a nod and spun with his full arms. Wading through the office, he hit his knuckle on the elevator call button. Keeping his focus on the doors as he waited, he could feel the eyes behind him.

Jake stepped onto the sidewalk of Main Street just as a man followed by a small entourage was walking by.

"Jake," the man in the lead acknowledged.

"Mayor," Jake gave a nod and a quick hello to the rest of the group. His eyes fell to a frown, "Say, Mayor Hammond. I notice the park tree isn't lit up with Christmas lights this year."

The mayor and the troop on his heels paused, "The shopping center petitioned us not to."

"Why?" Jake scowled.

"They didn't want the town's attention split with the activities out at the new shopping center," the mayor could see the dissatisfaction on his constituents' faces. "Look, the future of commerce in Wintergreen is the modernized shops and malls. Your firm is a case in point. It's just progress."

Jake watched the mayor and his team continue down the sidewalk. "Progress…" he muttered to himself as he pulled open the coffee shop door.

Aside from the small collection of regulars, the shop was eerily quiet.

"Jake!" Bea called from across the coffee bar. "It's good to see you."

"It's good to see anyone," Sara added from behind her grandmother. "Hello, Jake."

More resolute than ever, Jake strode to the counter, "I'm going to help. I already have a few ideas."

"Jake," Bea protested. "I appreciate your help, but I can't afford to pay for marketing."

"She can't afford to pay me. I'm just here to keep her company," Sara said.

"Well, let me show you what I have put together. On the house," Jake said.

Bea frowned, "No, Jake. I couldn't possibly…"

Leaning in, Jake pressed, "It would be my pleasure. Really."

Sara flashed a look towards Jake that he couldn't quite interpret.

Bea looked confused as to how to respond.

"Let me buy a round of coffee and show you what I'm thinking," Jake scanned the coffee shop. "It looks like you have a free moment."

Slumping her shoulders, Bea nodded. "Coffee is on *me*, however."

Knowing he was going to place a large order for his office before he left, Jake accepted the offer.

Finding a table they could huddle around, Jake placed a storyboard on the table. Before revealing it, he sat back in his seat and pulled out his notes.

Bea set a coffee in front of Jake while she and Sara sipped on tea.

"Every time I drive by Java Universe, there is a string of cars being paraded through by employees in bright-colored vests and headsets. It reminds me of trying to leave a concert parking lot. Their own marketing is all about speed, consistency and idle talk. While I suppose it has appeal for travelers who pulled off the highway for a quick stop or people heading to work and just want a quick coffee," Jake started.

"Okay, so far, not the best sales pitch. The other guys are fast, efficient and conveniently located. We on the other hand…" Sara frowned over her cup of tea.

Jake waved a finger in the air suggesting that he was just getting to it, "Getting a cup of coffee shouldn't be chaotic. It should be comfortable, relaxing. It shouldn't be impersonal. It should be about community. If all anyone wanted was a cup of coffee, why don't they just do it at home or at the office? There are machines that can churn that out, even fancy lattes."

Looking across the table at his small audience, he leaned forward, "The Coffee Corner is about community. It is warm and inviting. It feels like visiting a friend. And it *should* feel like that."

Jake flipped the storyboard over to reveal his vision, *Experience the Warmth of Coffee, authentic, friendly, hometown coffee - The Coffee Corner.*

Bea and Sara stared blankly as they listened to Jake's presentation. Finally, Bea let out a smile, "I love it."

"It's not bad," Sara admitted. Frowning, she asked, "But what do we do with it? Print flyers? There's no ad money at a coffee shop like this."

"I was thinking about that. I can lower the cost with a little help," Jake said.

"What kind of help?" Sara asked.

"I need an artist. I can work for free and I have a few media outlets that owe me a favor or two. Plus, I'm a huge fan of free advertising. But I can't use agency resources," Jake said. Looking directly at Sara, he said, "I need *your* help."

"Jake, I haven't produced any art commercially. I don't think…" Sara began.

"Of course, you can. I have seen what you can do. It's stunning. And expressing from the heart, it will turn out amazing. I promise," Jake said.

"I mean, I can try," Sara shrugged as she squeezed her grandmother's hand.

"There's one other thing," Jake said. "I want to invite local artists, musicians, and others from the community to present at the café. It will be a reason, if only for their own supporters to come on down to the café.”

Bea’s eyes brightened, “Jake that is a wonderful idea! Do you think that will work?”

“It will help,” Jake nodded. “But, we need a seed piece of artwork to get the concept rolling.”

Once more, Jake’s eyes fell on Sara. This time, Bea’s gaze joined his.

Sara’s eyes widened, “Oh, no. My work isn’t ready to go up on anyone’s walls. Never mind trying to launch an artist campaign.”

Feeling both pairs of eyes boring into her, Sara’s shoulders dropped. With a long sigh, she said, “Fine. I may have something that won’t scare customers away. I’ll think about it.”

“If it is anything like what I saw the other day, it’ll be a beacon for coffee drinkers far and wide,” Jake said.

Bea let out a smile and winked at him.

Sara gulped as her mind was clearly still wrapped around having to display her artwork.

“I need to run and finish some work projects. Would you be… available for lunch to go over some ideas for the campaign?” Jake asked.

Sara looked at her grandmother, who shot a knowing look back. Slowly, she nodded, “Yes. I can be available.”

“Great. I’ll swing by and we can go together,” Jake said. Gathering his papers, he asked, “Can I get an order for the office? A half-dozen egg nog lattes and a half-dozen peppermint mochas?”

Sara got up from the table, “I’ll get to work on the drinks if you ring him up, Grandma.”

Bea leaned across the table, cradling Jake's hands in hers, "Thank you, Jake."

"Bea, I sincerely mean it is my pleasure. You have been a gem in this community for years and I won't let a bunch of corporate types take that away," Jake said.

"I'll go down fighting, at least," Bea smiled.

Jake nodded, "Yes, you will. We can do this."

Seven

After making two trips to his truck, one for two full trays of coffee and one for his marketing projects, Jake plopped into his office chair.

Taking notice that Henry and Frank were no longer in the conference room and no more rush packets sat on the corner of his desk, he set to work.

Pulling open the restaurant chain project, he considered different ways to warm up the message and create an image of an experience for diners. A relentless string in his mind kept tugging him toward the Coffee Corner.

With a smile, he muttered to himself, "If they want straight forward, I will give them straight forward. Consistent, dependable, convenient locations, well… everywhere. Should probably leave out retread and uninspired."

A knock on his door broke his concentration.

Carol stood smiling, one hand wrapped around the door jamb as she leaned in, "If you are going to keep talking to yourself, you might want to consider closing this."

Jake offered a sheepish grin, "How much of that did you hear?"

"Let's say that I would agree with your proposed omissions," Carol said. "I just came in to say thank you for the coffee. It's way better than the Java Universe I picked up on the way in."

"You are one of those converts," Jake cocked his head.

Carol shrugged, "It's convenient. Right on the way in to the office. It does seem to be missing something. Almost worth the extra drive to the Coffee Corner. You alright?"

"Yeah. Just trying to get through these last two rush jobs," Jake said.

"Getting through is not your typical way," Carol frowned.

"I have a side project my mind seems to be distracted by," Jake said.

Carol hugged her cup, "Ooh, a Christmas project? For Tracy?"

Jake almost looked surprised at the suggestion and shook his head, "No. Just something to help some old friends."

"Well, I won't keep you. I will warn you that Henry and Frank were looking for you," Carol said.

"I figured as much. Thanks," Jake nodded.

"I'll let you get back to it. Thanks again," Carol lifted her cup. As she started to walk away, she paused, wrapped her hand around the knob and pulled Jake's office door shut.

Jake chuckled as he let his eyes land back on his work.

Rejecting his customary hours of creating unique and carefully crafted options, Jake cobbled together near boiler plate campaigns. Delivering the corporate lines the national chains were after in their messaging, it took him a fraction of the time to complete both projects.

Nearly wrapping up the second project, another knock on the door captured Jake's attention.

"Come in," he called. Not wanting another new project dumped on him last minute distracting him from the Coffee Corner project, he buried the completed proposals under the draft copies.

The door swung wide and Frank stepped in with Henry right by his side.

"There you are. Hard at work. How are those campaigns coming?" Frank asked.

Jake stammered knowing neither was to his liking, "I focused in on the direction requested by the clients given the timeframes we had to work with."

"Let's see what you've got," Henry said, stepping up to the desk.

Jake nodded and shuffled the papers on the desk to pull out the restaurant campaign. Handing the copy to Henry with Frank looking over his shoulder.

"'Wherever you are, we are here. A slice of home for the holidays. Insert a photo of their signature dish. I mean, that's a classic," Henry nodded.

"I like it. No matter what town you are in, if you see their restaurant, you know what you are going to get. I think that is just what they are after," Frank said.

"How about the other one?" Henry asked, handing the restaurant portfolio back to Jake.

"I still have a few finishing touches to put on it," Jake lifted the second packet for Henry.

Flipping through the storyboard, Henry hummed through his lips. Handing it to Frank who read aloud, said, "Simple never goes out of style. Familiar. Solid. Outlets nationwide."

"Not your most inspired work, but hits the chord the client was after," Henry said.

"That's what *we* are after. We usually have to wade through his artsy greeting card stuff to find the ones that hit the point so concisely. Nice job," Frank said, handing the packet back across the desk.

Henry leaned forward slightly, "We were hoping you would join us for lunch."

"Oh, I would love to, but I, uh, already have plans," Jake said.

"Are you all coming? The car's out front," a voice chirped.

Tracy's head popped up over her father's shoulder.

"It'll just be the three of us," Henry reported.

Pushing through Frank and her father, Tracey scowled, "You can't get away for lunch with me?"

"I'm afraid it's our fault," Henry said, placing an arm around his daughter. "We dropped some last-minute projects on Jake that need to be completed by the holidays. But I promise, these will be the last until after Christmas."

Jake shrugged, "Just trying to get the finishing touches on these campaigns. I'll have them done by end of day."

"Well, you are dedicated. That's what we appreciate about you," Henry said.

With a nod to Frank, Henry led his daughter out of Jake's office.

Jake sat for a moment as he watched them head toward the elevator lobby. Pulling out the completed ad campaigns, he set them on the edge of his desk while he gathered his notes for the Coffee Corner, slid them into his bag and left the office himself.

Stopping by Carol's desk, he handed her the completed proposal packets, "Would you do me a favor and put these on Jeff's desk later on this afternoon?"

Carol raised an eyebrow, "Off to your super-secret mission?"

"Something like that," Jake laughed. "Just trying to bring a little Christmas cheer to someone who needs it."

"Hopefully no one Tracy would object to," Carol cocked her head warily.

"Not unless she would be jealous of a sweet grandmotherly type," Jake said.

"Alright. This part of your mission is in good hands," Carol said.

"Thanks," Jake said softly and headed for the building lobby himself.

Eight

Jake pulled up to the curb next to the empty office space the marketing firm used to call home. Stepping out, he eyed the darker clouds rolling toward Main Street. With them, a breeze with a sharper chill hinted at impending snow.

Whistling a Christmas tune, he made his way down the sidewalk toward the Coffee Corner. An older couple huddle around a small table as Bea presented them with paninis.

Flashing Jake a smile, she said, "Sara's in back. She'll be out in a minute. Can I get you anything?"

"No, I'm fine," Jake returned a smile. "Thank you."

His eyes swept around the coffee shop. Noting the blank spaces and the generic prints on the walls, he made a reminder on his phone.

The door to the back room opened and Sara walked through. She almost seemed unsettled when she saw Jake who let out a wry smile.

"What?" Sara frowned.

"You just, you look nice," Jake said.

Sara blushed as she rolled her eyes, "You just aren't used to seeing me outside of a café apron."

"Not that they aren't stylish," Jake joked. "Are you ready?"

"Ready to hear those ideas of yours. But yeah, I could eat," Sara said.

Jake slipped in front of her so that he could hold the door.

"Take your time!" Bea called.

Jake and Sara each nodded.

Together, they walked down the sparsely traveled Main Street sidewalks. "Barely a month ago, this area would have been busy around the lunch hour," Jake noted.

"I can't believe how many spaces are empty," Sara said.

"The businesses were offered huge incentives to relocate," Jake said.

"Why would the town do that?"

"It was a tough year and they were trending toward a big deficit. The shopping center and commercial park developers offered the town a piece of the pie, but they had to hit certain occupancy goals by end of the year. Our firm got tax breaks and rent discounts for a year. That adds up to a lot of money," Jake said.

"Grandma said something about her being offered a deal but with Java Universe at the shopping center with an exclusive, she couldn't have moved if she wanted to," Sara said.

"Would she want to?" Jake asked.

Sara shook her head, "No. That shop is like her home."

"She and the shop are a big part of downtown," Jake said.

"The bakery is still here, for now. So is the book store, though Grandma says they have looked at moving," Sara said.

"Running a business is tough these days," Jake said as they turned up towards the Tavern on the River restaurant.

"You're going to fix all that, for Grandma, at least, right?" Sara grinned as she walked past Jake and the door he held open for her.

"Yeah. No problem," Jake said.

Greeted by a hostess, he smiled a hello and held up two fingers. Grabbing menus, she ushered Jake and Sara to a table overlooking the river.

Settling into their seats, Jake glanced at the menu and set it aside. Placing a leather folder in front of him, he looked across at Sara who was still studying her lunch options. Just rising above the menu, he noticed the freckles on the bridge of her nose that seemed to dance in the gauzy winter cloud-filtered light streaming through the window.

As she set the menu down, Jake averted his eyes to the river. The water looked cold as it flowed over the boulders that dotted the riverbanks.

"I haven't been here in a while," Sara said.

"So, accounting, huh?" Jake asked.

Sara shrugged, "Two years of art school, four years working at a museum with little room to move up and six years of pressure from my parents, I figured it was time to grow up. Get my 'real' degree."

"Excited?"

"I don't know if anyone is *excited* to go into accounting. It's stable, dependable, and I get to help people to improve their businesses. Kind of like you," Sara said.

"Every business needs a good accountant," Jake nodded.

"How about you? Were you excited to come back to Wintergreen?"

Jake looked thoughtful, "I was. I like it here. I think I always imagined working in one of the downtown offices. Having neighbors that operate their businesses alongside you. It's kind of the American dream. Work hard and prosper."

"You have an oddly romantic view of the business world," Sara beamed.

"I like to think so, but there are times when the romance of it all is stripped away. A lot of clients and certainly my bosses prefer a paint-by-numbers approach. Steady and dependable," Jake said.

"They'd make great accountants," Sara laughed.

They paused so the waitress could take their orders. "So, lay it on me. What do you think will help Grandma's coffee shop and somehow compete against Java Universe?"

Jake pulled open his notes, "First of all, I noticed when I delivered coffee to the office that there wasn't a logo on the cups. I think you need to take advantage of free branding. There is no marketing like having your product out there in the world."

"Let people know we still exist," Sara nodded.

"Remind people there is something better than Java Universe in town," Jake said.

"I don't know how soon we get logoed cups," Sara frowned.

"I have a sticker supplier. They could have a first shipment out in twenty-four hours," Jake said. "You want people Christmas shopping sipping hot beverages from Coffee Corner cups."

"Smart. Simple. Easy. I like it," Sara said.

Jake leaned back so the waitress could place their plates in front of them. "The trick is to get people to the café so that they do walk around with those branded cups. But first, we eat."

Sara looked across the table taking in the cheery marketing executive.

"What?" Jake asked, about to take a bite of his burger.

"Why are you going to so much trouble to help us?" Sara asked.

Jake set his burger down. "The reason I always imagined working downtown was a sense of community. To walk to work and be able to build relationships with the other businesses. To start the day with a visit to your grandmother's shop. Say hello to Karen, Lou and the other regulars while I wait for my coffee. When storms come to pitch in and help sandbags offices that are vulnerable. Help clean up branches after the storm has passed. Just be a part of something bigger," Jake shared.

"Don't you have lots of neighbors at the commerce park?" Sara asked as she stabbed her fork for a bite of salad.

"Yeah, but it's different. There isn't the vibe of entrepreneurs growing their businesses side by side but rather dutiful employees working for a corporation headquartered who knows where," Jake said. "There's no sense of belonging, just clocking in and clocking out."

"I guess. I don't suppose there's much difference in accounting. It's just numbers, right?" Sara said.

Jake shook his head, "I don't think so at all. The small business down the street walks to your parent's office for their appointment. They are both small businesses sharing their experience together. Going to the big building with a giant plaque of offices next to the bank of elevators in that sterile, marbled-clad tower is a disconnect. It's not *we*. It's the corporate accounting firm and my business instead of my fellow business owner that is a part of my neighborhood."

"I guess, but accountants have an arm's-length distance from our clients," Sara protested.

"I would argue you have a huge bond of trust. Who would you trust more - the guys in the marble tower or your fellow business down the block?"

"Never looked at that way. I wonder if my parents considered the change in their relationship with our clients. My dad just thought an office in the tower would make the business seem more prestigious," Sara said.

"And then there is town. They pulled all the funding for the traditional Christmas festivities," Jake said.

"I noticed the tree wasn't lit," Sara nodded.

Jake said, "I get it, to a degree. Cutting costs when you are up against the budget, but when you stifle existing businesses, they lose tax revenue. They should be doing everything they *can* to keep businesses healthy downtown *while* they grow out toward the highway."

"Don't suppose you want to run for city council… or maybe take over Mayor Hammond's seat?"

"No, I don't have the stomach for politics. I'm more of a behind-the-scenes kind of guy," Jake said. "You know… hmm."

Jake pulled out his pen and scribbled some notes on his pad.

"Care to share what epiphany you just had?" Sara asked.

"Not just yet. I have to think through a few things first," Jake said. Pushing his plate aside, he flipped his folder back open. "Now, to what we came here for."

Sara slid her plate aside so that they had the entire table to work with.

"So, branding. Does your Grandma have a logo?" Jake asked.

"Not really," Sara screwed her face into a knot. "Aside from the words *Coffee Corner* on the window and the sign, not really. But I can use the font and create something. Actually, it would be fun and super meaningful to do that for Grandma."

"Great," Jake said and scanned the list. "In the meantime, we need something that draws customers in and quickly. That's where you come in."

Sara looked wary, "Oh boy. I don't have to spin a sign out on the sidewalk or dance or anything, do I?"

Jake laughed, "No, nothing like that. I want to make the shop a destination. People need a reason to come downtown."

"How do we do that?"

"We create showcases for artists, musicians, poets, writers- you name it," Jake said.

"That will take some time. We'll have to reach out to people. Get schedules made, collect pieces..." Sara began.

"Except we already know where to get some pieces to seed the concept," Jake said, shooting a knowing stare across the table at Sara.

Her shoulders slumped, "Jake, my stuff isn't ready yet. Nothing worthy of putting on a wall for the public anyway."

"I've seen what you can do. The Coffee Corner has tons of blank space along with random reprints that can be replaced with true works of art," Jake pressed.

Sara's cheeks reddened, "I'm flattered you think so, but… there's a reason I am becoming an accountant. The best I could do in the art world was lead elementary school classes on museum tours."

"You belong in a museum, but not giving tours. Sara, your work, just what I saw the other day is stunning," Jake said.

"I don't know…"

"Go home tonight and look at your collection. See what sings to you. If that doesn't work, I'll come over to help you select a few pieces," Jake offered.

The waitress placed the check on the table. Jake pulled his credit card out and to hand to the waitress but Sara slapped her hand on the check and pulled it away. "You aren't buying me lunch. You are working for free to help my grandmother!" Sara said.

That waitress accepted Sara's card and walked away to run it.

"Jake!" a voice gasped behind him.

Closing his eyes tight, just for a moment, Jake slowly turned to see Tracy standing by their table, Henry and Frank were immediately behind her.

Jake stood up and offered a sheepish, "Hello".

Tracy looked cross, "What are you doing here? You said you couldn't come to lunch."

"I said I had a meeting," Jake said. "You remember Sara Bailey. Her grandmother owns a small business downtown and wondered if our firm might be an option for them. I wanted to get a feel for scale before I took up any of Jeff's time."

"Hmm, I like that you're always looking out for the business," Frank said.

Henry quietly observed the situation and gave Sara a scrutinizing scan.

"We were just wrapping up. Let me walk you out," Jake said. The look in Tracy's eyes melted from angry to a twinge of sadness. He hadn't seen that expression from her often. He didn't understand what triggered it this time.

"You go on ahead, I'll close out with the server," Sara said.

"It was nice to meet you, Ms. Bailey," Henry said with a nod to Sara.

"It's a surprise to see you here," Jake said as he joined the group heading for the restaurant exit.

"It was Tracy's idea," Henry said.

"Really?" Jake seemed surprised.

"You said it was good. I thought I'd try it. I haven't given this little town of yours a very fair chance," Tracy said. "If it is important to you, it is important to me."

Jake stopped and gave Tracy a gracious look, "Thank you. That means a lot to me. Dinner tonight?"

Tracy looked at Jake as if to size up his suggestion. Bursting into a warm smile, she nodded, "Yes. Daddy is that okay with you?"

"I have a dinner with Frank and Jeff tonight. You two are on your own. I do want to catch up with you two one night this week, though," Henry said.

"Great. I'll pick you up at the hotel at six," Jake said. Giving her a kiss on her cheek, he watched them pile into the black executive car that was parked waiting outside the restaurant and drive away.

"Interviewing a potential client for the firm, were you?"

Jake spun to see Sara descending the steps of the restaurant.

"It was the most efficient way to not explain that I am moonlighting my marketing expertise," Jake said.

"And put Ms…."

"Tracy."

"Ms. Tracy at ease."

Jake squirmed, "I don't know why she would have an issue."

"She seems like a nice girl. A bit uptight though. She always like that?" Sara asked.

"Not really. I mean, she has high standards for certain things and isn't shy to express it. She's been a bit off since coming to Wintergreen," Jake said.

As they started their stroll back to the coffee shop, the dark clouds began to shower snow over downtown.

"How did you guys meet?" Sara asked.

"A work party. I never would have asked her out if I knew she was the boss' daughter. Though, I guess, technically, she asked *me* out," Jake said. "She didn't like the spread at the party and asked if I knew a place. I said I did and she handed me her coat check."

"Swept off your feet," Sara giggled.

Jake shrugged, "Sort of. I mean, she's beautiful. A handful… Anyways, we should focus. Pull a few of your favorite pieces for the café. I'll stop in tomorrow morning and see what else we can drum up."

Sara eyed Jake warily with the abrupt change of subject.

"All right. I'll do it for Grandma, but I don't like it," Sara said. She sensed she should let Jake off the hook for talking more about his relationship with Tracy.

Arriving at the café, Sara turned, her hand falling to the crook of Jake's elbow, "It is very sweet what you are doing… for Grandma."

"I'm happy to," Jake said. Suddenly his eyes brightened, "Do you have a few more minutes?"

Sara shrugged, "I guess."

"Great! Let's go for a walk," Jake said cheerily.

Sara looked questioningly at the suggestion but followed along.

Nine

The falling snow drifted over Jake and Sara as they strolled down the sidewalks of Main Street. Jake drew a deep breath, "I love the snow. It's so peaceful."

"It's beautiful," Sara nodded.

Stopping, Jake held the door open for Sara to enter a building. Sara paused in front of Jake, "Are you trying to traumatize me?"

"I was going for inspiring," Jake said, urging Sara to continue inside.

"This is all stuff done by real artists," Sara scowled.

"Like you," Jake said.

Sara snapped with a forced, angry look on her face, "I am trying to figure out if I really like you or really hate you."

"And?"

"The jury is still out," Sara said.

Jake laughed, holding his hand out to motion Sara forward.

Slowly, they meandered through the gallery taking in paintings and sculptures. Different pieces would cause them to pause and linger a bit longer.

"You like Christmas," Sara noted. "You stop at nearly every Christmas piece."

"I do," Jake shrugged. "It's such a peaceful time of year. People are friendlier. Families and friends get to reconnect. How about you?"

"Christmas or art?" Sara asked.

"Both," Jake said, eyeing a painting of a carriage being drawn through the snow outside of a colonial home adorned with wreaths and candles.

"Christmas, I love. It is all about family for me. Almost every weekend in December we have some sort of gathering going on. Of course it all culminates at Grandma's for Christmas Eve and Christmas Day," Sara said. "Art… I like people. Not portraits, but people in some aspect of life. I like the painting to tell a story. Couples in love, families spending time together, communities gathering."

Jake smiled. Pointing to a painting of people walking alongside rainy streets.

Sara's eyes brightened, "There are lots of stories in this one. There is a younger man helping an older woman across the street. Probably his grandmother. Here is a man and woman arm in arm under an umbrella. Pretty sure they are husband and wife. I think they're in love. And here, a mom holds her daughter's hand while the child is mid-air, eyeing the puddle below. Her yellow galoshes will withstand the splash but I don't thinks mom's high-heels are going to fare so well."

"It is a fun one. Reminds me of an adult version of picture books I used to scour growing up," Jake said.

Sara smiled, "The one where you had to find the snail in each scene? I loved those books!"

"Oh, I really like this one," Jake said standing in front of an American piece depicting a Christmas village. Families shopped while others ice skated on a nearby rink or stood in line for hot cocoa or a wreath. "I kind of wish life was still like that."

"I don't know," Sara said. "Do people even want that anymore? Simple and old fashioned? They want modern, fresh, progressive."

"Do they?" Jake asked as they rounded the last corner and said goodbye to the gallery owner.

As they returned to the sidewalk to make their way back to the coffee shop, they passed several smiling faces and friendly waves. "Simple life seems to suit Wintergreen just fine," Jake smiled.

"Simple… and quiet… doesn't pay the bills," Sara sighed.

Passing Sara's parent's accounting firm, the door burst open, and a man nearly ran into them.

"Sara! And Jake. Fancy running into you two," the man said.

"Hello, Shawn. We were gathering ideas for Grandma's shop," Sara said.

"Oh, nice. Need some help?" Shawn asked, his eyes never leaving Sara's.

Sara rubbed her arms as the winter weather dropped a few more degrees as the early sunset neared. Jake stood back for several moments, watching Shawn and his obvious interest in Sara. As Sara shivered, Jake removed his coat and draped it over Sara's shoulders. Sara pulled the lapels tighter around her.

"Don't you need this?" she asked.

Jake shrugged her off.

"I'm sorry. I should have… Thanks Jake," Shawn said. "What are you guys working on? I'd be happy to help."

Sara opened her mouth to speak when Shawn's phone rang. Disgruntled, he reached into his pocket, "I'm sorry. I need to get this. We'll catch up later."

Shawn disappeared down the street, leaving Jake and Sara once more on their own. "Come on, let's get you something warm to drink. I know a place," Jake said.

"Do you?" Sara raised an eyebrow.

"Best in town," Jake beamed as he led her back towards the Coffee Corner.

"Hey, weren't you and Shawn an item in high school?" Jake asked.

"That was a long time ago," Sara laughed. "I'm surprised a senior would notice a couple of freshmen."

Jake's cheeks reddened, "You weren't just any freshmen."

"Oh?" Sara stopped and spun to face Jake head on.

"Yeah, you were the granddaughter of some of the best cocoa in town," Jake grinned.

Sara elbowed him in the ribs, "I may have had a little crush on you… back then."

"Hmm," Jake grunted as he held the coffee shop door open for her.

Bea poked her head out of the back to see who had entered the café.

"I've got it, Grandma!" Sara called.

"Just finishing up inventory. Kind of scared to order too much," Bea said as she retreated into the office.

Scrambling around the bar, Sara made a couple of steaming lattes.

"So, how come you didn't continue down the art path?" Jake asked.

"I wanted to keep going with it. I was even willing to come back and work with Grandma while I tried to make a go of it. Figure things out. I had so much pressure from my family to do something 'more practical'. I eventually gave in. So, I enrolled in Saint Mary's and got my accounting degree," Sara said.

"Will it make you happy?" Jake asked.

Sara took a long moment to respond, "I don't know. Maybe my parents are right. I can always do art for fun and support it from holding down a normal job."

"Well, I hope you find your happy, whatever that is," Jake said. Glancing at his watch, he stood up, "I should get going."

"Thank you for everything today, Jake," Sara said.

"My pleasure. I had fun," Jake said.

"Me too," Sara smiled. She watched as Jake filtered out of the coffee shop.

Ten

Jake stopped in front of Tracy's hotel. Climbing out, he wandered into the lobby and scanned for her. The chime at the bank of elevators caught his attention and he spun to spy the guests who streamed out.

He felt as anxious for the evening as he did on their first date. When the last guest had exited the elevator without Tracy among them, he couldn't tell if he was relieved for another moment to collect himself or disappointed.

A second chime broke the wonder as Tracy stepped out. Her blonde hair cascaded down one shoulder draping over a blue cable-knit dress. Jake smiled as he reached out to her and kissed her cheek.

"What?" Tracy asked, a wary tone staining her voice.

"My parents are going to love you," Jake said, taking her coat from her arms and helping her slide into it.

"Am I dressed okay? You said we were having dinner in, right?"

Jake nodded, "You're perfect. I'll be honest, I was afraid you were going to be overdressed for the occasion."

Tracy wrinkled her nose, "I tend to do that a bit, don't I?"

"It's alright. It's part of your charm," Jake said.

Tracy shot him a look, not sure whether she had just received a true compliment or not.

Helping her into the truck, Jake jogged around and slid into the driver's seat. With a big breath, he gripped the wheel, "Ready for this?"

"As I'll ever be," Tracy offered a half smile.

Jake could see that she was nervous.

"My parents… My parents are like friendly golden retrievers. They are happy to like everyone," Jake assured her.

Tracy scowled, "Did you just compare your parents to dogs?"

"I just meant they're friendly. They'll like you. You have nothing to be nervous about," Jake said.

Tracy breathed deeply, "I almost wish we were meeting at a restaurant. Neutral, formal, some simple polite banter over a dim candle lit table."

Jake squeezed Tracy's hand, "It will be fine."

Tracy settled into her seat as she watched Wintergreen flow by. "How was your meeting with… Sara?"

Jake subconsciously shifted in his seat, "It went fine. The café is a bit too small for us to take on as a client. I have known her grandmother for years. I'd like to see if I couldn't help in some way. The shop could really use it."

"Not sure if Daddy would like you spending time on a marketing project outside of the firm," Tracy said. Her voice softened, "But it sounds like the right thing to do. You are always looking to help people. It's sweet."

Jake shot Tracy a surprised look, "Thanks."

Pulling in front of his parent's house, Jake hopped out of the truck, He scurried around, nearly slipping on a patch of ice to reach Tracy's door and open it for her.

Holding an arm out, he held her steady as she stretched a high-heeled shoe to the thin layer of snow that accumulated along the curb. Stepping up onto the sidewalk, they surveyed the house. It was festive, adorned in classic string Christmas lights along the roofline. Candles glowed in each window and a large wreath with a brilliant red bow hung on the front door.

"Charming," Tracy said.

Jake couldn't help but wonder whether Tracy's comment was literal or cheeky. Tracy's parents' home would have taken up an entire block in Wintergreen and was professionally decorated. He was already nervous about the dinner, encouraging him to overanalyze each step of the process.

Walking Tracy up to the front step, he raised his hand to knock on the door, "Well, here we go."

Before the third rap, the door swung wide to reveal a squealing woman with arms wide and a curious man peering over her shoulder. "I'm so glad you came!" Jake's mother said, giving Jake a hug and then she studied Tracy.

"Mom, Dad… this is Tracy. Tracy, my folks," Jake introduced.

Tracy held out a nervous hand but was reeled in for a gut squeezing hug. She looked at Jake with wide eyes before she was released. Jake's father accepted her hand with a warm shake.

"Let's get you out of the cold," Jake's father said motioning them inside and shutting the door.

Jake took Tracy's coat from his father and hung it up in the foyer closet. His mother led them to the kitchen where a spread of meats and cheeses was laid out. Tracy glanced at it and shot Jake a look. His mother caught it.

"She doesn't eat meat or dairy," Jake said.

"I do like olives, though," Tracy perked up, stabbing an olive from a bowl with a toothpick.

"Oh, good," Jake's mother said, relieved.

Jake sniffed and looked around the kitchen, "It smells good in here."

"I tried my hand at fettuccini alfredo… with chicken," Jake's mother's face fell from proud to distraught. "Oh, dear."

Jake placed his arm around Tracy, "It's alright. I see you have some French bread. We'll make a simple tapenade out of these olives, and we'll make sure she doesn't go home hungry. I should have been more clear."

"I see you have chocolate for dessert. I definitely won't go home hungry. Thank you, Mrs. Myers," Tracy said.

Jake's mother beamed, "Thank you, Tracy. Next time, we'll make sure to set a proper menu."

Swatting her son on the arm and delivering a scolding scowl, she returned to her pleasant expression, "What *do* you like to eat?"

"I know so many people fear carbs, but I am a sucker for them. Breads and pastas and… cake and cookies," Tracy blushed.

Jake's mother gave Tracy a solid once over, appreciating her slender figure, "I wish I could eat like that. I'd give up meat and cheese too!"

Together, they laughed as Jake's father returned with a bottle of white wine in hand, "Jake, would you do the honors?"

Jake accepted the bottle and opened it while his father pulled out a stool near the counter for Tracy to sit. "I'm glad we could finally meet you. Jake has told us so much about you."

"He has, has he?" Tracy asked.

"You work for a non-profit?" Jake's father asked.

Tracy nodded, "An old friend of my father's runs it. He needed my help in planning events for the donors. Keep them happy and the dollars flowing, as my father puts it."

"He's quite the businessman, your father," Jake's dad suggested.

"He is. He works hard. He hires good people," Tracy cast a smile toward Jake.

"So, what does the Banks family do for fun?" Jake's mother asked.

"With Daddy's schedule, vacations have always been a way for us to catch up and reconnect. Europe, Aruba, Fiji…" Tracy said. "The past few years, solid internet has been a parameter, so somewhere close to civilization."

Jake's father handed Tracy a glass of wine, "And you get the holidays, right?"

"Sometimes," Tracy nodded. "The holiday season and the start of the new year have always been a busy time. So we sometimes just get a day or two before Daddy is back in the office. Jake has started to see that, haven't you?"

Jake nodded, "I have had a steady stream of rush projects lately. Mostly boiler plate stuff, so not so bad."

"You'll be here for Christmas, though, right?" Jake's mother asked, a tinge of concern in her voice.

"I was going to ask Jake, if he would join us for Christmas this year," Tracy interjected.

Jake's head turned sharply to Tracy.

She flushed, "I hadn't had a chance to ask you yet. Daddy was hoping you would come home with us after his business in Wintergreen was finished."

"I see. I mean, I can consider it," Jake said, shooting a wary glance toward his mother.

"Well, let's see if dinner is ready," Jake's father broke up the conversation. "I think I overheard something about a quick tapenade."

Jake nodded, "Grab me a cutting board and I'll get it ready."

Sitting back, Jake took in the dinner conversation as almost a third-party observer. Tracy was peppered with questions, most of which she handled with grace and answers which seemed to please his parents. The table even erupted into laughter on more than one occasion, if once or twice at Jake's expense.

When they were finished with their meal, Jake's father offered Tracy the remnants of the wine bottle while Jake rose to help his mother clear the dishes.

Placing a stack of plates on the counter, Jake's mother turned and whispered, "She's lovely, Jake."

"Thanks, Mom. I'm sure she was nervous to meet you and Dad."

"You should have warned me about her diet," his mother scolded.

"I know. I know. I've been busy and didn't even know if we were going to be able to sneak in a visit," Jake shrugged, running water in the sink to rinse the plates.

"She certainly is attractive," Jake's mother said.

Jake laughed, "She is."

"And charming," his mother added. She paused as she accepted plates from Jake and set them in the dishwasher, "You think she may be the one?"

Jake looked out at the moon swept, snow-sprinkled backyard, "I don't know, Mom. I'm not really thinking that way right now."

"*She* is," his mother snapped.

Jake looked surprised, "You think?"

"Why do you suppose going home with them for Christmas is on the docket?"

"I… I don't know. Didn't really cross my mind. Just figured she wanted a date for their annual Christmas Eve party," Jake admitted.

"It's in how she looks at you."

"What are you two jabbering about?" Jake's father asked as he brought the empty wine glasses into the kitchen.

"I was just going to offer Tracy some tea," Jake's mother said.

Tracy looked at Jake and then nodded, "I would love some."

Jake reached into the tea chest and produced a varietal that he knew she would like while his mother put a pot of water to boil.

"Thank you for a wonderful dinner," Tracy said, placing a hand on Jake's back.

"Well, I am sorry you had to have a plan B option," Jake's mother said.

"I didn't mind. Especially with such lovely company," Tracy said.

Jake placed cups on the counter and when the water was ready, he poured them full.

"It's snowing again!" Tracy said as the silvery flakes of snow flashed past the window.

"Why don't we take the tea outside? Mom, you still have blankets?" Jake asked.

"Right by the door," his mother nodded.

Leading her to the back door, Jake paused to grab a blanket and stepped out onto the back porch. The white snow picked up just enough reflection from ambient light to provide them with a peaceful backdrop.

Settling onto a bench, Jake spread the blanket around them as they cupped their warm mugs of tea.

"This is nice," Tracy breathed.

"And you survived dinner," Jake said.

"Your parents are sweet," Tracy said.

"Wasn't sure how it would go. Things have seemed a bit, tense lately," Jake observed.

Tracy looked at Jake in the modest blue light afforded by the dusting of snow which had just begun to properly cover the lawn. "I was nervous about this trip," she confessed.

"Nervous? We've been across the globe together," Jake said.

"Across the globe there is a sense of anonymity. No one knows you, no one really cares. We can relax and be ourselves," Tracy said.

"Wintergreen is pretty relaxing," Jake chuckled. "It's a pretty quiet town."

"It's a small town. *Your* small town. Everyone knows you. Everyone watches us like we are on a stage," Tracy said.

"I don't know about that. I mean, sure, I know most people…" Jake said.

"People you have a history with," Tracy said. "It's exhausting trying to keep up and be 'on' all the time. I don't know how you do it, going where everyone knows you."

"They are pretty friendly around here. I don't think anyone is judging. Outside of my parents, maybe," Jake teased.

"Even in the city, when you are at work, I need to get away. Find a place to hide, at least for a while," Tracy said. "I go to the library sometimes because I know none of my friends will be there. I started volunteering to read to the kids for story hour."

"I didn't know that. Why didn't you tell me?" Jake asked.

"You've been busy at work trying to get your promotion. I have just sort of slipped into the background. I'm okay with it. Well, sort of okay with it. I think sometimes it gets the best of me and I act out. I like being here. I'm sorry," Tracy said, looking sheepish over her teacup.

"I'm sorry you felt I had put you in the background," Jake said. "That isn't fair."

"Pretty sure between me and Daddy pushing you, we asked for it," Tracy admitted.

"Well, you deserve better," Jake said.

"When you get your promotion and we are back in the city where we belong, it will be better," Tracy said.

Jake's eyes shifted to the snowy backyard, his voice nearly absent, "Yeah."

Eleven

Jake felt a flutter of excitement as he pulled alongside the Coffee Corner. Getting out of his truck, he gave a wave to the travel agent who was arriving for work.

Holding the door open for a customer, Jake walked into the coffee shop. "Good morning, ladies!" he called to Bea and Sara who were finishing drinks for a couple waiting at the end of the coffee bar.

Bea gave Sara a quick nod. Taking off her apron and hanging it up behind the bar, Sara directed Jake to a table that had several wrapped items stacked on it.

"I've got something for you to try, Jake. If you don't like it, I'll make your usual," Bea called as she handed two cups to the couple and thanked them for coming in.

"Sounds intriguing," Jake said as he sat at the table with Sara. Scanning the contents of the table, he asked, "What's all this?"

"My homework," Sara said. Spinning her tablet around for him to see, she tapped a button. "Here is my first stab at a logo for the café. What do you think?"

Jake studied the image. It had a classic font dressed in gold. Silhouettes of a couple leaning over a table with steaming mugs of coffee were draped by the words *Coffee Corner* in gold font with *A Genuine Coffee Experience* and Downtown Wintergreen set below.

"Sara, this is fantastic. I think it sets the idea that the Coffee Corner is different. There is something special. It's classic. The silhouettes tell the story that the experience here is about people as much as it is the coffee. I like it," Jake said.

"Really?" Sara asked, her eyes wide.

"I don't think my team could have done any better," Jake said. "Send me a copy and I'll have stickers done by the end of the day."

Sara bounced with excitement. The moment abated as her eyes were drawn to the large items wrapped in craft paper between them.

"What do we have here?" Jake asked.

Sara nervously chewed her lip. With a sigh, she stuck a finger in the corner of one of the items and slid it between the tape and the paper, "The rest of my homework… but *only* until we find suitable replacements!"

"Sara, these are great!" Jake exclaimed, hoisting the first item in front of him. A painting of the town gathered around the tree in the park with strings of lights and garland laced around its branches gave Jake an instant sense of nostalgia.

The second was of Main Street in full Christmas regalia and a coating of fresh snow clinging to branches and awnings. The third depicted a family burdened with Christmas packages outside an elegantly decorated house.

"I have others, but these were the closest to what I saw you looking at when we visited the gallery," Sara said, her voice dripping with meekness.

"Wow, these… these tell the story we are trying to tell. Christmas isn't about fast and flashy and new, it's about tradition and family and memories. These are beautiful," Jake said.

"You really think so?" Sara wrinkled her nose.

With a hearty nod, Jake said, "Absolutely."

"Aren't those great?" Bea said as she delivered a mug to each of them.

"They are. I knew she was good, but these…" Jake swooned.

Setting the mugs on the table, Bea said, "I couldn't be prouder."

Jake eyed the frothy white concoction with a sprinkle of nutmeg floating on top, "What do we have here?"

"A new recipe," Bea said. Rocking back on her heels, she said, "I have had a little time to play around while things have been slow."

"I see," Jake said. Lifting the cup, he took a sip. "This is good, Bea. It's creamy, with a light sweetness but offset by the nutmeg. It tastes like Christmas. Not a peppermint mocha or pumpkin spice smack you in the face, but a subtle, memory-inducing taste of Christmas. What is it?"

"It is my version of a Tom and Jerry. Our family has them on Christmas Eve as we gather in the living room," Bea said.

Jake's eyes widened, "*That's* what it is. I haven't had one of these in years. Oh, it brings back memories. My grandparents used to make these- of course, virgin ones for us kids."

Bea chuckled, "Well, these are all virgin ones here. I experimented a bit to get the flavors right without the brandy. Those have coffee in them. I can make them without, and I think they taste even more authentic."

"Grandma, this is delicious. It does taste like Christmas. This is brilliant!" Sara said as she hoisted her mug in the air.

Jake brought his mug to the center of the table, "Cheers!"

Sara joined her mug with his and they each took a sip. As she set her cup down, she cocked her head as Jake had a grin on his face. "What?"

"You uh, you got a little froth…" Jake said as he leaned across the table and gently wiped Sara's nose with his thumb.

Sara reeled back a bit, "Oh!"

Looking sheepish, she shrank back and slipped out of her chair, "I'll… I'll just go clean up real quick."

As Sara disappeared, Bea studied her granddaughter's reaction and smiled. Turning her attention to Jake, she raised a brow, "Did I hear a spot on the Christmas station this morning?"

Jake grinned, "You did. I hope it was okay. I have a few friends down at the station that owe me some favors."

"I don't know too many people that listen to the radio anymore, but I liked it," Bea said.

"Oh, the same broadcast is online too. Like all businesses, they have learned to adapt," Jake said. With his face dropping more seriously and Sara still in the lady's room, he leaned forward. "So, what *is* going on, Bea? I get the slow down with Java Universe being open, but it shouldn't be so dire so quickly, should it?"

Bea took a long moment before sitting down and sharing, "Before I knew about all the changes, I was looking at expanding.

Downtown prices started to go down and I thought it was the right time. I purchased the space next door. More seating, more room to add in a bigger pastry bar and offer pressed sandwiches at lunchtime."

Bea scanned the room with most tables empty, "Seems like a silly idea now, huh?"

Jake's eyes followed Bea's before connecting. Shaking his head, he said, "Bea, I'm sorry. I assume no one in the process tried to steer you away or at least come clean with the bigger plans for the commerce center?"

"No," Bea shook her head. "The mayor even encouraged me. I got the keys two weeks ago and I have been afraid to go inside. No one even knows I made the purchase, save for the realtor, the mayor and the bank. Not even Sara."

Jake reached his hand out and placed it on top of Bea's. "The purchase is final?"

Bea nodded, "It is. Funny. The idea of expanding my business will likely be what ultimately sinks it. I don't want Sara to worry."

Jake straightened as Sara approached. His eyes alerted Bea that her granddaughter was rejoining them.

"What is going on here?" Sara asked.

"Just decided where to hang these amazing paintings," Jake said. "You should print little placards with your name and a price for them, if you are willing to sell them."

Sara let out an incredulous laugh, "I don't think anyone is going to pay money for my work."

"Don't sell yourself short. These are beautiful," Jake said, eying the canvases that were lined against the wall. "Come on, let's put them up!"

Rising from his seat, he looked at Bea, "You have a hammer around here somewhere?"

"In the backroom," Bea nodded. "On the shelf to the left as you walk in."

Jake walked as though he was on a mission, making a beeline for the storeroom.

Bea looked at her granddaughter.

"What?" Sara scowled.

Bea smiled a knowing smile.

Jake returned quickly with a hammer and some nails that he found. Scanning the room, he smiled as he spaced the paintings out where they would get the most view from people walking by. Tapping in nails for each corner of the canvases and measuring to ensure they were straight, he hung the art.

Taking a step back, he was flanked on either side by Bea and Sara. With a grin, he asked, "What do you think?"

"I think I should have thought of this a long time ago," Bea breathed, taken aback by her granddaughter's art on her walls.

"I don't see how these will bring in more business for Grandma," Sara shrugged.

"Just another reason for us to talk about the Coffee Corner and a reason for people to visit," Jake said. Walking up to each one, he took a picture with his phone.

"What are you doing that for?" Sara asked.

"One, capture them before they disappear," Jake said. "But, also, to post them on social media."

Sara crossed her arms and frowned.

"Come on. They are Christmassy. They are amazing and done by a Wintergreen artist," Jake said.

"Done by a Wintergreen barista soon-to-be accountant," Sara huffed.

Jake screwed his face into a twist, "Yeah, doesn't have the same ring. I'm going to stick with artist. Hashtag: Coffee Corner. Hashtag: A Genuine Coffee Experience Hashtag: Christmas Downtown Wintergreen."

"Whatever, you're the marketing guru," Sara sighed.

Glancing at his watch, Jake snapped his head up, "I need to go. Can I place another large order for my office?" Jake asked.

Bea put her hands on her hips, "Jake, you don't have to…"

"What?" Jake protested. "They drink a lot of coffee and I can't have them drinking that Java Universe gruel!"

Bea shook her head. With a glance toward Sara, she asked, "You wanna help?"

Sara nodded, slipping the apron back over her head. Her eyes locked on Jake's, her look expressing her gratefulness.

Twelve

The office parking lot became more sparse further into December and the holiday season. Jake noticed that some offices had begun closing for the holidays. The marketing firm was an exception. With the production teams scrambling to complete the projects he had designed, the energy only seemed to heighten.

As Jake stepped into the office, his armload of coffees was almost expected. Co-workers greeted him happily and selected one of two Christmas flavored drinks from the carriers that he toted in.

A glance across the office at an expectant branch manager Frank and an anxious sales executive Jeff waving him towards the conference room with frantic motions teased what kind of day he was walking into. Setting the drink trays on Carol's desk, he asked, "Mind sharing these?"

"As long as I get to select one of those. Looks like a long day for you and I," Carol agreed.

Jake offered a thankful nod and strode into the conference room, aware that he still had his jacket on and a bag slung over his shoulder.

"Jake, good for you to join us," Frank said with a stern glance at his watch.

Jake cocked his head, "Did I miss a meeting invite? I don't recall accepting one."

"No meeting. It just isn't like you. I'm unaccustomed to having to flip on the lights myself. You usually beat me to work," Frank said.

"It doesn't matter. We're all here. Well, almost all here," Jeff said as he craned his neck looking out into the office. "Henry… are you going to join us?"

Jake scanned the room trying to take the temperature. Jeff was always excitable, but he had never seen him quite this worked up. He could tell Frank was excited as well, but he held his demeanor with stronger decorum.

Henry strolled into the room as he always did. He had a steady stride, chest out, and an even smile on his face that didn't necessarily read happy. Seeing Jake, still draped in his wool coat, Henry said, "Oh, good. We're all here. Now we can begin. Jeff has some exciting news. Jeff…?"

Jeff eagerly stepped up to the table, "I got the big one!" Looking at each set of eyes gathered in the room like a father anticipating his children opening the largest package on Christmas morning, "Java Universe! I got Java Universe!"

Clearly, Henry and Frank had already heard the news but cheered Jeff as though it had just been revealed. Jake felt a flip in his stomach as he heard the words stream from Jeff's mouth. "They want a campaign from our crack marketing team. That's you, Jake. And they want it by Christmas Eve. If they like what they see with the first ad, we will get a national campaign contract for the entire new year!"

Frank looked at Jake, "We are going to need ad copy, radio spots, digital media, television, billboards- the works. And not just for the Wintergreen market or even the country, but this could take us international."

"This is the big time, Jake. This campaign paints a bright future for you and Jeff. For all of us," Henry said.

"It's, uh. going to be quite the honor to put this together," Jake swallowed. "Nice work, Jeff."

"Ah, the work has just begun, buddy. Don't let me down. I'm counting on that genius brain of yours!" Jeff said, slapping Jake on the shoulder.

"Frank and Jeff will fill you in on the client parameters. Sorry, this will make your holiday season a bit more hectic. It will for all of us. I'm heading back to corporate to spin up the national production teams. I had wanted to spend some time with you and Tracy, but that will have to wait. We'll have lots of time to catch up in the new year," Henry said as he looked Jake square in the eyes. "Well, I am off to catch my flight. I look forward to seeing what you come up with, gentlemen."

Henry exited, leaving Frank and Jeff to hold court. Jake set his bag on an empty conference room chair and draped his wool outer coat in an adjacent chair before slipping into one himself. Pulling out his laptop and his notebook, he set up to hear Jeff's project requirements.

"Alright, here's the pitch. None of that warm fuzzy, greeting card stuff here, Jake," Jeff began. Spreading his hands in the air to frame his message, he said, "Modern. Fast. Convenient. We're talking Jetsons stuff. No waiting. No mind-numbing talk with a long line of customers or with those coffee people…"

"Baristas," Jake said.

"Right, baristas. Anyways, they want a cohesive line that runs through all of their campaign stops that is as consistent here in Wintergreen as it is in New York City or Topeka. That is their brand. Solid. Consistent. No hassle," Jeff said.

"What do you think, Jake? Have a few ideas?" Frank asked.

"I can think of a few," Jake muttered. "Let me take all of this to my office and give it some solid thought before I go off the cuff."

Frank nodded, "Fair enough. But we need some pitches and we need them quickly. Henry wants to produce some sample spots before the Christmas Eve pitch."

"Counting on you, Jake," Jeff looked him square in the eyes before releasing a cheeky grin. "We've got this! Remember, streamlined. To the point. Fast and bother-free, just like they are."

"Got it," Jake nodded. Grabbing his things haphazardly in his arms, he shuffled out of the conference room. Shooting a desperate glance toward Carol, he ambled toward his office.

Dumping his load, he sorted it all out and assembled himself properly at his desk. His notebook and laptop were centered in front of him.

Carol bounced into the room. With a wince, she said, "I wanted to warn you, but they were all about the surprise news. Yaaaay!" Carol shook her fists in feigned excitement.

"I do love a good surprise," Jake mumbled.

"So, what's the big news?" Carol asked.

"Java Universe."

Carol's eyes went wide, "That's huge! Wow! It says a lot they are leaving it in the hands of the Wintergreen team. I'm surprised they aren't bringing it to corporate."

"Production will come from corporate. I think this is like a final exam. For all of us," Jake said.

"The long-promised promotions?" Carol asked.

"And moves to the city," Jake said.

Carol's lips tightened before musing, "Big city, big paychecks."

"Yeah," Jake nodded.

Carol's eyes brightened, "You can do some amazing things with this!"

"I could," Jake laughed. "But not if I want to keep my job. I believe the word Jeff used was 'Jetsons'."

"I like the Jetsons," Carol countered.

"Yeah, but coffee should be warm, cozy, social. Cold, impersonal and on the fly belongs to energy drinks and fast food," Jake said.

"Coffee is fast food these days, Jake. I have no doubt you will come up with something wonderful within the client's expectations. You always do," Carol said. Her eyes seemed to see that Jake was yet to be convinced. "What?"

"And the entire campaign with production samples needs to be presented by Christmas Eve," Jake said.

Carol's shoulders sank, "Of course it does."

"Well," Jake flexed his fingers together and stretched his arms out in front of him. "I'd better get to work or we'll have to let Santa know to deliver our gifts under the fake tree in the office foyer."

"Let me know what I can do to help," Carol said.

Jake looked up from his laptop, "You know what? Let's go on a field trip."

"A field trip?"

"Let's see what this Java Universe is all about," Jake said.

Jake pulled his truck into the busy shopping center drive. Waiting for several rushing cars to drive by, he edged his way in line.

Tapping the steering wheel, he suddenly wheeled out of line and parked.

Carol shot him a look.

"Let's get the whole experience. I mean, I get the drive-through line. Headset-wearing Java Universians walking out to the cars in line to process their orders even faster... speed, organized, in and out. But what is the Java Universe *experience?*" Jake asked.

Carol gave a quick shrug, "Guess we'll find out. I've never actually been in."

Jake led the way, opening the door for Carol only to have a man brush by, coffee in hand and phone pressed to his ear mid-conversation. "You're welcome and Merry Christmas," Jake called as he held his hand out for Carol to step inside.

The inside of the coffee shop was like stepping into a science fiction movie set. Everything was neat and orderly. Modern lighting and gleaming metal shelves displayed Java Universe merchandise. Like outside, a headset-clad employee stepped up to take their order. Staring blankly with digital pen in hand, the young lady waited.

"Oh, our orders... Let's see what you've got..." Jake craned his neck at the menu. It was neatly organized and easy to follow. "You have anything seasonal?"

"Seasonal?" the coffee house employee asked.

"Yeah, you know, Christmassy. Like egg nog or something?" Jake asked.

The woman looked cross, "We have our winter menu, if you like pumpkin spice. And of course, our famous peppermint mocha Frappuccino. Which would you like?"

Jake frowned as the woman bounced anxiously eyeing the customers beginning to form a line behind Jake. He considered his options out loud, "I'm not much of a pumpkin spice guy, or mocha… Can you do a vanilla latte with a splash of peppermint?"

The woman let out a sigh and tapped in his order. Her eyes met with Carol's who blurted, "I'll have the pumpkin spice!"

Appreciating Carol's response, the coffee house employee said, "Your order is number 132."

"Thank you. I'm Jake and this is Carol," Jake smiled.

The woman looked at Jake with a blank expression before forcing a weak smile, "132. Next!"

"Merry Christmas!" Jake smiled" but the woman was already looking over his shoulder and entering the order for the irritated customer behind him. Carol looked at Jake with a mixed expression on her face.

As Jake stood by the section of the counter dedicated to receiving their coffee orders, he gazed around the room.

"What?" Carol asked.

"No Christmas decorations."

"They have snowflakes," Carol shrugged.

"No Christmas music."

"They have peppy pop music, if a bit loud," Carol said.

Jake scanned the shelves of Java Universe souvenirs. He eyed how many customers had Java Universe travel mugs, bags and even phone cases.

"Number 132!"

Jake continued surveying the room, "There are hardly any tables."

"Number 132!"

"That's us," Carol said, tugging on Jake's arm.

"Right. Do I go by that all day or just until I receive my ration of coffee?" Jake teased.

Carol punched him in the arm and delivered a hoarse whisper, "You are going to have to find the bright spot!"

Jake accepted the coffees and offered a smile at an attendant who abruptly turned away. "Merry Christmas!" he called.

The attendant, along with a few other coffee house employees paused for a moment. They turned their heads in near unison as the attendant returned in a low voice, *"Happy holidays."*

"Right…" Jake said as the employees instantly snapped back into their duties.

Nudging Carol toward one of the empty tables, he asked, "Wanna have a seat?"

Carol looked around at the stream of coffee goers moving like a conveyer belt through one door and out the other. "I'm not sure that is a good thing. You might get us thrown out and off the account," Carol sneered.

Jake laughed. Suddenly his eyes brightened and he snapped his fingers, "You know what? I figured it out!"

Carol looked up at him unsure if she wanted the answer, particularly given they were still in the Java Universe environment.

"It reminds me of an amusement park. Like when you get off the ride and they force through the gift shop? Its theme is fun, it wants to be fun but… it really kind of isn't," Jake said, looking over his shoulder as he heard the order numbers being called out were already up to 156.

"Yep, we're out of here," Carol tugged Jake on the arm and led him toward the door.

Taking a sip of his drink, he swished it in his mouth and considered it as one would while wine tasting. As he started to remark, Carol gave him a stronger tug, "Nope!"

Jake willingly followed as he studied his Java Universe cup with its highly identifiable trademark purple lid.

Once outside, Carol said, "Alright, let me have it!"

Jake wrinkled his nose, "It's coffee but almost like forced. A charred hammer hitting my head with a growl, 'I'm coffee'. The vanilla is largely lost, though expressed in an almost medicinal aftertaste and the peppermint is layered in with the nuance of a lawn care guy spraying fertilizer. Other than that, it's pretty good."

Carol scowled, "It's coffee. It tastes like coffee. I mean, the pumpkin spice is classic. It's pumpkin spice."

Jake accepted the cup that Carol held up for him. He drew in the aroma from the small hole in the lid and handed it back as he considered it. "Reminds me of a drug store candle in October."

Carol scanned the parking lot as they neared Jake's truck. "We better get you out of here!"

"Well, I think we understand the vibe a lot better now, don't you think?" Jake asked, his tone not concealing his disappointment.

"It was fast," Carol winced as she shrugged her shoulders.

Thirteen

Jake settled in behind his desk. Scanning his notes and leafing through the photos he snapped of his and Carol's trip to Java Universe. To his right sat a blank storyboard. His eyes shifted, trying to come up with something that would send an enticing message to caffeine seekers.

Plopping his head in his hands, he knew in his heart, the contents of the cup weren't what the local coffee shop was about. It was about the people, the atmosphere, the experience.

Carol popped her head in. Seeing Jake buried in his hands, she stepped in.

"Making progress?" she asked meekly.

Slowly, Jake lifted his head from his hands, "Yeah. Sure. I mean, I think we understand the Java Universe vibe a lot better, now, right?"

Carol winced and shrugged, "It was fast."

"Number 132…" Jake muttered.

"Yeah, well, you have to guess that appeals to some people. Java Universe is in all fifty states, fourteen countries. They must be doing something right," Carol said.

Jake thought about all the Coffee Corners that were booted to the curb with each Java Universe grand opening.

"Here's the point. Java Universe isn't for everyone. You need to appeal to those it is for and allow those who haven't visited it yet to form their own opinion. That's fair, right?" Carol said.

Looking into Carol's eyes, Jake let out a smile, "Yes. You're right."

Carol beamed and swayed back in forth with her illuminating message.

Jake's face fell and he ran his fingers through his hair, "Any idea what that appeal is?"

"It's fast. You can be in a half-a-sleep daze and not care who's in line or taking your order because, frankly, they don't seem to care either," Carol said.

Jake laughed. "I'm not sure I can spin that into a message. Alright, the whole thing is built on speed and technology. The commuters who just want a copy of coffee and can't pull out of the fast lane long enough to swing to the Coffee Corner."

Carol froze. Her head turned slowly at the realization. Looking directly at Jake, she asked, "Is that the real issue? You don't want to bury your friends at the Coffee Corner?"

"I don't like to see any small business, mom and pop shop shuttered because a corporate giant comes to town and guts them," Jake admitted.

"It's a free market," Carol shrugged. "The little guys need to step up their game and fight back. It's not the giant's job to tread lightly. You need to share the giant's message and give it all you've got because that's the job you signed up for."

Jake stared blankly at Carol's strong and true message.

Carol laughed, softening the mood, "Besides, if you stop and buy coffees for the office each day, you'll single-handedly keep them in business."

Letting out a laugh, Jake said, "Thank you for the reset. And you're right. I will build the Java Universe campaign that they deserve."

"I know you will. And it will be great. Remember that gutter leaf system commercial with the family playing in the leaves? We got fan mail. Over gutter covers! You've got this!" Carol said.

Jake nodded and watched Carol leave.

Tapping his pencil on the desk, Jake pulled out a second storyboard. On the first, he scribbled *Java Universe*. On the second, he wrote *Coffee Corner*. They were two different worlds. His job wasn't to have one beat the other, but allow them to stand on their own merits.

With a deep breath, he began working on an impactful campaign.

Hours ticked by, with Jake hardly noticing the time. A knock on his office door broke his attention. Looking up he saw Frank standing in the doorway.

Quickly stuffing his Coffee Corner work under the pile of Java Universe spreads, he smiled and said, "Afternoon, Frank."

"Working hard, I see. Took a few knocks to get your attention," Frank said.

"This is a big deal, right?" Jake asked.

"Biggest our firm has ever had," Frank nodded. "I bumped into the developers of this business park, the same ones that put in the shopping center. They asked if they could meet with you and Jeff about putting a campaign together for them."

Jake's eyes went wide as he looked at the growing hill of papers and marketing slicks on his desk.

Frank waved his hands out in front of him and he laughed, "Don't worry. I told them it would be after the holidays. They were fine with that."

"Good," Jake breathed a sigh of relief. "Yeah, sounds great."

"Jeff is pretty excited about it. Could be another national campaign for us," Frank said. Tapping the door frame, he started to turn.

"Hey, Frank," Jake called.

His manager turned back.

With a slight squint, Jake asked, "About how many people would you say work out of this complex?"

Frank pursed his lips and shrugged, "In this building alone, I'd say roughly two hundred. Three buildings in the complex, though they aren't all full yet… Four hundred total maybe?"

"Thanks," Jake said.

His boss' eyes brightened, "Already thinking about the developer's campaign, aren't you? Atta boy. You are going to do great things with Banks Marketing, Jake."

Jake watched Frank walk away. Chewing his lip, he pulled out the Coffee Corner note page and jotted a new idea.

Fourteen

As Jake swung the door open to the Coffee Corner, he nodded and exchanged "Merry Christmas" with two couples as they streamed out. Entering the café, he was pleased to see several tables occupied by customers.

Bea and Sara perked up from behind the coffee bar, "Good afternoon, Jake!"

"Good afternoon, ladies," Jake returned. Holding up a large packet of stickers in his hand, he smiled, "I have something for you."

Sara raced from behind the bar leaving Bea to complete an order for a couple standing at the end of the bar. "Our stickers!" she squealed.

Nearly ripping the packet from Jake's hands, Sara studied the printed design. "I love these!"

"They'll look great printed on cups, too," Jake said.

Sara looked at Jake as she hugged the stickers, "Thank you."

"I'm glad to help," Jake smiled.

Scurrying back behind the coffee bar, Sara tore the packet open and readied them for use. Peeling a sticker off, she carefully placed it on a cup and held it up for her grandmother to see.

Bea's eyes grew wide, "Those are wonderful! Why haven't we thought of that before?"

"Because we make coffee. Really good coffee. That man makes…" Sara began.

"Stickers?" Jake quipped.

Sara's face fell serious, "Business owners' dreams come true."

"I only share the business' vision and message," Jake put his hands out in humility. "I'm a messenger."

"Well, for me, you are an angel. Look at this place," Bea said.

Jake scanned the shop, which was busier than it had been, "It's nice to see."

"But…" Sara sensed Jake was not as enthusiastic as her grandmother.

"How do today's receipts compare to last year's?" Jake asked.

Bea shuffled, her face almost in a pout.

Sara tapped a few buttons on the register terminal and said, "Down by… roughly sixty percent."

"We still have work to do," Jake acknowledged.

Bea sighed and nodded slowly, "You have ideas?"

"Some," Jake admitted. "How about I buy a round of coffees and I share? If you have a moment, that is."

Bea glanced toward the door which hadn't opened since the last guests left with their lattes, "We have a moment. What can I get you?"

"Surprise me," Jake said.

"Careful what you ask for," Sara quipped.

"You two get started, I'll be right over," Bea said.

Taking seats around a tall table, Sara leaned in and whispered as she looked directly into Jake's eyes, "Thank you."

Jake smiled and nodded. "I really am glad to help."

"Those radio spots and website banners seemed to help. Customers said they almost needed to be jolted into remembering the Coffee Corner was here," Sara said.

"Out of sight, out of mind. With so many businesses pulled out towards the highway, people don't drive by anymore. They aren't within walking distance. They aren't even the easiest exit off the freeway. The Coffee Corner needs to be a destination for them," Jake said.

Sara wrinkled her nose and spoke low so that her grandmother couldn't hear her, "But it's just coffee."

Jake smiled, "Is it?"

Sara looked confused.

"The stuff that comes out of the machine is just coffee. But if wine was just wine, California wouldn't need hundreds of wineries. Can Wintergreen sustain two coffee shops? We'll see. But what Bea creates out of her machine is… special," Jake said.

Bea placed cups in front of everyone, "Pulla latte."

Jake wrinkled his brow.

"Like the Finnish bread. Try it," Bea beamed.

Jake studied his mug. On top of the froth was a dusting of a soft powder and the mug itself was ringed with coarse sugar. Taking a sip, he looked like he might have been at a winery sampling a new varietal. His eyes opened, "This is good, Bea!"

"You like it?" Bea smiled. "My grandmother used to make this bread every Christmas. For me, the scent of cardamom and the baking of bread is as Christmas as pine needles and cinnamon."

"I like it. It's light. It's different, but very good," Jake said.

"She has been like a mad scientist since things have slowed down," Sara laughed.

Jake held the mug up, "This is one of my ideas. Your Tom and Jerry drink, this…"

"Pulla," Bea said.

"Pulla," Jake nodded. "These are special and unique. Sara, you said coffee is coffee. But is it?"

Sara looked confused, "So we advertise new drink recipes?"

"We can," Jake shrugged. His eyes widened. "It would be better to get these flavors into the hands of customers who have forgotten that the Coffee Corner is worth the detour into downtown. It's worth taking a moment to sit and actually *enjoy* their coffee. Have a meeting downtown. Go on a date downtown."

Both Bea and Sara smiled at how Jake embraced the essence of the little downtown coffee shop with such zeal.

"You paint such a picture. Not just of my lowly little coffee shop, but the downtown experience," Bea smiled.

"It's not just downtown. I have been to plenty of downtowns that I kind of don't particularly enjoy. *Wintergreen's* downtown is… something special. It is a hometown. I think the mayor and his council have forgotten about that. I think the people have forgotten that. We need to get them to remember," Jake said.

"Okay, so how do we do that?" Sara asked, cupping her mug in both hands.

"No one thing will work. It is a multifaceted effort. I had an idea with the Tom and Jerry drink and maybe now this Pulla latte- which is delicious, by the way. The radio spots, the digital ads are just the start. They are great reminders. We need to get the Coffee Corner coffee into their hands. Remind them in a cup what they are missing," Jake said.

Sara and Bea sat silently listening to Jake. Neither knew what direction he was pulling them in.

"The Commerce Center, where our office moved to. There are over four-hundred people who work there every day. Who slog to work through sleepy eyes to clock in for another day. How about you set up a stand, one day in each building, and hand out samples? Bea's unique flavors that they can't get anywhere else! And, you get four hundred advertisements walking around with those fancy new stickers of yours," Jake suggested, commanding Bea and Sara's attention like a storyteller over a campfire.

"How do we do that?" Bea asked.

"Each building has a kiosk. An attendant gives directions, redirects visitors when they are in the wrong building, and provides de facto security. They love treats. I would bet that if you bring them some treats from the Coffee Corner and tell them it is a gift from you to the patrons of the Commerce Center, they'll let you set up shop. If you have any issues, let me know. I just… I can't be directly connected," Jake said.

Sara cast Jake a questioning glance.

Bea broke in, "You think that will work?"

"It will grab people's attention. Remind them you are here and give them a taste of something they can only get if they visit the Coffee Corner. Will that get them to break their routines and make coming here a regular thing so that you can have a lasting, thriving business? No," Jake admitted.

Bea's face fell, "Then what can we do?"

Jake confidently smiled, "It's a step. We need to make the Coffee Corner and downtown a destination. I have an idea."

"Of course, you do," Sara laughed.

"We need events that people have to come downtown for and low and behold, the Coffee Corner will be conveniently open for," Jake said. Turning his gaze directly to Sara, he said, "We start with an art class."

"An art class?" Sara's look of confusion quickly melted into one of horror. "Oh, no. No, no, no, no!"

Jake cocked his head to suggest she should consider it.

"That would be wonderful! You can share your gift!" Bea said enthusiastically.

Sara looked through scowling eyes, "I'm not good enough to teach people. My stuff shouldn't be on these walls."

Bea's eyes grew wide and she spread her hands out to lay atop Sara's, "In all the bustle, I forgot to tell you. You sold one of your paintings!"

"What?" Sara looked incredulous. "To who? Which one? Was it Fred from the city council? Pretty sure he's nearly legally blind?"

Bea's eyes fell to the table and she shrugged, "I'm not sure. There was an envelope on the bar with a note requesting the painting of the town."

"It was Fred!" Sara gushed. "Or the mayor… or…"

The front door to the coffee shop opened. A man in a camel hair wool coat strode in.

"Or Shawn," Sara's final guess had a great air of confidence in it.

Jake watched as the man walked up to the table.

"Good afternoon, all!" Shawn beamed. "Jake, how're you doing? I'm surprised to see you here with the new office in the Commerce Center building and all."

"I find coming to downtown… worth the trip," Jake said.

"Well, visiting these two ladies certainly is," Shawn said. "And these winter scenes on the wall just make it feel like we're in an old postcard or one of those towns a little train runs through by the Christmas tree."

Jake laughed, "Well, said. Might have to hit you up for ad copy once in a while."

"Being on the mayor's team, I am here to serve," Shawn beamed as he tugged at his lapels. "You wouldn't mind me stealing these ladies for a moment? The mayor has a late meeting and I think it is going to run long."

"I've got it," Sara stood up and headed behind the bar. "You two keep plotting coffee shop domination."

Jake watched as Shawn followed Sara over to the coffee bar. Their friendly banter was twinged with flirting as she prepared his beverage. Jake tried to return his full attention to Bea, but a fraction remained distracted with Sara at the bar.

Shaking his head, he looked at Bea who sat back in her chair observing the scene.

"What?" he asked, trying to interpret the coffee shop owner's look.

Bea's eyes danced on her granddaughter before returning to Jake, "I always thought you two would make a great couple."

Jake looked shocked, "Who, Sara and… me?"

Bea's gaze only grew more fervent.

"No, I, uh, I mean there's Tracy. My promotion. There's Shawn, and they have a past. No. We're friends. Friendly. We're friendly," Jake stammered. He looked at Bea, unable to resist a cast over his shoulder. He spied Sara smiling behind the counter as she handed Shawn his cup.

Jake's gaze back to Bea was met with raised eyebrows. His own grew flat and serious, "Let's focus on filling your coffee shop with customers."

Fifteen

Jake arrived at the firm to see Bea in the office lobby. Her cheery smile brightened the room as soft Christmas carols played in the background. Even the desk attendant had been lured in the action handing out samples of her Christmas concoctions.

Bea smiled at Jake, "Ben, here, told me to get in especially early to catch the investment group."

"They do like to jump ahead of the markets," Jake nodded. Rubbing his neck, he scanned the lobby, "I'm usually the first in from my office. How's it going?"

"Great. I think they were happy to get a shot of something before they started their day. Most wore some pretty serious expressions until they tasted one of my holiday drinks," Bea said.

"What's this?" Jake asked, picking up a flyer from a stack on the coffee cart. Scanning the page, he studied the pictures and the bold messaging about local artists. "Sara's work. Nice job."

"I told them they needed to get down there because the first showcase was selling fast," Bea said.

Jake chuckled, "Any developments on this mysterious buyer?"

"No," Bea shook her head. In almost a disappointed tone that threw Jake aback, she added, "I have a pretty good idea how you did it, though."

"Oh?" Jake asked.

"It's no secret that Shawn has been trying to rekindle that old high school flame that he had with Sara. Nice sentiment, though. Giving her a boost with her art out of the gate," Bea said.

"Hmm," Jake nodded. "Maybe by doing anonymously, it could appear genuine instead of a gesture of... courtship?"

Bea handed a passerby a drink and a flyer, "Merry Christmas! Come see us downtown at the Coffee Corner! We have a new local artists showcase."

"You're a natural at this," Jake said.

"When I opened the café, many years ago, I would stand out on the sidewalk during slow periods. Talking to folks as they walked by. Little Sara even helped me back then. No one could resist the bright-eyed four-year-old barking for her grandmother's coffee shop," Bea said.

"Well, you'll look back on this period many years from now as one of those slow periods on the way to better times," Jake assured.

Bea looked at Jake, and for a split second, her cheeriness fled her eyes. As she handed out another cup and received a gracious thank you and a hearty Merry Christmas, the excitement returned.

"You love serving people," Jake said.

"The community is an extension of my family," Bea nodded.

Turning toward the elevators, Jake said, "I should head up. It throws everyone off when I'm not the first one to flip on the lights."

Bea stopped him, and looked up in earnest, "I hate to do this, but… could you do me a favor?"

"Sure, what do you need?" Jake asked.

"I know you're busy," Bea began.

Jake could see the wheels busily churning in Bea's head.

"Sara is holding down the fort at the café. I don't think I brought enough of my Tom and Jerry mix. I called her and said that you might be willing to pick some up for me. I'd be so grateful. You were right. This was a great idea to remind folks about the shop. I'd hate to leave so early," Bea said.

Resisting a chuckle at Bea's masterfully crafted plea, he simply nodded. "I'll put my stuff upstairs, shuffle a few things around in my office and head out right away," Jake said.

Bea's eyes brightened, "You are a lifesaver."

Jake just smiled and shook his head as he pressed the call button for the elevator. "Watch out for this one, Ben. She'll have you under her spell soon."

"She's sweet. And her drinks… Oh, my they remind me of holidays with my grandma," Ben said.

"See, it's already starting," Jake said as he slipped into the elevator.

Jake was pleased to see the coffee shop busy. Sara lobbed a cheery hello over the coffee bar as she assembled several drinks and handed them out. Jake took the moment to assess the shop. Only two tables remained empty. Customers waiting for their drinks stood in front of Sara's artwork, often pointing out something in the scene that tickled a memory.

Sara did her best to ignore the attention on her paintings and rather focused on the craft of making coffee drinks.

After the line dwindled, she stepped out from the counter, "Grandma said you'd be stopping by."

"I'm here. I guess she needed some more mix for her drinks?" Jake asked.

"Her Tom and Jerry mix. I'm not sure why she didn't bring more," Sara shrugged. "I'm sure you're busy and Grandma has you running errands for the coffee shop."

"I don't mind," Jake said.

The admission caught Sara for just a moment as she paused to look at Jake. Softening into a smile, she said, "You really have been so good to us… to Grandma."

Sara's cheeks grew rosy. Snapping her head uncomfortably, she suddenly walked towards the back storeroom. Over her shoulder, she called, "I'll get the mix."

Jake watched her walk away. In a flood, his conversation with Bea popped into his head. For a moment, he was captured by the idea there could be romantic interest between them. As Sara turned to shoulder her way into the backroom and their eyes met, Jake shook his gaze from her and filed the notion away.

Returning with a sealed container, Sara handed it to Jake. "How's it going down there?"

"Great," Jake admitted. "No one is slipping by her. It sounds like she is even flipping sour morning faces into examples of Christmas cheer."

Sara laughed, "Yeah, Grandma has a way of doing that."

"Well, thank you for getting this," Jake said, lofting the container in front of him.

Sara scowled, "Thank *you* for coming all the way down here to get it."

Jake nodded and turned to leave.

With a hand placed on his arm, Sara stopped him. Slowly pivoting to face her, Jake looked at her.

Her face was meek and the rosy color in her cheeks had faded, "Do you really think the art class will help?"

"It won't hurt," Jake admitted. "The truth is, it's another step. The entire downtown area needs to be reawakened. We need the rest of the businesses on board to really do that."

"How do we do that?" Sara asked.

"I have an idea," Jake grinned.

"Of course you do," Sara laughed.

For a long moment, they explored each other's eyes. Neither knowing exactly what they themselves were thinking, never mind the other.

The sound of the café door opening broke their gaze. Sara pulled away from Jake. She looked over her shoulder as she slipped back behind the coffee bar, "Will you come back later?"

"I'll come by this afternoon," Jake said.

"Okay. I'll do the art class, but I want to know what else is churning in that head of yours," Sara said as she prepared to greet her new customers.

For a brief moment, Jake wasn't sure what train of thought she was speaking. He almost felt as though Bea had put a spell on him with wild, unfounded notions. "Yeah, I'll share," Jake nodded.

Turning, Jake left the shop as Sara took a set of coffee orders.

Sixteen

Jake climbed out of his truck. Encumbered with work papers and ideas for the coffee shop, he stepped up on the curb. He frowned as he felt an odd combination of excitement and reticence. Brushing it off as a mix of hope to save the coffee shop and the fear that their efforts might not be enough, he approached the café.

Pushing into the coffee shop, he was pleased to feel the buzz of afternoon coffee conversations. It was nearly as busy in the latter part of the day as it had been in the morning. He gave Bea a wave as she smiled from behind the counter.

Jake saw Sara come out of the backroom. She froze for a moment when she saw him and then relaxed into a smile, "You came back."

"As promised," Jake said. "Things are picking up."

Sara nodded, "A far cry from the not-too-distant past, but yes, your heroic efforts seem to be paying off."

"*Our* efforts. I'm just the idea guy," Jake said. "And occasional delivery boy."

"Grandma, a couple cranberry spritzes, please," Sara called.

Jake looked curious, "Something new?"

"Not everyone wants coffee late in the day. So, she came up with something refreshing. A cranberry spritz. She wanted you to try it," Sara said.

Absently placing a hand on Jake's arm as she got up to retrieve the sparkling drinks, she slid into a chair opposite of him and leaned. Her eyes sparkled as she spoke, "So, what master plan do you have for us?"

"Well, the first step was exposure. Getting people to remember why the Coffee Corner had become such an institution in the first place. The next step is giving them a reason to come downtown and visit the shop," Jake said.

Sara's face twisted nervously, "Like hanging a fledgling artist's paintings on the wall and making her go way outside of her comfort in teaching an art class."

"Yes," Jake grinned. "Just like that."

"Okay. I sense a *but* in there," Sara said as she took a sip of her drink.

"It won't be enough to sustain traffic. We need the other downtown businesses to pull together. We need to create reasons for people to go one more exit down and visit Main Street as part of the Wintergreen experience," Jake said.

"What do you have in mind?" Sara asked.

"To start, I think we need to have the tree lighting event- just like we used to. Just like we had as far back as I can remember," Jake said.

"It is weird to not have it this year. But, they are doing it out at the new shopping center," Sara protested.

"They are. In the middle of a shopping mall. It is a celebration of shopping, not the season," Jake said.

"You think people will actually come," Sara screwed her face into an expression that clearly stated her doubts.

Jake leaned in, "People may not be excited to shop downtown anymore, but the tree lighting was Christmas in Wintergreen. It *is* Christmas in Wintergreen."

"I think that is the campaign slogan right there," Sara nodded, clearly warming to the idea. "But the town didn't even decorate the tree this year. There aren't lights. They moved all of their energy to the shopping center."

"So, we do it ourselves," Jake grinned.

"Ourselves?" Sara's eyes widened.

"Well, not just you and me… and your grandmother. We gather support from all of the businesses downtown. We come together as a downtown community and make the tree lighting happen," Jake said.

Sara frowned, "But it's not just the tree. There are vendors and gingerbread building and snowmen contests."

"We do it all," Jake shrugged.

Sara sat back in her chair, studying Jake. "You are something else. No wonder Grandma has always spoken so highly of you. This isn't even your fight…"

Sara's hands landed on Jake's arms as he leaned further and further across the table in excitement as he laid out his plans. Their eyes locked. For a moment, their chests seemed to settle into harmony as their breaths matched.

The café door opening broke them from the moment. A small crowd marched through with Shawn in the center of the activity.

Jake peered over his shoulder at the entourage, his heart taking an inexplicable plunge as he observed.

Sara hopped out of her seat and rushed to join the group. "Mom, Dad!" she called.

"I found these two wandering the streets and I decided to join them," Shawn announced, his voice cheery.

"Always good to see you, Shawn," Sara's father bellowed as he clapped him on the back.

"We came down to see these paintings of yours on display," Sara's mother said.

Sara's face fell for a moment and then revived. She nodded toward Jake, "It was Jake's idea. He has been amazing in helping Grandma with the café."

"So, we heard," Sara's father glanced at Jake. "Everything has its season, right?"

Jake looked at the man trying to interpret his message.

"By the time you come aboard in January, we'll have moved to our new office suite," Sara's father added.

Sara looked at him, almost stunned before nodding slowly, "Yeah."

"Sara, these are so lovely. It reminds me of when you used to paint Christmas ornaments for family presents," her mother said.

"They are much more than that," Bea said, slipping her way into the center of the conversation. "She has already sold a painting."

"Really?" Sara's mother gasped.

Her father leaned closer to the placard. His eyes grew wide, "For *that* much?"

Sara snapped her head towards her father.

Jake walked up, "Sure. At the gallery, paintings that I would argue don't measure up to these sell for three times as much."

"I will never understand the art world. That's why I like accounting. Straight and true, not based on subjectivity," Sara's father said. After receiving a punch on the arm from Bea, he stammered, "I mean, these are beautiful. You clearly have talent. Selling art can be a nice supplement to your accounting salary."

"I, in particular, like this one," Shawn said, stepping forward and pointing at the piece with the "sold" card on it.

Sara looked at Shawn with a look of appreciation.

Shawn placed a hand on Sara's father's back, "You're right, Richard. Sales like this would add some substantial play money into your daughter's bank account."

Jake sank to the back of the room to let the family and their longtime family friend have their conversation. Bea noticed and quietly followed him. Retreating to the table that he had shared with Sara, he tidied up his notes.

"A lot of history there," Bea said.

"Hmm?" Jake looked up, appearing not to understand what Bea was saying.

"Shawn and Sara and her parents. They have a long history," Bea stated.

"Hmm," Jake nodded, not taking particular note of the conversation.

"Sometimes that's all there is— history," Bea said, glancing around the café. "Richard isn't completely wrong. Everything has its season. Sometimes the old is just that -old. New needs to be able to grow."

"Are we talking about the café?" Jake frowned.

"Are we?" Bea asked.

Jake looked at Shawn and Sara and her parents. They gathered and laughed and shared stories. Occasionally, Sara's gaze would fall on Jake and her grandmother. With a slight nod of his head, he tried to dismiss Bea's insinuation.

The spry coffee shop owner merely offered an undeterred shrug.

Giving her parents hugs and placing a firm hand on Shawn's arm, Sara abruptly pulled away and strode toward the table with Jake and Bea.

"You ready to go?" Sara asked.

Jake looked surprised.

"We have work to do, don't we?" Sara pressed.

Nodding, Jake stood, "We do."

"Then let's go!" Sara urged. "I'll get my coat."

Emerging while pulling her coat on, Sara moved through the cafe.

"You guys need help?" Shawn asked.

Sara smiled politely, "No, Jake and I've got it. Thank you."

Grasping Jake's arm, she tugged him towards the door. Over her shoulder, she called to Shawn, "When it comes to needing the city's help, I will be calling!"

"You didn't have to leave your family… and Shawn," Jake said as they moved down the sidewalk and paused outside of the first business.

Sara looked up, realizing she was still holding Jake's arm. "What? I'm going to let you single-handedly take on the effort to save Grandma's business? Nope, we're in this thing together!"

With a hearty push, they made their way in to make their first downtown business pitch. The aromas of dough and sugar and cinnamon welcomed them. Jake eyed the displays that used to be packed with cookies, cakes, and pastries. They were still there but sparsely arranged.

"Sara! When did you get back into town?" a woman behind the counter asked.

"Hi, Jennifer!" Sara smiled. "I've been back in town for a few weeks. I had been meaning to stop by, especially since I've been pitching in to help Grandma at the café."

"Well, it's nice to see you, just the same. And Jake, wasn't sure I'd see anyone from the firm since you all moved. I have to admit, your coworkers were some of my best customers," the baker said.

Jake nodded, "Some Wintergreen growing pains."

"Boy, you're telling me! I used to sell out of each item by the end of the day. Now, if it wasn't for my specialty cakes, I'm not sure where I'd be," Jennifer said.

"Grandma's shop has been struggling," Sara said.

"I think everyone along Main Street has," Jennifer added.

"That's kind of what we came in to talk to you about," Jake said. "We want to bring people back to Main Street."

Jennifer leaned across the counter, her head cocked, "How are you going to do that?"

"We want to start with the town tree lighting," Jake said.

"The one out by the shopping center?" Jennifer frowned.

Jake laughed, "No. The real one. The one that the town has enjoyed for decades, right here along Main Street."

"You got the town to change their mind?" Jennifer asked.

"We're going to do it ourselves," Sara grinned.

Jennifer stepped back and considered the proposition. Wincing, she asked, "You think we can pull that off?"

"If we all work together? Yes. It was Jake's idea," Sara said casting Jake an appreciative smile.

"Hmm. I bet Donna at the boutique would pitch in. Jill at the gift shop, she'd be all over this. Oh, and Howard, his little hardware store isn't on Main Street, he's a block up. He has been hit hard by the new superstore along the highway," Jennifer mused.

"What do you think?" Jake asked.

"I think… I think we are going to light up downtown again!" Jennifer grinned. "What about the vendors and the contests?"

"We are going to have all of it. Tap into every small business, crafter, garage hobbyist, whoever. We'll make this the best downtown Christmas lighting ever," Jake said.

"If we all work together, he's right. I think we can pull this off," Sara said.

Jennifer began scribbling a list, "Then we have no time to waste. I'll get ahold of all of these people on the list so you can focus on the others!"

Sara took the list and scanned, "Jennifer, this is great. And it was wonderful to see you."

"Don't be a stranger!" Jennifer called.

Jake was staring at the display case. With a sideways grin, he held up two fingers, "Before we go, can I buy a couple of those gingerbread cookies?"

"You bet!" Jennifer said. Slipping the cookies into a baggy, she handed them across the counter. "On the house. For what you are doing for downtown businesses."

Jake shook his head, "No. Your cookies are a Christmas memory. I remember picking one out each year as my family made our way to the tree lighting. Cocoa from Bea's in one hand, a cookie in the other. These are worth every penny, and more."

Jennifer reluctantly accepted the bills Jake pulled out of his wallet.

"Merry Christmas!" Jake said as he held the door for Sara.

They looked at each other as they made their way to the next stop. Sara leaned into Jake as she looked up, "Thank you for doing all of this."

Jake smiled back, "This is my community. Besides, I haven't had this fun on a marketing campaign since… well, ever."

"Come on, we're going to need all of your marketing prowess for this one," Sara said, giving Jake a quick tug toward the next business.

"Old man Fuller," Jake muttered. "Used to scare me as a kid. I think I'm still scared of him."

Opening the door to the drugstore, Jake was happy to let Sara go in first. The little bell above the door rang like an alarm that made Jake wince.

"Eh?" a weathered voice called from the back of the store. "You call in a prescription?"

"No, sir. We are working on a project to help the businesses downtown," Sara called.

"I ain't buyin' nothin'. I ain't placing no ad. I ain't donating to some charity that I never heard of or subscribin' to any magazines that I'll never get." A man, whose appearance matched the gravelly voice sauntered down the aisles to greet Jake and Sara.

Pausing for a moment to eye them, he squinted, "Do I know you two?"

"I'm Bea's granddaughter, from the coffee shop. This is Jake Myers. He is the marketing genius that is helping her store and all of Main Street get some of its customers back," Sara announced.

"Bea Bailey's granddaughter, huh?" Mr. Fuller considered. "She makes the best coffee. Not like that gut rot stuff along the highway."

"I haven't seen you in the café since I've been back," Sara said.

Mr. Fuller looked at Sara under his bushy eyebrows, "Well, I don't get around as well as I used to."

"What's your favorite? I'll bring you a cup the next time I pass by," Sara offered.

"You don't have to do that," Mr. Fuller waved a hand defiantly at her.

"I'd love to," Sara said, her voice soft and sincere.

The old pharmacist paused, raising one of his eyebrows at Jake, "So, what's your story? Let me hear this supposed genius of yours?"

Jake stammered for a moment before sharing his plan, "There's no one thing that will return steady busy to downtown. Working together, we can weave together a community along Main Street that gives people of Wintergreen consistent reasons to come downtown. To shop. To pick up their prescriptions conveniently while they are down here."

"How are you going to do that?" Mr. Fuller scowled.

"We are going to start with the tree lighting. Whether the town officially endorses it or not, we are going to host it ourselves, as downtown businesses. Sara is doing art classes and we have a few more ideas to encourage families to come downtown instead of the big shopping center near the highway," Jake said.

"So, what's in it for you?" Mr. Fuller eyed Jake.

Jake's face softened, "I get to keep my memories and ensure that other Wintergreen families get to keep them too and make new ones. I get to visit with friends and neighbors at Bea's shop. I get to find homemade treats like gingerbread cookies that remind me of my grandmother's instead of some boxed factory cookie at the supercenter."

"Out of the goodness of your heart, eh?" Mr. Fuller asked, his voice dripping with skepticism.

Jake shot a glance at Sara and then back toward the pharmacist, "It started with Sara's grandmother. Then, as I walked down Main Street. How beautiful it is. How everything feels connected down here. I don't want my town to lose that."

Mr. Fuller looked at Jake. His bushy eyebrows intensified his scrutinizing glare. With a deep breath, the pharmacist said, "You remind me of my son, Jonathan. You might know him. Seems roughly your age. I had always planned on him taking over the shop when I retire. I saw things begin to turn long before the new center came in. I encouraged him to get a job at a hospital or one of those residential pharmacies you see on every corner. He talks about this place the way you do."

"Jonathan Fuller. Nice kid, always carried that backpack with the medical patch on it," Jake said.

"That's right!" Sara snapped her fingers. "We always fought to have him as our chemistry lab partner!"

Mr. Fuller took a deep, proud breath, "So, what do you need from me?"

"Only what you want to give. We are going to decorate downtown like it used to be. Bring in vendors. And of course, light the tree," Jake said.

Fuller nodded, "All right. You're going to need a lift to decorate that tree. I've got a buddy who owns the warehouse at the edge of town. I'll call in a favor."

"That would be wonderful. Thank you. I'll admit, that was a piece of the puzzle I hadn't figured out yet," Jake admitted.

"Well, get out of here. I'm sure you have more stops to make and I've got prescriptions to fill," Mr. Fuller said with a wave of his hand.

Jake and Sara began to leave but Jake paused and spun on his heel, "It was nice to visit, Mr. Fuller."

"Eh?" the old pharmacist scowled from behind his bushy eyebrows. He nodded, "Indeed, it was. Indeed, it was."

"Merry Christmas!" Jake called as he led Sara back out on to the sidewalk.

Sara nudged Jake as she pulled her coat tighter to fend off the intensifying breeze, "See, that wasn't so bad."

"Not bad at all," Jake said thoughtfully.

Seventeen

Jake and Sara's jaunt down Main Street continued as did their first stops. Businesses feeling unsettled and unsure of their futures were becoming fueled with optimism after their visit.

Looking at the shops crossed off on their list and the sun dipping out of sight, Jake led Sara to their final stop. With a deep breath, they pushed their way in. The moment was like déjà vu as they had just stood in that spot together a few days earlier.

"Hello?" an elegantly dressed woman called as she approached from the back of the art gallery.

"Mrs. Marcom?" Jake called back.

"You can call me Debbie. How can I help you? You two were in a couple of days ago. See something you liked?"

"Well, yes," Jake admitted. "But that's not why we are here this evening."

The gallery owner's eyes peered above the rim of her glasses, "Oh?"

"We, uh, we are on a mission to bring people back to Main Street. Starting with the tree lighting in the park," Jake said.

"It was disappointing to hear the lighting event had been moved this year, but what does that have to do with the gallery?" Debbie asked.

"Jake is helping my grandmother's coffee shop, Jennifer's bakery, even the pharmacy rekindle their relationship with the families of Wintergreen," Sara said.

Debbie stared at Jake and Sara for a moment, "An admirable task, but the gallery is a bit different. We get less volume of people looking, I suppose. But it really doesn't impact our business. People who come, come to buy. It has been quieter, but not necessarily a bad thing. I get to focus on curating and working with artists more rather than nervously watch children with jelly on their hands."

"I see," Sara said, her words coming out soft.

Jake could see in the corner of his eye, Sara's shoulders slump.

"For the retail shops, increasing customers is key," Jake admitted. "For other businesses, that aren't impacted by traffic, they miss the spirit of downtown. They miss walking down Main Street and greeting neighbors. They miss gathering at the coffee shop or seeing what new confection they can take home to their kids from the bakery. Mostly, they miss the feeling they used to get when they were here."

Walking over to one of the Americana paintings with a scene depicting a simpler time, he said, "They miss this. Having it in a painting on the wall is wonderful, for those who were able to experience it or something like it. For those where it isn't a memory, their opportunity to experience this life, this community… it's fading."

Debbie looked at Jake, unmoved as she stared above her glasses at him. With a slight lean back, a smile slipped through, "I should have you help sell for the gallery. You paint a picture that almost makes me want to take that home."

"Wintergreen is special. I don't want it to turn into 'just any other town'. Bland and lifeless," Jake said.

"All right, all right. I'm sold. What do you need from me?" Debbie asked with a soft laugh.

"First, we are asking businesses along Main Street to help us host the tree lighting. Vendors along the sidewalk, decorations just like we used to have, and of course, culminating around the tree," Jake said.

Debbie shrugged, "Tell me what you need."

"You clearly have an eye for decorating. If we get a team of volunteers, would you help orchestrate them in placing decorations?" Jake asked.

"I can do one better," Debbie smiled. "I have a shed full of exquisite decorations I have accumulated over the years that I don't have room for at my house. I'll bring them and have the gallery staff on hand when you guys are ready."

Jake wrinkled his nose, "Would tomorrow be too soon?"

"Well, they'll be a day less dusty, might as well," Debbie laughed.

Jake's eyes brightened, "Oh, if you happen to know of any budding artists, Sara will be hosting an art class at the café tomorrow night. It's a free event though participants are encouraged to bring a toy for charity."

"An art class… I may have to come down and check it out. See who the next great Rembrandt or Picasso is in our midst," Debbie said. "If you need easels or display lighting, let me know. We have plenty in the back.

"Thank you. I am sure it will be a cozy and casual affair," Sara blushed.

"The offer stands," Debbie shrugged. "Thank you for coming in. And thank you, Jake, for sharing the romanticism of Main Street Wintergreen. You are right. We need to hold on to these fading glimpses of Americana as long as we can."

Thanking her, Jake and Sara left the gallery as Debbie closed up behind them. The street lamps had come on as the sun had long since set.

"That was a good day," Jake said, pulling his collar tight.

"It was," Sara nodded, huddling her arms close to her body.

The pair shuffled side by side down the sidewalk in silence for several long moments. Sara looked up at Jake and grinned.

"What?" he scowled. "Did I do something wrong?"

"No," Sara laughed as she shook her head. "'Bringing the romanticism of Main Street'. Who knew a stretch of businesses in a small downtown could be romantic?"

The words, an innocent reflection of the gallery owner's sentiment, suddenly took on a different meeting. Jake and Sara paused. Pivoting ever so slightly towards one another. Their eyes explored the meaning as they fought to understand the moment.

Sara gasped, "I mean, the town. The businesses, the people…"

Her mouth remained open for just a moment as the words tumbled out. Their bodies leaned in. Their breathing deepened.

"There you guys are!" a familiar voice called from down the sidewalk.

Jake and Sara turned to see Shawn approach with his hand in the air. "Your family and I thought it would be fun to go to the new restaurant that just opened for dinner tonight," Shawn said.

Jake and Sara shared a brief, awkward glance.

"I mean, you can come too, Jake. I'm sure it would be fine," Shawn shrugged.

Jake took a deliberate look at his watch, "No, it's okay. I have a lot of work to catch up on."

"Maybe next time," Shawn said.

"Yeah, next time," Jake echoed. Looking at Sara, he said, "I'll see you tomorrow?"

Sara smiled, "See you tomorrow. Big day!"

Shawn frowned trying to interpret what they were talking about. With a shrug, he put an arm around Sara, "Come on. Your family is already getting us a table."

Jake watched as Sara was whisked away.

Once again, Main Street was quiet.

Jake could almost have enjoyed it, if he didn't know that quiet meant the slow, spiraling death for many of the businesses. An end to an era and a way of life that made Wintergreen, *Wintergreen*. A special speck of a town where people shared as part of a community.

Shawn and Sara disappeared into the night. Jake walked slowly back toward his truck. Pulling out his phone, he sighed. Six calls from the office, three from Tracy. His email marker was in the high double digits.

"Well, at least I didn't fib about having lots of work to do," Jake muttered to himself as he shoved his hands in his pockets and walked on.

Eighteen

Jake's phone buzzed and email chimed all morning long. Downtown business owners donating decorations, volunteers offering their time and Mr. Fuller's friend wanting to schedule time with the lift to work on the tree kept the workday lively.

"Everything okay?" Carol asked. His eyes were creased with worry, "You have barely left your office since you got here. That isn't like you."

Shoving his plans for the tree lighting aside, Jake tapped the storyboard for Java Universe, "Just trying to get phase one for the campaign done."

"Jeff and Frank were not happy with how long you were gone yesterday, especially without any email updates on the proposal," Carol said.

"Yeah, I imagine," Jake nodded. With a sigh, he pulled the campaign papers to the forefront. "I'm working on it. Trying to get their message into something meaningful that works for not just the local store but nationally is taking a bit of time."

"What was it you said after our visit? The experience reminded you of getting off a ride at an amusement park and being funneled through the gift shop? Are there any positives you can take away from that?" Carol asked.

Jake tapped his pencil thoughtfully against his lips, "I mean, it isn't terrible. They can handle a massive crowd. Maintain a theme throughout and flow so many people can filter through in a reasonably pleasant and orderly manner."

"It sounds like you just described the Java Universe experience," Carol smiled.

Jake nodded, "Maybe. I'll have to put some polish on it, but there might be something there."

"Here to help," Carol said, about to walk away.

"Are you sure you don't want to switch seats? You're pretty good at this," Jake said.

Carol turned and leaned back into the office, her fingers hugging the door frame, "I'm good at nudging you from time to time. Seeding an idea. You paint these wonderful landscapes out of that seed. Besides, I can handle working with you. I am not the one to work with the Jeffs and Franks and Henrys of the world. I'll leave that to you."

"Thanks," Jake said.

"Speaking of which," Carol looked over her shoulder. She gave Jake a look and then slipped away.

Jake straightened and glanced to ensure the downtown plans were tucked away.

"Jake, you're here!" Frank's voice boomed as he entered the office. Jeff bounced on his heels, his head peering over his boss' shoulders. "We need an update, Jake. The big wigs at corporate are starting to get anxious."

"I have a storyboard that I'm working on," Jake said. His phone buzzed. Instinctively, Jake swiped the "decline" button.

"Great, let's see it!" Jeff urged.

Jake winced, "It's not quite ready yet." His phone chimed with multiple messages in a row. Jake let out a sheepish shrug and flat smile.

"Lay it on us anyway," Frank said, his brows creasing as he eyed Jake's phone.

Shifting in his seat, Jake held his hands in the air, "Think of a wild, rolling, twisting, turning amusement park ride as a metaphor for life– getting the kids ready for school, getting ready yourself, traffic, the ticking clock each morning. And then pan to Java Universe. The staff is ready and waiting. The service is fast and orderly. It is that little bit of painless and easy in the day."

Jeff scratched his chin and nodded. With a scowl, he said, "I don't get it."

"Have you been to one of the big amusement parks?" Jake asked.

"Sure. I went with my nephews. Aside from the lines and the ridiculous prices on everything, it was great. Why?" Jeff asked.

"When the wild ride is over, what happens next?" Jake asked.

Jeff looked thoughtful, "You kind of get funneled through the obligatory photo wall and then popped out into a gift shop."

"Exactly. The wild ride is life. And despite how many people they cram into those lines and onto those rides, the flow once you are off is smooth. Orderly. Consistent. They carry the theme throughout the experience," Jake said.

Jeff pointed excitedly, "That's kind of like Java Universe."

"Exactly," Jake nodded.

Frank cast a wary look, "I see where you are going. It needs some work. If you have to explain it…"

"I know. That's why the storyboard isn't ready yet," Jake admitted. "But here's the pitch. Life is wild and busy and hectic. Getting your coffee at Java Universe isn't."

With a nod, Frank smiled, "It is a general theme that can be carried through a long campaign with countless life examples of where you get off the busy freeway to get your hassle-free cup of Java Universe coffee. I like it. Good work."

"I see it now. Yeah, good work, Jake," Jeff chimed.

"Now get us a clean first draft– storyboards, visual mocks, ad schedules… and today," Frank said.

Jake's phone rang.

"You need to get that?" Frank asked, staring at the phone that Jake tried to swipe at without looking.

"No," Jake shook his head. "Probably just my lunch order. So much work to do. Planning ahead."

"Hmm," Frank huffed. Turning to head out of his office, he called, "Today, Jake!"

Watching the branch manager and sales executive exit his office, Jake sighed. Scribbling hasty notes on his ill-conceived though strangely viable campaign pitch, he turned his attention to his phone.

The decorations were beginning to pile up. The gallery owner had another truckload on the way. Volunteers started showing up and didn't know where to begin. Bea had called and texted a dozen times.

His head spinning, Jake glanced at the clock on his computer, eyes landing on the blank storyboard and then on the equally blank ad campaign timeline. Finally, his eyes fell on his phone.

Picking it up, he walked to his office door and closed it. Hitting the call button, he returned one of Bea's many and increasingly urgent phone calls.

"Jake! Oh, thank goodness. When are you going to be here?" Bea asked.

"I'm trying, I have a few things that I need to finish here first," Jake said.

"Sara was going to start organizing people and things, but good news, helpers need cups of coffee in the morning, so she has been stuck behind the bar with me," Bea shared.

"That is good news," Jake said. "I'll get a hold of Debbie at the gallery. She said she would help direct the decorating. I'll be there as soon as I can."

"Okay. We'll see you soon," Bea said as the whir of the burr coffee grinder spun in the background.

Jake hung up the phone, staring at the papers on his desk, arms spread wide to encompass the mass of storyboards, design specs and notes. Scooping them into a single pile, he revealed his decorating plan for downtown. Glancing at his watch, he shot up from his desk. Shoving his Java Universe campaign items in with the Christmas tree lighting to-do list into his bag, he hoisted it over his shoulder and strode defiantly toward his office door.

Feeling guilty, he craned his neck around the office to see who was in his line of sight. Other than a curiously raised brow from Carol, he had a window to escape. Grabbing his overcoat, he closed the office door behind him and walked confidently towards the elevator lobby. Tapping the call button with his knuckle, he shuffled impatiently as he waited.

As the doors opened, Jake saw Frank and Jeff emerge from the conference room. With one big stride, Jake disappeared, willing the elevator doors to close. Letting out a sigh of relief as the elevator shook to life, lowering him to the ground floor, he let out a smile to himself.

When the doors opened and Jake took a step out, he froze.

"Jake?"

"Tracy. What are you doing here?" he asked.

Tracy gave a wary look at his bag and overcoat, "I was told you would be locked in your office all day. I thought I would stop by and bring you some coffee." She raised a pair of Java Universe cups in the air.

"Ah," Jake said, flustered. "I had a major breakthrough on the campaign. I was just heading out for a bit. Get my head straight before I finished the draft. It's due today."

"I see," Tracy said.

Jake's eyes brightened, "Why don't you come with me? I am helping the businesses along Main Street decorate for their tree lighting. It will be fun, get you in the Christmas spirit."

Tracy wrinkled her nose, "That's not really my scene."

Jake looked dejected.

"Look, that is your thing. Those are your people. It really has nothing to do with me," Tracy shrugged, reading Jake's reaction.

"You could be a part of it. Maybe you *should*," Jake said.

Tracy let out a long sigh and paced a few steps away before turning back, "Why, Jake? Why is this downtown… *distraction*… so important to you?"

"Those are my neighbors. My friends. My community," Jake shared.

"You have friends, Jake. And they aren't here in Wintergreen. Your *future* isn't here in Wintergreen," Tracy said.

"My family is here. It will always be a part of me," Jake protested.

"Sure," Tracy choked a hoarse laugh. "As your past. A place to visit your Mom and Dad. But your life and opportunity are in the city. An opportunity you are supposed to be working on, to my understanding."

"I'll get it done. It's not like there is any soul, nuance or romance to the campaign. Fast, efficient, on to the next is not a hard concept to hammer out," Jake said.

"Then hammer it out before you go off for playtime!" Tracy snapped.

The lobby fell quiet. In the corner of his eye, Jake could see Ben try and look busy.

Tracy turned back and breathed, "I'm sorry, Jake. That was out of line. I'm worried about you. I'm worried about us. I think… I think we should take a break. I'm going back to the city."

Jake looked at Tracy for a long moment before nodding slowly, "Maybe, that is for the best."

"You need to get your head out of this place, Jake. Out of the past," Tracy said.

"Tracy…" Jake started but realized he didn't know what to say. He had nothing to say.

"Goodbye, Jake. Take this time to figure out what it is you really want. Have your little project. Your Wintergreen friends. When you are ready to move on, you know where to find me," Tracy said.

Tracy set the Java Universe cup she had brought for him on the counter.

"Goodbye, Tracy," Jake replied, his voice soft.

As Tracy reached to push open the door, Jake's phone burst with another volley of urgent messages from the downtown decorating committee. He watched her leave before dropping his head to scroll through his phone. With a deep breath, he pulled his coat over his shoulders, slung his bag on his back and started for the door himself.

"Oh, uh… Jake. Your coffee!" Ben pointed toward the cup on the stand.

Jake just laughed, "You can have it, Ben."

Ben looked across the counter at Jake, who slipped out of the building into a bright and sunny, yet chilly day.

Nineteen

Jake arrived downtown to witness a wonderful, yet chaotic scene. The sidewalks were lined with boxes. People had come out of the woodwork to help decorate. Jake recognized people from the travel agency, the local insurance agent, and the tavern restaurant all listening to Debbie from the gallery give tips and assignments.

Looking up, she saw Jake and her eyes widened, "Oh, good. Jake is here! Jake, share a few words and set the overall stage. I have the decorations covered, but… I don't know the rest of your plans."

Jake nodded, smiling and waving to the crowd as he approached. Slipping the clipped packet of ideas he had mapped out for the tree lighting event, he stood beside Debbie.

"First of all, thank you everyone for coming out to help. The downtown tree lighting has been a tradition for as long as I can remember and from the tales, way longer than that. I get that times change, but it doesn't mean that some things aren't worth holding close and preserving. I think the town coming together as a community and celebrating Christmas, together. I think it is one of those things we should cling to and make happen, even in the face of change," Jake said.

In the corner of his eye, he saw Bea and Sara poke their heads out from the café. He saw Jennifer emerge from the bakery and Mr. Fuller lean his head against the pharmacy window to get a glimpse of the scene out on his sidewalk.

"This," Jake swirled his hands in the air to draw an imaginary circle around the crowd. "This is what it is all about. We'll put in some hard work today. We'll have some fun and create something special that the whole town can enjoy."

"Thank you, Jake for doing this. If we all kept our heads down, change would have rolled right on by us," Debbie said.

"Thank you. And Bea and Sara. And Jennifer and all of you for loving this community as much as I do," Jake said. Holding out his diagram for the event layout, he started calling out, "We need eight spots for booths set up. The area for snowmen building, the cocoa cart, the gingerbread houses and the wreath making. The rest of you are in great hands with Debbie on sprucing up Main Street for one of the most festive Christmases downtown has ever seen!"

Handing out sheets describing the layout for each booth and work area, Jake made his way through the crowd. Landing in front of the coffee shop, he found a smiling Bea and Sara waiting outside their door.

Bea grinned and pulled Jake in for a hug, "This is magnificent. Whatever happens from here on, this will be a lasting tribute to what we all know and love about downtown."

Jake pulled back and looked at Bea, "This will be more than a tribute, Bea. We are going to *save* Main Street Wintergreen."

"I like your confidence," Bea laughed. With a look toward Sara, she said, "Well, don't just stand there. Help the man. You have Main Street to save!"

"Don't you need her at the shop? It's pretty busy down here," Jake suggested.

Bea shook her head, "For the rest of the decorating party, there won't be any sales. I'm just going to be hauling out carafes of coffee and cocoa while providing a space where workers can shake the chill off."

Jake gave her a questioning look.

"One day won't make or break the café. Me giving back to those willing to give is the least that I can do," Bea said.

"You heard the woman. Let's get to work," Sara said with an excited bounce in her step.

Casting a glance toward Bea who nodded, Jake clapped his hands, "All right! Let's do this!"

He and Sara spun in unison. Watching the group of volunteers work on Debbie's instructions as a cargo van pulled down Main Street and stopped in front of the gallery owner. With a grin, Debbie stepped away from the decorating and approached Jake.

"Where would you like these?" Debbie asked as a man hopped out of the van and with a flip o the latch, swung the doors wide.

Jake and Sara looked inside to see the entire van filled with Christmas trees. With their eyes wide, Jake pondered for a moment. "Wow, Debbie. You have… You have really come through. These are great," he said.

"Indoor or outdoor, they are fine," Debbie said. "Use them however you see fit."

"What do you think?" Jake nudged Sara.

"A Christmas tree walkway leading to the town tree, or whatever we call it now, would be delightful," Sara said.

"Yeah," Jake nodded. Biting his lip, he said, "Give me a minute."

Jogging off toward the café, he left Debbie and Sara to instruct the van to pull to the side of the street awaiting further instructions. In moments, he returned dangling a key from his fingers. "Let's put some in the vacant space, maybe half a dozen of them and then the rest can line the path to the entrance of the park," Jake suggested.

Handing Sara the key, Jake grabbed a pair of trees off the van and set them on the curb outside the empty storefront next to the coffee shop. By the time Sara had turned the key and pushed her way into the building, Jake had returned with another pair of trees, hauling them all the way inside. As Sara pulled the original set into the store, Jake returned with the final two and sent the van to distribute the remaining trees along the pathway to the park.

Sara looked at Jake, "What are we going to do in here?"

Jake grinned, "Honestly, I don't know yet. But, I am running through some ideas."

Jennifer walked over from the bakery to help, pulling the second tree from the sidewalk inside, "I have an idea."

Jake and Sara's heads swiveled towards Jennifer. The baker's eyes went wide as she set the tree down and used her hands emphatically while she spoke, "How about a Christmas Cookie Bake-off!"

"I like it!" Sara heartily agreed.

Jake chuckled, "I do too. I was thinking the gingerbread house contest could be held in here. Anything to bring people downtown and on the night of the tree lighting, encourage them to visit the entire expanse of Main Street."

"That would help," Jennifer nodded.

"I'll talk to the people at the Tavern Restaurant. They are really the last bit of downtown along the river. Maybe they could end the night with a special dinner or something to get some much needed attention as well," Jake said.

"I like it. Main Street coming together like this," Jennifer said. She looked at Jake as she straightened branches on one of the trees, "With the city pulling out and encouraging businesses and shoppers out of downtown, as an owner, I just felt kind of helpless. I'm not sure any of us would have thought to tackle this ourselves or pull everyone together the way you have."

Jake shrugged, "This is just a step to help the businesses. But, I've been to towns where they followed the bright glow of progress. They let all of the character seep out of their town and became another collection of stores along the highway looking and feeling just like the towns a few exits either direction from them."

"Wintergreen has something special," Jake continued. Walking to the storefront window, he held his arms wide. "Wintergreen has this."

For a moment, he stood quietly watching the volunteers string lights and adorn garland and bows along Main Street.

"Well, I think these are all set. They are all pre-lit. Now, we just need decorations," Sara said.

"I can ask my parents if they have any they can spare," Jake offered.

Sara nodded, "I'll check with Grandma and my family too."

"I have a better idea," Jennifer stepped forward. "Why don't we host an ornament making night?"

"I like it," Jake agreed. "The more reasons we have for families to come downtown, the more it will become a comfortable thing to do."

"There is one thing downtown can't do as well as the new shopping center, and that's parking," Jennifer mused.

Jake nodded, "It is one of the biggest challenges downtowns struggle with. I guess we just need to make parking in the adjacent blocks worth it for the downtown experience."

"So, let's make Main Street amazing!" Sara grinned.

"Let's see what Debbie's team needs help with," Jake said.

Pushing out onto the sidewalks lining Main Street, they paused. Amidst the bustle of decorating activity, the sounds of classic Christmas carols filled the downtown area, and decorators hummed and sang along as they worked.

Nudging Sara, Jake pointed out the source.

Turning her head, Sara saw what he was looking at and smiled, "Mr. Fuller."

"Old Man Fuller," Jake nodded. The pharmacist shuffled out of his shop, a basket in his hands. Curious, Jake walked up. "Good morning, Mr. Fuller."

"Morning, Jake. Candy cane?" Mr. Fuller asked with a slight shake of his basket.

Jake laughed, "I would love one. Thank you. The music is just what we needed."

Grabbing a candy cane for himself and handing one to Sara, Jake asked, "What do you think?"

"At first, I thought it was a bunch of commotion. Seeing the street come to life brought back a lot of memories," Mr. Fuller said, his eyes welling a bit as he spoke.

Jake smiled, "Yeah. It sure does."

"You should have seen this place. It was so beautiful. The town was so cheerful. I don't see that much anymore. Catching a glimpse of that, well, that's something else," Fuller said.

"Let us know if there is anything we can do for you," Jake said, holding his candy cane up as a nod of thanks.

"You just make sure those decorators touch up the pharmacy a bit. It could use a little more Christmas cheer," Mr. Fuller said.

"We sure will," Jake promised.

A suit and overcoat-clad entourage made their way down the sidewalk. Casting frowns and scowls at the activity along the street, the man in front bellowed, "Who is in charge of all this?"

Most eyes fell on Jake who shuffled, "I guess that would be me, Mr. Mayor."

"What is going on here?" he grumbled.

"The downtown businesses are struggling. We wanted to remind people that they were here," Jake shrugged.

"By blocking our sidewalks?" the mayor asked.

"By decorating Downtown Wintergreen the way it had been in the past. All with the businesses' own expense and manpower. No cost to the city," Jake said.

A backup alarm caught the contingent's attention as a large cherry picker on a flatbed was being unloaded near the entrance to the park.

"And what in tarnation is going on over there?" the mayor snapped.

Swallowing hard, realizing he may have missed a step or two in his downtown plans, he admitted, "Stringing the town Christmas tree, Mr. Mayor."

The mayor's head slowly swiveled to face Jake, "We aren't lighting that tree this year. We have the one in the Commerce Center."

"That tree has been lit every year for the past fifty years, Wyatt!" a voice called from behind them. His basket still in front of him, Mr. Fuller stepped into the fray and offered, "Candy cane?"

The mayor scowled, "We have a deal with the developers of the Commerce Center. The town tree lighting is to be held there."

"Okay. So, this isn't the *town* tree lighting. This is Main Street Wintergreen's tree lighting," Jake countered.

"You have a permit for this?" the mayor growled.

A voice pushed through from the rear of the entourage, "Yeah, it's pending, sir. They asked me to do it and we have been so busy with the plans for the Commerce Christmas I hadn't filed them yet."

The mayor cast a disbelieving glance at Shawn who shared quick looks with Jake and Sara. "Hmph, I guess a few decorations won't hurt anything. Just don't do anything outlandish or that will take away from the *town's* plans."

"I wouldn't dream of it, sir," Jake grinned, shooting a knowing grin toward Sara.

As the mayor spun to head back toward town hall, Sara mouthed a "thank you" to Shawn, who nodded with wide eyes and a shrug.

"Well, there's that," Jake breathed. "Remind me to thank Shawn later."

"Rushing ahead without all the pieces put together, are we?" Sara teased.

Jake laughed with a shrug, "Better to ask for forgiveness than have the town deny the businesses of Main Street by asking?"

"I suppose. We better get to work before they uncover the rest of our plans!" Sara urged.

Twenty

With each completed phase of decorating, Main Street looked more and more the part of a Christmas postcard. It had quickly become a glimpse of the past sprinkled on top of a present day downtown.

The decorating volunteers became increasingly giddy throughout the day. Singing Christmas carols together, they enjoyed breaks with holiday cookies, coffee and cocoa. There were multiple occasions when Jake would look up from his work and just stop. Seeing the folks of Main Street come together as they did warmed his heart.

"You okay over there?" Sara asked, feeding a volunteer on a ladder a continuous flow of garland.

"Yeah," Jake nodded. Holding a large reel of lights, he said, "Just… just admiring Main Street at Christmas."

"It's pretty amazing, isn't it?" Sara said.

Snapping himself back to focus, Jake completed another strand of lights at the same time Sara finished her last bundle of garland. Meeting in front of the gallery, they nearly collided.

Glancing over his shoulder, Jake said, "The garland looks great."

Sara smiled looking in the direction Jake had been working, "Nice work on the lights."

"They're, uh, they're not on yet," Jake said.

"Well, I can imagine them," Sara said, her face turned a rosy hue. "The whole area is looking beautiful."

"A winter wonderland. We just need to snow," Jake said as he scanned the clouds slowly creeping in over Main Street.

"Someone say snow?" Debbie asked, her arms laden with two large bags. "There's two more behind me, if you don't mind grabbing them."

Jake and Sara saw the bags on the sidewalk. Each grabbing one, they followed the gallery owner, into the empty space near the coffee shop. "Bea told me you were decorating this shop for small events. I thought this would be fun."

Taking one of the bags, Debbie dumped its contents, allowing them to spill on the floor. "It's not exactly snow, but we used this for simulated snow at one of our events a few Christmases ago," she said.

"You are an amazing cultivator of fun things," Jake said.

"I would love to explore your storerooms. I bet it's almost as fun as combing through your gallery," Sara said.

"I'm just excited to see all of this stuff get some use," Debbie said. "Besides, this is the most fun I have had in a while. Thank you for putting this together."

Jake scanned the busy streets of downtown, "I don't know how much I did."

"It takes an idea and someone to act on it. You know how many of us were disappointed about the downtown tree lighting but did nothing?" Debbie said.

"Grandma's coffee shop wouldn't stand a chance without Jake and his help," Sara said.

"Bea's coffee shop…" Debbie mused. Her eyes grew wide. "Those are your paintings that were hung up? I saw them on social media. I have been meaning to come down and check them out."

Sara winced, "They probably seem like they're done in crayon compared to the works by the real artists you have in your gallery."

"The moment you put brush to canvas, you are an artist. Never let yourself think differently than that," Debbie said. Her voice was direct and serious.

Still blushing, Sara offered in a low voice, "Thank you."

"I think they are great. They kind of remind me of a few paintings you have in your gallery. Different styles and color use, but I mean, they kind of grab your senses in the same way," Jake said.

With a handful of fluffy white material, Sara scowled, "Can we get back to decorating, please? Or I will begin singing carols loudly and I promise you, singing is not a talent I have."

Jake and Debbie laughed, each taking an armful of fabric and spreading it along the trees dotting the interior of the space. With a wary eye, Sara grabbed part of the bunch Jake was struggling with and began working it to more resemble organic snow as opposed to crafting material. They met in the center, their foreheads inches apart.

Jake looked slowly up at Sara and offered a meek smile, "Thank you."

"You're welcome," Sara smiled back and abruptly pulled away. "Come on. We have another five trees to snowscape!"

Hours ticked by. As the sun gleamed off the windows of town hall, Jake knew that was a sign in December, that it was not long from setting. He looked at his list with most boxes checked and a few new ones added as other décor and ideas filtered in throughout the day.

Glancing down the street, he was more than pleased with the day's results. "Results!" his eyes grew wide in alarm. With an exasperated shout to Sara, he waved, "I'll be back in a few!"

Sara nodded. She walked with Debbie eyeing anything that required finishing touches.

Jake streaked into the café, a hasty hello offered to Bea as he pulled his laptop out and began hammering on his keyboard as quickly as he could. He had admittedly forgotten about the Java Universe campaign. There were a few brief moments of inspiration before he was completely swept up and immersed in decorating downtown.

Cramming his thoughts into the pre-set pages as quickly as he could, he scanned his work. It was perhaps the sloppiest proposal he had ever submitted, but his thoughts were there. And it did cover the elements Jeff had requested in the proposal. He had enough flourishes of his own creativity, he was confident enough to hit send.

Staring at the screen, he was surprised. He thought he would feel a lot more trepidation in the weak submission. But, he didn't. Instead, he matter-of-factly closed his screen and slipped it back into his bag.

Looking up, he noticed Bea glancing over at him. "I certainly hope that helping me, helping us, hasn't caused you problems at work," she said.

Jake said, "Not at all. In fact, I think working to help the Café has only brought more clarity to my job."

"Good. I would hate to think we were an unwarranted distraction," Bea said.

"Some distractions are healthy, Bea," Jake smiled. "And I am grateful that I have the opportunity and that it turned into helping out the entire community. This is fun stuff."

"That it is," Bea chuckled. "It has been a long time since I have seen so much concerted effort by the businesses down here."

"I'm glad," Jake said, slipping out of his chair. "That said, I should get back out there. We are almost finished. You should come see."

Bea set her apron down, "You know what? I'll join you."

Jake waited for Bea to slip around the counter and escorted her out to the sidewalk. Dusk had overwhelmed the sky, chasing the sun home for the evening. The busy sidewalks had largely quieted. The empty decoration bins and boxes had been cleaned up and stowed.

Jake and Bea saw Sara wave to them as a small crowd had huddled just outside of town hall. Flanked by Debbie and Jenny, Sara urged them to join in. Mr. Fuller poked his head out of his pharmacy as Jake and Bea walked by, and smiled, "Evening, Bea."

"It is a beautiful evening, Francis," Bea said, her arm tucked in her young escort's.

"Mr. Fuller," Jake nodded. "Thank you again for the music today. It was just what we needed."

"Glad to be a part of something, even if a little," the pharmacist said.

Meeting with the small contingent that gathered, Sara said, "We thought you might like to have the honors."

"The honors?" Jake asked.

The crowd parted revealing a large power switch on the face of town hall, just at the corner near the small alley that separated it from the building next door.

"We couldn't think of anyone that should flip that switch as much as you," Sara said, supported by nods from Jennifer, Debbie and the remaining volunteers who stayed until the end.

Jake looked at the faces in the small crowd, a wave of emotion cascaded over him as he walked up to the electrical panel. The solitary switch that served as the master breaker for the auxiliary exterior lighting along Main Street beckoned. With a deep breath, Jake gripped the switch. With a slight glance over his shoulder, he pulled down on the lever.

Even without facing the street, he could see the glow radiate over Downtown Wintergreen.

Turning, he joined the cheers as the group enjoyed their work.

The entire stretch of Main Street was lit with garland strung in a wave from storefront to storefront. The trees in the park twinkled along a path that led to what was historically known as the town tree.

The tall pine that served as a sentry to Downtown Wintergreen dazzled in colorful lights that stood against the small white lights used throughout the rest of the decorating effort. It was a grand beacon for the town. It was a hallmark of downtown Wintergreen.

Jake's chest swelled with pride. Bea and Sara instinctively wrapped their arms around him.

"This… is… amazing," he breathed.

Sara and Bea subconsciously squeezed.

"It is splendid," Bea said.

"Spectacular," Sara exhaled.

Together, they joined with the rest of the group to do a visual tour of Main Street with their eyes. Each held their mouths in awe.

A voice from down the street began singing. Low at first, but then rising, "Silent night. Holy night…"

Soon, everyone was linked arm and arm singing from their hearts along with Mr. Fuller who led the effort. Jake could see from the shine gleaming from the newly strung lights, a teary sparkle in Fullers' eyes, a surprising sentiment from the man he had always held as grouchy and unyielding. Here he was in the bright light of humanity, leading a Christmas carol on the streets of Downtown Wintergreen.

When the song concluded, Mr. Fuller waved a "good evening" and slipped back within the interior of the pharmacy.

"Okay, now we need to flip that switch… right there," Debbie pointed. Jake complied and the large tree in the park went dark leaving the remaining trees lit in their silvery splendor.

Jake continued to take in their efforts of the day. His heart somewhat saddened to extinguish the beautiful centerpiece of the park tree. He knew its slumber held a greater meaning as they invited the town to rally around its awakening.

Quickly, the exhausted crowd diminished. Bea told Sara that she would close down the shop.

All at once, Jake and Sara were left on the elegantly decorated main street of Downtown Wintergreen. Neither could bear to pull themselves away from the wonder they were experiencing as their eyes and hearts took in the beauty of the scene.

Suddenly realizing they were lost in their own moment, Jake shook himself. "Nice, uh, nice work today."

"Jake, this is amazing," Sara said.

"We have to give credit to Debbie. Her decorations are magnificent," Jake said.

Sara laughed at Jake's adjective but nodded in agreement.

"Well, we should probably get going," Jake said.

"I hate to leave," Sara admitted. "This is so lovely."

"Yeah," Jake said. Taking a deep breath, he glanced at Sara. He could see the lights of the trees and strands of garland reflecting in her eyes like jewels. "This was," he began softly, "A good day."

Sara looked up at Jake and smiled, "It was."

"Shall we?" Jake asked.

Sara nodded and walked in step with Jake. They remained a distance apart as though a force was keeping them separate.

Jake considered Shawn.

Sara was keenly aware of Jake's relationship with Tracy.

So, they walked. Together. Apart.

From the window of the coffee shop, Bea watched the pair as they ambled down the sidewalk toward the coffee shop. A soft smile swept across her lips.

Twenty One

Jake arrived at work with a bounce in his step. He smiled as he saw several workers entering the building holding Coffee Corner cups mixed in with the handful toting Java Universe coffees.

Inserting his key to unlock the office, Jake was surprised when it didn't need to be turned and instead, opened straight in. "A few early risers," Jake muttered as he made his way to his office. The moment he entered, he heard a pair of heavy footsteps steadfastly making their way toward him.

Barely setting his things down and slipping into his seat, he eyed the door. It didn't take long before Frank's concerned face was standing in his office, a stack of papers in his hand. Striding forward, Frank tossed the papers on the desk in front of Jake.

For a moment, he just stared. With a bite on his lip, Frank lout out in an exasperated torrent, "You have always done good work, Jake. Great work, in fact. Attention to the greatest detail. Providing multiple solutions almost ad nauseum. On our most important project… ever… for the entire firm… you mail in this work?"

Jake looked up at his direct supervisor and shrugged, "You wanted a rough draft, and while it is a bit rough, it has all of the elements of the campaign that were requested *and* a few artistic embellishments thrown in."

"Rough?" Frank scoffed. "I have seen rough drafts before. I mean, to be honest, this looks like a rough draft from *anyone else* on our marketing team. But for you, Jake, this is *way* below expectations."

Frank leaned forward, "Jake, what is going on with you lately?"

"I'm not sure what you mean, sir?"

With a perturbed purse of his lips and scowl, Frank said, "Don't think I haven't heard about your coffee cart lady in the lobbies of the Commerce Towers or your antics downtown from the mayor. And don't think Henry hasn't heard an earful. Jake, this is no time to be taking philanthropic ventures, as well intended as they may be. Not while we have a national, if not, multi-national opportunity dropped in our laps. We need your full attention. Do you hear me?"

Jake looked into his boss' eyes. For a moment, he didn't speak. He didn't blink. Finally, he said, "I will deliver what is asked of me. Like I always do."

Frank blinked at Jake. With a large sigh, he said, "Be sure you do, Jake. We *all* have a lot riding on this."

Jake nodded and pulled out his laptop and storyboards. With a glance up, he said, "I'm on it, Frank. I will not let you down."

Frank stared for a long moment. Finally, he nodded, pivoted and left Jake to do his work.

Jake took in a large breath, stretched his arms with his fingers laced and got to work.

Twenty Two

Jake left the office late. Spending hours cleaning up his presentation and adding to it, he hit submit on a package that he could be reasonably proud of. Given the client parameters, it still wasn't in the top tier of work that he was especially happy with or proud of, but he was confident it would satiate Frank and Jeff.

Most of the office did not have a habit of staying past five o'clock, he was able to sneak out without any fanfare. Jabbing at the elevator button, he urged it to come faster as he could see the shadow against Frank's door indicating his boss was heading out as well. Jake got the job done but was not in any mood to enter a lengthy discussion about it, or about his much-harangued absence from the prior day.

He relaxed as the elevator doors opened. He slipped inside and hammered the lobby button encouraging the doors to once again close and begin moving to the lobby. As soon as they opened, Jake burst through, bid a pleasant evening to the night attendant and disappeared into the night.

Starting his truck, Jake was happy to hear the Christmas song through his speakers. Putting the truck through its paces, Jake made his way downtown. He was both excited and frustrated to have to hunt for a spot near the Coffee Corner.

Wheeling in next to the curb, he walked briskly through the gorgeously decorated and lit streets. Seeing Sara pace back and forth through the coffee shop window, he craned his neck to see a full house in the space next door. Adults and children alike sat in front of canvases perched on easels waiting for the event to begin. The space looked brilliant with art stations scattered throughout the Christmas trees.

Pushing into the coffee shop, Jake saw the panicked look on Sara's face.

Sara wrung her hands in worry as she looked up at Jake. He offered a comforting smile, "You've got this."

"No, I don't. I think I'm going to be sick," Sara said, her face genuinely pale.

"You aren't going to be sick. Because there are people *wanting* to know your work, to catch a glimpse of what you know and how to paint amazing pieces like you do. That is why they had to move it to the new space. There wasn't enough space in the coffee shop to host everyone," Jake said.

"That makes it worse!" Sara spat.

Jake was unrelentingly calm, "That is what makes it so wonderful. Just be yourself. Tell them about how *you* approach a painting and assure them that there is no one way. Help *their* visions come to life. Sure, there are techniques and tips you can share. Art comes from within. Have fun with that. Send them home with that notion."

Sara looked at Jake, still clearly unconvinced. With rapid, shallow breaths she said, "I'll do it if you do it."

"What?" Jake reeled.

"If you paint. I know it isn't your thing, I remember you from art class," Sara said.

"Okay, fine. Let's do this," Jake said, his voice defiant. "Remember, have fun."

She let her shoulders soften. With a nod, she lifted her chin, "All right. I'll have fun. Encourage them to have fun."

"There you go," Jake applauded.

The café door opened and Bea pushed through with an empty cocoa carafe, "They are all there and ready for you, my dear."

The panic returned to Sara's eyes. Her head snapped to Jake, her face wincing, "Will you introduce me?"

Jake was taken aback.

"I don't know how to start. If someone can get me going, I think… I think I can take it from there," Sara said.

Jake smiled, "I'll introduce you."

Sara immediately looked relieved.

Bea looked over her efforts to put together a new vat of cocoa offering her own knowing smile.

"Come on. Your audience awaits," Jake said.

Reluctantly, Sara followed.

As they entered the event space, all eyes turned towards the front of the room. The buzz of excited conversation came to an abrupt stop.

Sara danced in place as her breathing became choppy and her heart raced.

Seeing Sara's anxiety, Jake stepped forward, spreading his arms wide and addressed the room, "Welcome. Thank you for coming to the first of many holiday events on Main Street leading up to Christmas Eve. In addition to art, it looks like you have the opportunity to paint what looks to be an amazing snowman. I can see that coming back out as Christmas decorations in your homes for years to come."

Jake nodded toward Sara's sample painting on the easel in the front of the room.

Clapping his hands together, he continued, "In this same space, we will have a Christmas Cookie Bake-off sponsored by Jenn's Bakery. There will be exciting events, right here in this space, every day until Christmas Eve. It all culminates in the Wintergreen Main Street tree lighting. An event our families have looked forward to and enjoyed for years. We will have snowman-building contests. Don't worry about the snow, we have a plan regardless of the forecast, a gingerbread-making contest, carols and more. Bring your families, tell your friends, invite your neighbors. The Wintergreen community is alive and well."

With a glance and arms held out toward Sara, he said, "And with no further ado, I turn over tonight's exciting program to our very own Sara Bailey. Many of you know her from the coffee shop next door. A few of you from high school might remember her as an award-winning artist. Her own work is on display in the Coffee Corner, I encourage you to visit and check it out. It is... beautiful."

Jake turned his full attention to Sara who blushed. "And with that, I have nothing further to say. Let amazing holiday art commence!"

Sara took a deep breath and looked at the crowd. "Who is ready to paint? Thank you, Jake for that introduction, I hope I can live up to it. I certainly hope you all attend the Christmas events along Main Street. Our Christmas traditions mean so much, not just to us, but to generations before and those we get to introduce it to. That is what I get out of painting. I take the memories and the images and emotions that go along with it and I do my best to apply it to a canvas. What do you think? Want to paint along with me tonight?"

The room cheered. Jake retreated to a corner with Bea. Bea leaned in and gave him a big sideways hug.

With the ice broken, Sara tackled the room with aplomb, sharing her strategy for getting started. She encouraged the painters to pick a background color. It could be any color they wanted. It could fill the entire canvas. It could be a shape with clean lines or like her example, it could fade at the edges in rough lines like the sun peeking through the trees.

Taking a seat in front of the class, she readied herself at her own blank canvas. With a stern nod toward Jake, she held him to his word as he grabbed an extra easel and canvas setting up in the back of the room.

He enjoyed watching Sara's transformation as she slowly became engulfed in the moment. Seeing the smiles on the participating painters as they began to put paint to canvas. She would tackle a phase on her canvas and then work the room, helping each painter, and encouraging them from the first brush stroke to the last.

She stifled a giggle as she approached Jake's spot. He didn't see her at first as he concentrated hard on attempting to make clean lines with his brush. His tongue poked out of the corner of his mouth as he focused.

"Not bad. A bit of suggestion, this is art. Let it flow. You are so concerned about making a mistake. That's what the rest of the colors on the palette are for. Kind of like your marketing projects. Don't see what's on the surface, the flat image in front of you. Tell a story on the canvas. Make it come to life," Sara said, guiding Jake's brush to make softer strokes.

Letting go, she allowed him to make the next swipe of the brush.

"Good," she said. Trying not to over-focus on Jake, she pulled away and returned to working with the other students.

Bea smiled from her vantage in the corner.

As the class was well underway, Debbie walked in, glancing at the group's efforts. Seeing Bea in the back, Debbie nodded at Sara with a smile as she made her way through the room. Pausing at Jake's painting, Debbie frowned before seeing Jake look up, his eyes wide.

"Hmm, not quite gallery-worthy yet, Jake. Keep at it. Maybe working without the look of sheer terror would help," Debbie said.

"Oh, there is no help for me. I am just wasting this canvas in a show of moral support," Jake whispered back.

"A worthy effort, then," Debbie said.

In the back of the room, Bea observed the eager painters hard at work as she kept vigil on the beverages and treats. Seeing Debbie admire the artwork in motion, Bea smiled.

"You made it," Bea said.

"Just had to shut the gallery down for the night. This is a great turnout. I thought you'd be in the coffee shop," Debbie said.

"We couldn't have fit them in there. Besides, this makes the space all Sara's for the evening," Bea said.

"But they can't see her paintings on the wall," Debbie said. "I can't see them. I keep trying to make it down there."

"We can go now," Bea said.

Debbie scanned the room.

"They'll be fine," Bea assured and led Debbie out the door and into the coffee shop.

Debbie stopped in front of the first painting. "Bea, this is really good," she said.

"I think so," Bea nodded.

Debbie took her time, her eyes dancing all over the piece. "Mixed techniques, but that doesn't take away from the depth and beauty," she said. Moving to the next painting, Debbie had more of the same superlatives to share. "Bea, these could be in my gallery. These *should* be in my gallery. They are better than some of my other paintings. Really."

"Don't tell me. Tell Sara," Bea said.

Debbie looked thoughtful and nodded. Stopping at the final painting, she noticed the tag in the corner. "Someone bought one," Debbie said.

"Second day it was up on the wall. I think I have a buyer for the first one, too. They had to measure space for a Christmas present," Bea said.

"I'll have paintings in my gallery for years that don't sell," Debbie said. "I want these. Does she have more?"

"I believe she does," Bea nodded.

"Right under our noses in our community," Debbie said. "I really like all of this working together stuff. We should have been doing this all along."

"Some of us might not be struggling so much," Bea admitted.

Debbie slung her arm around Bea, "We'll come out of this stronger than ever."

"I'm too old to start again," Bea laughed. Nodding toward the door, she asked, "Shall we?"

"We shall, but I need to have a serious conversation with your granddaughter," Debbie said.

As the art class was showing signs of wrapping up, Jake peered over the shoulders of budding artists to see some surprisingly nice snowmen. Looking at his own, he decided it would make decent refrigerator fodder for an elementary schooler.

Titling his easel so that his somewhat eerie-looking snowman wasn't so easy to see, he set his brushes down and hopped out of his seat.

Sara drew a crowd of participants asking her questions and reveling over her painting that she completed in between walking the room and helping students. Sara congratulated the students for their personal works of art.

As one eager woman spoke to Sara, Jake was waved over to join the conversation.

Sara looked at Jake as she rocked on her heels, "Mary here wanted to know, if within the weeks' worth of activities already booked, there would be room for a chocolate pop-up. She also has a friend that makes homemade jewelry. She thought this space would work great for them."

"In *this* space," Jake repeated. "Yes, I think we can make it work. While downtown Main Street has activities planned all week, there is room for them to share the evening. In fact, I think it would only bolster a stronger showing."

Sara gave Jake a look before breaking into a smile, "Well, there you go. I'll arrange it with my grandmother. She owns the space now."

"Wonderful. I can't wait to tell my friend," Mary said. "What should I do with this? I am afraid to smudge the paint."

"You know what, Mary? If you all like, you can leave them here and pick them up later in the week. What would be wonderful is, if they were set up in the front window. Everyone could see the beautiful work that you all did this evening," Sara said.

"That is a great idea. I'll invite more friends to see my work on display. It will be so fun!" Mary said.

As Mary scurried off, another woman took her place, "I'm sorry. What evening did you say the tree lighting was?"

"It is our big event Friday night after a week of fun activities down Main Street. Saturday, the tavern is having a special Christmas feast. It should be amazing," Jake said.

"I see," the woman looked a bit crestfallen. "That is the same night as the High School choir concert. Though it might work out, they are limiting tickets since the auditorium can't hold everyone."

Jake cocked his head, a finger raised in the air, "What if… what if the choir concert was here, *at* the tree lighting.

The woman's eyes went wide, "That would be spectacular! I'll bring it up to the choir director first thing tomorrow. Thank you."

Jake nodded and watched the woman filter out with the rest of the students.

Sara was boiling over with energy.

"Fine, right?" Jake asked.

"It was so much fun. Thank you, Jake. For pushing me," Sara said.

"You were great! The class loved you. I can't believe you created a masterpiece in that short bit of time especially since you spent most of it working the room," Jake said.

Sara perked up, "I didn't get to see your finished product."

"Oh, it, uh… I'm going to leave art with the artists. There is a special trash can behind every gallery that deserves my work," Jake said.

Sara peered around him, trying to steal a peek, "It's, it's not *that* bad. I mean it isn't the worst."

"Little Johnny is three. And I'm pretty sure from an abstract perspective, his is better than mine," Jake said.

"Well, you tried," Sara smiled up at him.

"For you," Jake gritted his teeth.

Sara's eyes widened with his choice of words.

Bea and Debbie approached them before the conversation could continue.

"I have the most fabulous idea," Debbie said. "How about we have a gallery event where we invite local artists? Painters, sculptures, metalworkers…"

"That would be great. I know some terrific artists who are just trying to make a name for themselves," Sara said.

"I know a few as well," Debbie said. Slinging her arm around Sara, she said, "I would like you to come down to the gallery tomorrow. There is something I would like to talk to you about."

"Yeah, sure," Sara said with a shrug of her shoulders. Looking at the otherwise empty room, she said, "Well, it is getting late. We should get this cleaned up."

"I'll help," Debbie offered.

"Nonsense. We'll get all this," Bea shooed Debbie away.

"You'll notice she didn't refuse my help," Jake said.

"You got us into all this!" Bea snapped before breaking into a smile.

"Well, I will leave you to it then," Debbie said. She turned to Sara, "I'll see you at the gallery tomorrow?"

Sara nodded, "Right after the morning rush?"

"See you then."

Jake, Sara and Bea watched the gallery owner walk out into the night.

Bea wore a knowing smile.

"What?" Sara winced.

"You just did a great job tonight," Bea said.

"It was fun," Sara admitted. With thankful eyes, she looked at Jake.

"Come on," he said. "Let's get this cleaned up. It sounds like you have a big day tomorrow."

Twenty Three

Jake arrived early. Beating the rest of the team, he flipped on the office lights and retreated to his office with the door shut.

Pulling up the Java Universe spread, his eyes scanned the updated work he had turned into Frank and Jeff the evening before. It had all the elements. He knew he needed to add more, but his mind drifted.

Opening up a new file on his laptop, he began plotting out the days leading up to Christmas Eve. He went backward to accommodate decorating Main Street and the art class. He noted the Christmas cookie bake-off, the chocolate and jewelry pop-up, the gallery event, the tree lighting and the tavern Christmas feast. He couldn't help but smile at the level of involvement and activity that had sprung up in such a short time.

Checking his email, he read that the choir director was checking with the school to ensure they could entertain a location change. Three more requests for pop-ups followed. A local author wanted to do a signing for one of their children's books they had launched. Wintergreen's own Parks and Rec Department asked if they could use Bea's space before the tree lighting for an arts and crafts class.

Jake chuckled to himself, "I wonder if the mayor knows about that one."

A knock on his door snapped Jake to switch gears, toggling the pages on his laptop to display the Java Universe campaign. Straightening up in his seat, he called, "Come in."

The door pushed open. Frank entered with Jeff on his heels.

"Got the revision. I'd say draft number two is a huge improvement over the first draft," Frank said.

"It has all of the elements that the client requested. And I think you struck the chord they were trying to share. Had to think about the scenario a bit, but I think they'll like it," Jeff said. "Can you spin up drafts and life cycles for local, regional and national versions of the campaign?"

"I can," Jake nodded.

"Great! I think we can win with this," Jeff said. "We'll need the finals as soon as possible. They left a window before Christmas

Eve to make the presentation. I feel like I've been working through the holiday."

"I know the feeling," Jake said, his lips flat.

"Anyway, I am going to run with this," Jeff said, pivoting to leave the office.

Frank's stance suggested he had no inclination to leave. He looked at Jake with a heavy expression on his face, "The mayor says you were quite busy yesterday."

"I did some philanthropic work while trying to capture the essence of the Java Universe campaign," Jake said.

"I've been shown some local social media campaigns," Frank turned his phone over and scrolled through posts. "Here is one for the café and the local artist showing."

Jake chewed his lip, wanting to update his schedule of downtown events. He couldn't believe that he had forgotten that one.

"Here is an art class. Great little ad. Ooh, my kids would love this one, a Christmas cookie contest. That sounds fun," Frank said.

"They *do* sound fun," Jake admitted.

"The style of the ads looks familiar. They are reminiscent of our well-paid, on-the-clock marketing executive, who is on the biggest project of our firm's history," Frank said.

"Mimicry is the best form of flattery," Jake said.

Frank's already furrowed brows became more severe, "Jake…"

Changing his stance in the conversation and his posture to match, he asked, "Was there something wrong with the Java Universe pitch?"

"No, like we said, it has everything that the client asked for. It was a pretty good pitch overall. What it wasn't, was your best effort. It wasn't even your usual effort," Frank said. "Jake, we need your head in the game."

Jake blankly looked at Frank as though he were waiting for the punchline.

Leaning closer, Frank asked in a low voice, "Is everything okay between you and Tracy?"

"Why?" Jake asked, his tone expressing his irritation with the line of questioning.

"Something is up with you. It isn't lost on Henry, either. He has big plans for you. I want you in a position to be able to capitalize on those plans, Jake," Frank said.

"I appreciate that Frank. You know, part of it is, the Java Universe project, especially given the client's parameters on messaging and the timeline, it didn't allow for a lot of creativity. I figured giving you the single solution in this case was the best idea," Jake defended.

"Your downtown activities didn't factor in?" Frank pressed.

"Sometimes the job is the job, Frank," Jake replied.

Frank studied his marketing executive for a long moment before offering a weak nod, "All right. Just know there are a lot of eyes on this one, Jake. Important ones."

"I got it, Frank. I appreciate the looking out for me, I really do," Jake said.

With a sigh, Frank slipped his phone into his pocket and left Jake's office. His slumped shoulders clearly displayed that he did not take the conversation as a win.

Jake stared at the open, empty door way for a solid minute before he sighed. Flexing his fingers, he began working feverishly on the marketing life cycles Jeff had requested. As he tried to condense his focus, he let out a slight smile, muttering to himself, "I guess my social media marketing is effective."

Jake worked into the late afternoon. His focus remained unbroken until he received an urgent call from Bea. Leaning back from his work, he was satisfied that he had given it more of a taste of his usual effort. Tapping into his email, he pulled up the calendaring function. Setting each phase of the marketing plan to send a draft to Jeff and copying Frank, he began to tidy up his desk.

Thinking twice of it, he packed his laptop but left his Java Universe notes strewn. Leaving his chair untucked, he grabbed his jacket and headed out, offering a sheepish smile to Carol.

She hissed, "If you come back, bring one of those Christmas lattes!"

"If I can," Jake nodded.

Slipping through the office doors, he waited for the elevator. As the doors opened, he froze when Frank stepped out. Snapping into action, Jake stepped in as his boss scowled, "*Now* where are you off to?"

Jake had to park several blocks away from the Coffee Corner. Shoppers dotted the sidewalks and bakers were already prepping their stations in the extra space by the café.

Holding the door open for a stream of customers, Jake made his way into the coffee shop. Bea looked up, "I'll be right with you, honey."

Jake nodded as he watched Bea and Sara work through the line of customers.

When the line had dwindled, she stepped out, "It's been like this all day. It's a Christmas miracle."

"Maybe a miracle. Maybe just a town remembering how good they have it with special people like you, Jennifer and the rest," Jake said. Settling around a tall table, he asked, "What's going on?"

Bea sat in the chair across from him, "I got a call from a woman who wants to rent the space next door. She and her husband were looking for a place for a small book store. They have enjoyed downtown so much, they decided it would be a great place to set up. I thought it might buy me time to see how things work out with the café, long term."

Jake looked at Bea, "How do you feel about it?"

Bea shrugged, "I really liked the idea of expansion, but I don't think I can afford it. Not right now."

"All right," Jake leaned back. After a thoughtful moment, he leaned forward, "You could work together. The coffee shop leading into the bookstore. You could share customers. Make it more of an experience. I bet you could find a way to make Jennifer's bakery a part of the equation."

"Yeah, that would work," Bea said. "You think I should do it?"

"I think taking pressure off yourself, while Main Street rebrands itself would be a good decision. You still have options for the future, but then again, if you opened space with the bookstore, you might not need anything more, plus you'd be financing the extra space through the lease," Jake said.

"They are really nice couple," Bea said.

"Well, how can I help you?" Jake asked.

"I don't know the first thing about leasing, contracts or any of those things," Bea said.

"We'll set aside some time and go through it. I bet Sara could help you put together the financial side of things. She is an accountant after all, if by education, at least," Jake said.

Bea smiled, "Yes, she is. Thank you for coming all the way down here. I don't know what I would do without you this year."

"Sell coffee, but maybe a few cups less," Jake winked.

Bea laughed and shook her head, "You are something else."

With a shrug, Jake pulled out his wallet, "Speaking of coffee, I would love one of those cardamom lattes."

"Pulla," Bea said.

"Yeah, one of those, please," Jake said.

Bea stared at the bills in his hand and wandered off. Jake slipped out of his seat and stuffed the bills in the tip jar.

"Causing trouble, Jake?" Sara asked from behind the bar.

"Not with any intention, but yeah, most likely," he said.

Sara's eyes went wide, "You are never going to believe this. I sold another painting! No mystery this time, the man came in and actually took it off the wall. He said it was the perfect gift for his wife."

"I believe it," Jakes said.

"Oh, I need to tell you," Sara said. Glancing at Bea , she asked, "You got the bar for a bit, Grandma?"

"Go on. Get out of here," Bea said. "It is almost time for the Christmas Cookie Bake-off. You two check it out. I'm going to hold down things here at the café."

Sara shot her an "Are you sure" look only to have a look of irritation volleyed back.

Sara slipped off her apron. Grabbing her coat, she paused when Jake reached out to help her slip it on. "Thanks," she said softly. "Let's walk and talk."

Leading Jake out of the café, Sara stepped out onto the sidewalk. Taking a few strides down the street, Sara looked at Jake, "I met with Debbie today."

"Oh? How did that go?" Jake asked.

"She said she wanted my art work at the gallery. Not just for the local event, but as part of her artists collection," Sara said.

"That's great!" Jake said.

Sara looked up at Jake, her eyes dripping with trepidation.

"It's not great?" Jake asked, confused.

"I'm afraid she is doing it to be nice. I mean, we are all caught up in Christmas and revitalizing Main Street…" Sara trailed off.

Jake nodded slowly seeing where the conversation was going. "Do you think of Debbie as a sound businesswoman?"

"Yes," Sara shrugged. "She is likely one of the few that would survive a downturn if we can't get people down here regularly."

"I think you just answered your own concerns," Jake said.

The pair walked in silence as each other's words resonated in their own minds.

After several minutes passed, Sara looked up at Jake, "You really think…"

Jake's stern glare was all the response she seemed to need.

A few more steps in silence, Jake offered, "I love your work. I may be a bit biased."

"Biased?" Sara swayed a step toward Jake.

"I mean," Jake flustered. "We're friends. Your grandmother and I are close…"

"Right," Sara nodded, her voice almost disappointed in the response. "We should… We should go and see if Jennifer needs any help."

"Yeah," Jake agreed.

Steering in unison, they remained the same parallel distance apart until they reached the cookie competition. Jake held the door for Sara to slip inside. Jennifer looked up, her cheeriness unrelenting despite the near pandemonium breaking out in the room.

Half a dozen stations had been set up. Mini ovens were spread out in parallel with heavy-duty electrical outlets supplying them. The baking teams scurried assembling their ingredients and tools. Decorative platters and tiered stands were ready to welcome fresh baked goods for judging.

Jennifer was trying to coordinate the teams, guide the judges and welcome guests. Standing directly in front of her, Jake and Sara asked, "What can we do to help?"

"One of you entertain the guests. The other can prep the judges. I am trying to make sure the teams have what they need," Jennifer glanced at the clock. "We kick off in less than half an hour."

"Got it boss!" Jake clicked his heels together. With a glance toward Sara, he asked, "Judges or guests?"

"Flip for it?" Sara asked.

"Know the rules?" Jake asked.

Sara frowned, "Choose which cookie you think is best?"

"Perfect, you work with the judges," Jake said.

Clapping his hands together, Jake approached the crowd, "Who's ready to taste some cookies?"

The gathering applauded and cheered.

"First, a big round of applause for Bea Bailey and the Coffee Corner for brewing up some of the most delicious coffee and cocoa in Wintergreen!" Jake rallied the crowd. "And to Jenn's Bakery for hosting this incredible event!"

Jennifer slipped an index card into his hand.

Giving it a glance, he said, "All right. Here is how tonight's inaugural Christmas Cookie Bake-off is going to work. There will be two prizes awarded tonight. The first for the audience choice and the second for the judges' choice. Each winner gets a giant Yule cake from Jenn's Bakery and, of course, bragging rights. If the decision is unanimous, the winner gets a weekly goody basket from Jenn's Bakery for a year and their recipe with their family name gets a spot on her shelves with profits going to their charity of choice. I'm second-guessing not entering myself now."

The crowd laughed. Jake looked at the clock, "Only fifteen minutes and the cooking will begin!"

With a glance toward Sara, Jake saw her setting up the three judges with scoring cards and plates. Each judge received a beverage of their choice from the Coffee Corner.

Jennifer seemed to have the final contestants ready to go. Giving Jake a warm smile, she indicated they were ready to go when the clock hit the top of the hour.

Jake yielded the floor to Jennifer who eyed the clock. She welcomed the crowd and thanked them, the contestants and the judges for making it such a special night. At right on the hour, she started the timer letting the bakers know they had just one hour to produce their best Christmas cookies.

Huddling together with Jake and Sara, Jennifer beamed, "This is great! What a showing. I think we'll need a bigger venue next year."

"I hope so," Sara said.

"They seem to be having fun," Jake added. "These are all home bakers?"

"Just families that thought they had a winning recipe," Jennifer said.

"I'm sure they will all be wonderful," Jake said. "Glad I don't have to judge."

"You can put in for an audience vote," Jennifer suggested.

Jake nodded, "Why not?"

Jennifer walked off to check on the contestants and root them on.

Sara nudged close to Jake, "The café did better today than any day in December over the last three years."

"That's great!" Jake said.

"Yeah. Thank you," Sara said.

"You guys need to stop thanking me and just know… just know I'm doing what I think is right. I care about you. I care about all the people here, I mean, look at them!" Jake said.

"Think they are having this much fun at the shopping center?" Sara asked.

"I'm thinking right now. They are wondering where all of their customers went," Jake said. "But, no. There is no way they're are having this much fun, even if they are teeming with shoppers."

Sara looked lost for a moment, her eyes glazed.

"What's wrong?" Jake asked.

"This time, next year, I'll be working at the accounting firm," Sara asked. "In a few weeks I will be."

"And?"

"I don't think I want to," Sara said, her voice flat.

Jake shrugged, "So, don't. What do you want to do?"

"I don't know," Sara shook her head. "My parents have my role set up already. They have a client base for me. I'll walk in with a stable foundation. Not many accountants fresh out of school get a book of business like that."

"I'm sure there are options," Jake said.

"My family is counting on me," Sara said.

Jake rubbed his chin, "Don't you think they would rather have you happy over financially stable?"

"They're accountants," Sara smirked.

Jake laughed, "They love you. Somewhere in that love, your happiness is their ultimate happiness."

"What about you?" Sara asked.

"What about me?" Jake winced.

"You've been avoiding your work lately," Sara said.

"I haven't been avoiding work. I have just…" Jake sighed. "I've just found my time downtown here more meaningful."

He looked Sara in the eyes. His lips quivered slightly as he was lost for a moment in the pools reflecting the Christmas tinsel and glitter of the world around him. The sight made his chest tighten.

Jake swallowed hard as he realized his words carried more weight than he even cared to admit.

"Distracted, annoyed, disheartened and I am still the best marketer in the firm. My role is safe even if my boss wants my full attention. They have gotten used to me working seventy hours a week relentlessly. Maybe it was time that I gave to something else," Jake said.

Sara looked around the room and out the window at the brilliantly decorated Main Street, "That something else has turned out pretty terrific."

"I had amazing help and inspiration," Jake said. "I need to tell you…"

"Bakers, stop! Put down your cooking utensils!" Jennifer called out. "Place three cookies on a plate of your choice, they will be presented to the judges. The rest can be set out for the guests. If you have extras still baking in the oven, you are free to pull them and serve them as well when they are ready."

The crowd watched excitedly as the cookies were plated and delivered to the judges. The judges wriggled in their seats but resisted the urge to dive into the cookies set in front of them. They wanted the spectators to begin their own tastings and not be swayed by the judges.

"Come on, let's taste some cookies!" Sara tugged at Jake's arm. Following the line, they stopped at each station, complementing the bakers on how their cookies looked. Taking a bite, they looked at each other without sharing their initial impression. Repeating the process from station to station, they sampled each cookie. Scribbling notes on the scorecards they were given, they made their final assessments and placed them in a large cookie jar to be tallied.

Once the crowd had largely run through the gauntlet of Christmas cookies, the judges began their own tasting. One by one, they studied each cookie, inspecting the color and caramelization on the bottoms before taking a bite. Some would close their eyes, others stared at some nebulous blank spot above the crowd as they allowed their senses to completely focus on the flavors that entered their mouths. After several bites of each, they scribbled furiously on their scorecards. One judge paused, took bites of two cookies and made a notation on their card before handing them over to Jennifer.

At the cookie jar table, Sara and Jake tallied the spectator scores while Jennifer took to the center of the room. With a glance over, Sara nodded, handing Jennifer the final results.

"Wow, this was a close one. Only a few points separated the bottom score from the top score. It makes sense. All of the cookies looked amazing, tasted even more so, and most importantly, reminded me of Christmas," Jennifer said. "With that, the winner of the spectator award in the first annual Wintergreen Christmas Cookie Bake-off is… the Jensen family with their spin on a traditional shortbread cookie. Delicious, buttery, and, I know, had me wanting to reach for another. I may need to borrow your recipe for the bakery."

Moving over to the judges' table, she stood beside them and picked up the tally sheet, "The scoring from the judges was equally tight! But there can only be one winner and it is… the Hart family. Congratulations!"

The crowd cheered, giving applause for all of the contestants and the judges.

The remaining cookies were doled out and the crowd slowly made their way into the night. Jennifer sought Jake and Sara out, "Thank you for your help tonight."

"Thank you for putting this together. You had a great turnout," Jake said.

"Business has taken a huge leap forward the last couple of days, thanks to you, Jake," Jennifer said.

"I had plenty of help. We are all in this together," Jake said. "You've had a long day. Let's get this cleaned up and get you home."

Jennifer scanned the room. Napkins, cookie crumbs and plates were scattered like confetti. With a nod, she grabbed a trash bin and started collecting items. Jake broke down the stations while Sara gathered the items from the café.

In minutes, Jake was taking the trash out, Sara removed the table linens and Jennifer was running the vacuum. When Jake returned from the dumpster, the room looked good as new.

"Thanks again, guys!" Jennifer called. "I'm going to lock up the bakery and go home. I am beat."

Jake and Sara waved. Shutting off the lights, they made their way out of the extra space and locked the door behind them. Once more, the streets of Wintergreen had fallen silent. A few scattered snowflakes drifted in the air, making the lights and décor of downtown even more magical.

Taking a deep breath of the cold night air, Jake didn't say a thing. He just let his senses absorb the moment.

"Well, I should go. I have to help Grandma open bright and early tomorrow," Sara said.

"Yeah, I…" Jake started.

Sara looked expectantly into Jake's eyes, but he could only swallow hard.

"I, uh, had fun tonight," he finally said.

"Yeah, me too."

"I wanted to tell you earlier that…" Jake started.

The rattle of keys behind them as Jennifer closed and locked the bakery door stopped him. "Thanks again, you two!" Jennifer called.

"Goodnight, Jenn!" Sara said. A shiver suddenly struck her as she pulled her coat tight.

"I, should… I should let you go. It's freezing out here," Jake said.

Sara looked at him for a long moment before offering a slight nod and pivoting on her heel. Moving in the opposite direction, Jake suddenly spun, "I should walk you to your car!"

Sara froze for a moment and turned to look at Jake, "That's sweet, but it's just around the corner."

"Still…" Jake insisted. "It's beautiful out here."

"It is," Sara said.

Reaching her car, she looked into his eyes. His lips quivered but no words came out.

"Goodnight, Jake," Sara said opening her door.

Jake slumped. He wanted to blurt out to her that he and Tracy were broken up. That all he could think about was how much he enjoyed working with her and her grandmother. How much his heart raced when they were together.

Biting his lip, he said, "Goodnight, Sara."

Squeezing his eyes shut, Jake turned and walked back to the sidewalk. Only when he heard Sara start her car did he open them. Turning slightly, he could see Sara's taillights driving away.

With a sigh, he turned, taking solace in the breathtaking sight of Downtown Wintergreen in all of its Christmas glory.

Twenty Four

"Long day, yesterday?" Frank asked.

Jake shot him a curious look and then remembered his staggered emails. The last one was well after everyone would have gone home. "Yeah, just wanted to make sure everything was done right."

Frank studied Jake for a moment, his eyes searching for answers as though he might find them on somewhere on Jake's forehead. With a slow nod, he said, "Yeah, it was all there. An 'A' effort for just about anyone else. Jeff is happy. I came by your office a few times to talk with you about it."

"I was in and out. You know us 'creative' types. Have to get fresh perspectives," Jake smiled.

"Well, see to it you are available. Jeff is doing a first pass with the local client. He presents to regional and national over the next couple of days," Frank said.

"Sure, of course," Jake nodded.

Jeff's voice cut through the office, "Hey guys, great news. The local was in the pitch with his district manager. They love it. They know the national team will have a few ideas, tweak here and there, but they are all in. The district guy said he knew it would sail through regional."

Frank pursed his lip as he glanced at Jake before revealing a big smile and 'atta boy pat on Jeff's shoulder.

"And there is more. I got wind of this gallery event downtown, I turned these guys on to it as a great opportunity to launch themselves in the Wintergreen community. They called up and the gallery owner sounded like she was in. Helping them grow their business even from the grass roots level," Jeff said.

"That's great. Nice work," Jake said, unable to hide the curiousness in his tone. Almost before he could get the words out, his phone buzzed. Pulling it out of his pocket, he saw Debbie's number pop up. "I have to get this. Great work, Jeff!"

Jogging to his office, he shot a glance toward Carol and closed his door. "Hello?"

"Jake, it's Debbie. Hey, I just got a call from someone who works at your firm…"

"Jeff," Jake said.

"Right, Jeff and those Java Universe guys. Anyway, they pitched this whole catering the gallery event with coffee and cocoa and cookies. I'll give them credit, but there is no way. It did give me pause, though. I was going to have it catered, like I usually do, but why not? Why not coffee, cocoa and cookies? But using Bea and Jennifer instead. What do you think?" Debbie asked.

"I love the idea. Does that work for your clientele?" Jake asked.

There was a clear pause on the line, "I mean, they are used to charcuterie and Champagne."

"What about the tavern? Could they do it?"

"You know, I'll ask. I'd love to support them, too," Debbie said. "Thanks, Jake. Will I see you downtown today?"

"Yeah, I'll be down there at some point," Jake said.

"Great. Stop in, say hello."

"I will," Jake said. About to close the call, he asked, "Hey, I was wondering, did, uh, did Sara bring in any of her work?"

"I asked," Debbie said. "And I genuinely want some, but no. Not yet. I haven't heard back from her."

"Hmm. Okay. Thank you for sharing," Jake said. "I will see you later, Debbie."

Jake ended the call and gazed out onto the parking lot. A light flurry had begun to descend. His mind swirled. His life had been so uncomplicated. It had a clear track. He was dedicated to moving forward. Suddenly, nothing seemed clear. His heart was full and yet conflicted. The path was there, but he felt oddly hesitant about taking it.

With only minor tweaks to the Java Universe presentation, Jake slipped out of the office quickly at the end of the day. Heading downtown, he found a spot and enjoyed watching the sidewalks and streets beginning to look busier.

Making his way into the coffee, shop, he gave Sara a quick wave as she prepared a drink behind the bar. Finding Bea at the back table going over her order for stock, she eagerly waved Jake over.

"How's it going today?" Jake asked.

"Great. And, I spoke with Debbie. She wants us to provide coffee, cocoa and tea for the gallery event. I don't know what they are used to, but she ordered so much. I'll have to wrangle some additional carafes," Bea said.

"That's great news!" Jake applauded.

"Come, sit," Bea said. As Jake settled in opposite from her, Bea looked over his shoulder and smiled.

"There is an energy between you two. I see it," Bea said.

"Who?" Jake gasped.

"Don't play dumb. It doesn't become you. You and Sara," Bea said.

Jake didn't reply. He shuffled in his seat, with his eyes drifting downward toward the table. Subconsciously, his gaze drifted to Sara but just for a moment before returning to Bea.

"I see the way she looks at you when you aren't looking at her. She has feelings for you. And unless I am just a blind old woman, I see it when you look at her, too," Bea pressed.

"I don't know," Jake twisted in his seat. "There's her and Shawn…"

"Pfft! Shawn. Nice kid. Sure, they were high school sweethearts. But, there is a reason they have never become more," Bea said.

Jake remained unmoved.

"How about you and your lady friend?" Bea asked.

"I'm pretty sure we broke up. If I'm honest, it had been trending that way for a while. Dating my boss' boss' daughter- the boss who would ultimately be *my* boss someday just doesn't seem like a good idea," Jake said.

"Love is always a good idea. If it isn't a good idea, then it isn't love. Love doesn't come with reservation. It comes with your whole heart. When I see you and Sara together, you are both working from your whole hearts," Bea said.

Jake glanced over at Sara whose eyes averted as they met.

Drawing in a deep breath, he looked at Bea, his expression revealing nothing of what he was thinking or feeling.

Bea smiled as she sent Jake and Sara on a mission to the gallery. Calling ahead, she had Debbie hasten some notes about the numbers of attendees and desired beverage flavors. Her grin grew wicked as she knew full well, Debbie could just email the list over.

Jake and Sara walked down Main Street, their eyes focused on their path and largely avoided contact with one another. Jake could swear he could hear snowflakes touching down on the sidewalk in front of them as they walked in silence.

Arriving at the gallery, Debbie was waiting for them.

List in hand, she waved it as she greeted them. Sara's eyes followed the piece of paper. Her hand even gestured toward it, but

Debbie lured them further inside. Spinning, she smiled with a hopeful expression in her eyes.

Before Debbie even spoke, Sara knew what she was going to say.

"I hope you have considered bringing some of your paintings to the gallery, Sara," Debbie said.

"I don't know, Debbie," Sara swayed self-consciously back and forth. "You really think people want to see my art?"

"I *know* they will," Debbie said, her voice exuding confidence.

"I hear people admiring your paintings in the café every time I am in there. You are already selling them. Debbie is right, people love your work, Sara," Jake said encouragingly.

Sara's eyes danced along Debbie's earnest expression. With a brief glance toward Jake, Sara blushed and offered a hesitant nod, "Fine. If you are sure."

"I am sure," Debbie says assuredly.

Sara swelled her chest with a deep breath. "Okay. I will select a few to bring in."

"Great!" Debbie clapped her hands. "I can't wait to host an exclusive showing after the New Year. You will, of course, be a part of the holiday gallery event."

Sara blushed and nodded.

"You'll do fantastic," Debbie assured her.

"Thank you." Chewing her lip, she said, "I will see you tomorrow."

With a glance toward Jake, Sara said, "I could use some air."

Leaving the gallery, the air they found was cool and crisp. The light flurry continued, just barely coating the ground and the trees as it fell.

Jake cast an expectant look. Sara started to take a step towards the heart of Main Street but as the lights turned on at the cusp of dusk, she instead swung her foot towards the park. They walked slowly side by side. Jake felt a different feeling inside him as they walked. It was warmth, hope and fear.

His frown wasn't missed by Sara. "What?" she asked.

Jake bit his lip as he shook his head, "Something Bea said has me thinking."

"Careful with the ideas that Grandma puts in your head. She has a plan for the world and likes to corral everyone along that path," Sara laughed.

"Yeah," Jake said softly, "I got that."

Sara looked up at Jake as they entered the park, bathed in the light of the small trees placed along the main path, "You okay?"

Jake nodded, "Yeah. I'm at a crossroads. I think I am a little surprised by the paths I see in front of me."

"Care to share any of them? I am happy to listen," Sara said.

Jake looked at Sara, a soft smile spreading across his face, "I'm glad. I'm glad I have had the opportunity to spend time with you these past few weeks."

"I am, too," Sara nodded.

Jake paused as he began to speak. The snow fell heavier, making its way through the trees of the park. He was enamored with the way the light shone through the bows and made the snow sparkle. Showering like glitter over Sara, he was taken aback for a moment.

Sara took a slight step forward and looked directly into Jake's eyes. "What?" she asked nearly in a whisper.

Biting his lip, Jake said, "All of this. Every bit of it, has made me rethink everything."

"Everything?" Sara asked.

Jake inched closer, "Everything."

Their lips hovered close. Through the cool night air, they could feel each other's warmth radiate, drawing them closer still.

Jake's mind whirled. He felt dizzy, flushed.

Sara's phone chimed. Fumbling, she fought for the alarm. At first, she didn't take her eyes off of Jake. Fumbling for the phone as the alarm continued to chime, she huffed in frustration as she was forced to focus on her phone. With a sigh, she said, "It's Grandma. With the homemade vendor event tonight, she is overwhelmed."

Jake nodded, "Bea needs our help."

Sara cocked her head, "You are something else. You know that?"

"As long as 'something else' means something good, I'll take it," Jake said. "Come on," Jake extended his arm escorting Sara back through the park.

When they reached the entrance to the park and began to mingle in the view of others, they shied apart. With rosy cheeks, they marched together down Main Street to help Bea with supporting the *Chocolate and Jewels* event.

Jake rolled up his sleeves, "How can I help?"

"Jake, you don't have to do that," Bea protests.

"I am a full-service marketer, Bea," Jake said.

"You are an unpaid marketer, Jake," Bea said.

Jake stood up, his face serious, "I have been paid in-kind so much more than you could ever know this season, Bea."

Bea stopped and looked at Jake. Her smile was met with tears welling in her eyes.

With a laugh, Jake leaned in and gave Bea a sideways hug, "We're a sappy pair, aren't we?"

"'Tis the season," Bea laughed.

"Did you just end this moment on a Christmas tree joke?" Jake asked. "Had style to it, I'll give you that."

"Uh, you two? Wanna get to work? These cocoas aren't going to serve themselves!" Sara teased holding a tray full of cups.

"Yes, ma'am," Jake clicked into position grabbing another tray to follow Sara over to the spare room.

As a trio, they made their way into the space next door where two ladies captivated their audience with luxurious homemade chocolates and a sparkling display of handmade jewelry.

"I love that we can not only help local businesses but local entrepreneurs, too," Bea said.

Jake nodded, "Every business has to start somewhere."

"Look at those chocolates!" Sara set her tray down and made a beeline to the chocolatier.

Each chocolate was glazed to look like glass gems. Eyes wide, she readily accepted a sample. After one bite, she said, "That's it! I want three boxes. Two for stockings, one for me."

"Do you make these all year long?" Bea asked. The woman behind the table nodded. "I would love to visit after the holidays and see if you would like to sell some out of the café."

"Really?" the woman beamed. "I would love that!"

"Stop by in January. I'll treat you to a coffee and we can talk about it," Bea said.

Jake watched the interaction. He chuckled to himself to see how many relationships had begun with just the slightest nudge.

Sara had migrated to the jewelry table where a mother and daughter displayed their handcrafted jewelry. A clip from a Christmas movie with an actress wearing earrings made by them was on prominent display.

"Well, that's impressive," Jake said.

"What do you think?" Sara asked, holding them up to her ears.

"They look… They look beautiful," he said.

Sara blushed, handing them back to the proprietor.

As she moved on to another end of the table, Jake discretely handed a few bills over and slipped the earrings into his pocket. For a moment, he watched as Sara looked at the wares and giggled with the ladies on the other side of the table. She was so light, so radiant that she made others around her shine. He had to admit, she certainly had an effect on him.

Turning, she saw Jake observing and smiled, "Silly girl stuff, right?"

"Not at all," Jake said. His usual jovial voice came out rather pensive.

Sara took notice but returned her attention to the woman displaying what she thought would be a good match for Bea's style.

From across the room, Bea watched Sara and Jake. A thin smile formed across her lips.

Twenty Five

Jake was hardly present at the marketing firm. His mind was focused on the Main Street Wintergreen Tree Lighting. Emails flew into his inbox and texts invaded his phone throughout the day about vendors, volunteers and how the choir should set up.

Town hall had even reached out, asking if the mayor should make an appearance and address the crowd. Jake contemplated his response. His knee-jerk reaction was a hard no. Being more shrewd and thoughtful, he elected to make the arrangements to allow the mayor to speak. He even bestowed him the honor of lighting the tree himself. The second lighting for him that holiday season.

Frank poked his head in several times throughout the day. Jake questioned whether he had a genuine need for most of them. He would look up from his desk, his increasing ire beginning to sear through the veil.

Inspired by the final interruption, Jake asked, his voice cheery, "Going to attend the tree lighting tonight?"

"Hmm?" Frank frowned.

"The Main Street Wintergreen Tree Lighting. The community has really come together to make it happen. Would be great for the executives of Banks Marketing to be present. Bring their families. I had Carol blast it out to the staff, I hope you don't mind," Jake said.

Frank looked shocked, "Mind? Pssh, not all. I think it is a wonderful celebration of the holidays. I mean the Commerce Center celebration was packed. But you can never have too much Christmas, right?"

"Right," Jake nodded. His stare was vacant as he watched his superior exit his office.

Jake tapped his fingers against his desk. His work was complete for the day. He decided he'd had enough for the day. Grabbing his bag and his jacket, Jake stopped by Carol's desk.

"Are you bringing your family downtown to the tree lighting tonight?" he asked.

Carol smiled as she brushed her long brown hair back over her shoulder, "I told my kids about it. They can't wait. I am so glad the town is still having it this year. I had heard they weren't. We went to the shopping center tree lighting but it just wasn't the same."

"The town isn't hosting it this year. The Main Street businesses are," Jake said.

"With no help from a certain marketing executive, right?" Carol asked.

Jake shuffled back looking surprised.

"I love what you have been doing. Don't think I don't follow on social media. You have your fingerprints all over this thing," Carol said.

"Thank you for covering," Jake said.

"I knew what I was doing. I'd do it again. I trust your judgment, Jake. You always have everyone else in your best interest. Seeing you sneaking out of here, doing something for yourself, even if it benefits others has been… refreshing," Carol said.

"Thank you," Jake had no other words.

"Just let me know if there is anything else that you need from me. How can I help "Operation Save Downtown"?" Carol said.

"It has a name?" Jake winced.

"Not really, I just made it up. Sounds good, right?" Carol grinned.

Jake nodded slowly, "Sure. You will be writing copy in no time."

Carol frowned, straightening her glasses, "You're teasing me."

Jake shrugged, "You're still coming downtown, right?"

"Wouldn't miss it," Carol smiled.

Downtown Wintergreen was as bustling as Jake had remembered seeing it. The sidewalks were packed. Families were already visiting vendors. Businesses had steady streams of shoppers. People were having fun– together.

Sara scooted around the coffee bar to greet Jake, "This is amazing!"

"It's pretty good, right?" Jake smiled.

Without thinking, Sara placed her hand on Jake's chest as she watched family after family walk by the coffee shop. Realizing her faux pas, she quickly reeled her hand back in. "This is just so exciting and the official event hasn't even started yet. Vendors are still getting set up," Sara said.

"You guys have a good day?" Jake asked.

"We had a great day," Sara nodded. "Can I get you anything?"

"I'll have a cocoa later," Jake shrugged.

Sara's eyes were once more glued to the heavy traffic outside the shop. "I think with the choir coming, we are going to have a parking problem."

"I may have a plan," Jake grinned. As the sound of jingle bells ringing approached Main Street, Jake asked, "Right on time. Care to take the inaugural ride?"

Sara's eyes went wide, "Are you kidding me?"

"Come on," Jake urged holding the door open for Sara.

"All right!" Sara could barely contain herself. Turning, she glanced at her grandmother.

"You go, or I'll take your place!" Bea called from behind the coffee bar.

"We should probably go," Sara smiled.

With his hand out, he helped Sara climb into the carriage. A driver urged two draught horses to embark on their maiden journey. Behind that carriage, awaited two more.

"This... is... amazing," Sara said.

Jake cast a glance at her and then at Downtown Wintergreen, "Yes, it is."

Sara frowned, "Wait, where did you come up with horse-drawn carriages? You know what? Never mind. I am just starting to believe in Christmas miracles."

"So am I," Jake said quietly.

"What about the town? Did you have to get a permit?" Sara asked.

"Even better. I accepted the mayor's request to steal a moment of limelight," Jake grinned.

Sara wrinkled her nose, "Why would you do that?"

"He and Town Hall are now complicit in the Wintergreen Main Street Christmas Tree Lighting event," Jake said.

"Wow, you are positively wicked!" With a smile she added, "But I like it."

Jake nodded toward Jennifer's bakery. She waved as they rode by. "She's hosting a bake sale as a benefit for the choir. They have a trip in January," Jake said.

"That's wonderful!" Pointing and waving, she called, "Hi, Mr. Fuller!"

"Even he showed out. It looks like he got some more candy canes," Jake noticed.

Nearing the park, the driver leaned back and said, "Normally, we'd go down that street and loop around. I'm just going to bring you guys right back up Main Street."

Jake nodded, eyeing the contest areas all set up. Volunteers stood by, ready for their event. The entire area sparkled with twinkling lights and overflowed with a festive atmosphere.

"Is that a chestnut booth?" Sara asked. "I have always wanted a bag of roasted chestnuts while walking around a holiday fair."

"It looks like you'll get your chance," Jake said. "I noticed your painting in the gallery, by the way."

"You did?"

"Debbie has it right up front. It looks great," Jake said.

"I haven't seen it up yet," Sara's eyes went big. "I don't think I want to see it up."

"Of course you do. It's amazing," Jake assured her.

Sara shook her head in wonder, "I don't know. I think I'll just bury myself in holiday festivities and pretend it isn't there."

"While a good plan, I bet Debbie is not going to let you off so easily," Jake said.

Sara slumped, "You're probably right. Still a good try. You don't think I could just get lost in bags of chestnuts, delicious Christmas cookies? Ooh, I can build a snowman. I'll need a partner for that."

"I'm in. But I will warn you, I'll be in it to win it!" Jake said.

"All right folks. End of the line. I believe I have some passengers to bring to Main Street," the driver said.

"Thank you, good sir," Jake said.

"That was fun. Thank you," Sara called.

Stepping down, Jake held his hand out to help Sara out of the carriage. Her heel caught causing her to stumble. Jake held onto her hand and spun her safely free, catching her in his arms. Face to face, they stood, collecting themselves. For a moment, the world was a blur around them. Their chests heaved in rhythm.

Suddenly they were acutely aware they were not alone. Clearing her throat, Sara exclaimed loudly, and tapped the side of the carriage, "Yep, a successful test. I think this will work."

Ignoring the crowd for a moment, Jake said, "Sara…"

Sara stopped and looked Jake in the eyes.

As Jake collected himself to speak, a voice from the crowd shattered the moment.

"Jake!" Carol called with her two children each grasping a hand.

"Carol, you made it," Jake said. "Sara, meet Carol, the most amazing marketing assistant ever. Carol, this is Sara Bailey. Her grandmother owns the Coffee Corner."

"I see," Carol smiled. For a moment, she took Sara in before extending a warm handshake. "It's nice to meet you, Sara."

"Likewise. And who are these two cuties?" Sara asked.

"Tanner and Bethany, my everything. Well, almost my everything. My husband Eric will be joining us in a bit," Carol said.

"Can I buy you guys a coffee or a cocoa?" Jake offered.

"No, we're fine…" Carol started. Seeing the insistent look on Jake's face she relented, "Fine. Yes, fine."

"What does your husband like to drink?" Jake asked.

"He's a coffee and creamer kind of guy, but I want him to try one of those Pulla lattes you've been bringing to the office," Carol said.

"Sounds great. Come on," Jake said leading them into the very busy shop. Calling to Bea, he said, "Whatever these guys want, Bea. It's on me, please!"

"You got it, Jake!" Bea sang, her voice cheery despite the volume of orders she was filling.

Sara scanned the busy café, "I should probably get back there and help her."

"You won't miss the lighting, will you?" Jake asked.

"No. We are going to shut down a half an hour before show time," Sara said.

"Mind an escort?" Jake asked.

"From you, good sir? I'd be honored," Sara curtsied before slipping behind the bar.

Jake laughed. He couldn't help but take a moment to watch her. She was absolutely radiant. The night was setting up perfectly until- the café doors swung open once more.

"I thought I would find you here!" a voice called through the crowded coffee house.

The voice made Jake wince. Taking a deep breath, he turned to see Tracy striding through the crowd directly toward him.

"Tracy, what are you doing here?" Jake asked, his brows furrowed.

"It seems if I want to find you these days, I need to come here," Tracy said. Taking a step back, she said, "I've missed you. You look good, Jake."

Jake couldn't help but see Sara watching the conversation unfold.

"Daddy is coming back to town. He wanted me to come meet him. He said he wants to make sure you are giving the Java Universe account your full attention," Tracy said.

Jake paled further with each sentence uttered.

Sara spun her head at the conversation.

"Your future, *our* future, is riding on this Jake. He wants to take us to dinner, you know, as a couple," Tracy said.

Sara's head did another pivot.

Having had enough of the conversation blasted in public, Jake said in a low tone, "How about we go for a walk and discuss this?"

"I know. It's crazy busy around here," Tracy said.

Jake cast a glance toward the coffee bar. Bea looked at him with a slight shake of her head. Sara wouldn't look his way. Her face was as hard as stone.

With a sigh, he led Tracy out of the coffee shop. Carol stood with her children wanting to thank him, but seeing Tracy, she did an abrupt about-face. She herself glanced at Sara and whispered, "Oh, no, Jake."

Tracy looked at Jake and frowned, "You don't look happy to see me."

"I'm not a big fan of my personal life being broadcast in public. Besides, the last time we spoke, you said we weren't a couple," Jake said.

"I said we were on a *break*, Jake," Tracy said.

"It felt a lot more like we were fundamentally going in different directions," Jake said. His shoulders slumped as he looked at Tracy. "It is good to see you. But what I don't need is being babysat by your father or anyone else."

Tracy nodded. Jake could read that something was on Tracy's mind.

"What aren't you telling me?" Jake asked.

"I sort of didn't tell Daddy that you and I broke up. So, with him coming to town I was hoping we could call the break off," Tracy said. "At least for the holidays."

Jake paced a few steps away and then turned back, "Tracy, I'm not so sure it wasn't the right thing to do. I don't want to play pretend. If that harms my status in the company, so be it."

"I'm just talking dinner. You can come up with a hundred reasons why you can't spend the holidays with us," Tracy said. "Please, for me?"

"Fine," Jake sighed. "Just dinner."

"Thank you, Jake!" Tracy threw her arms around him and kissed his cheek.

Instinctively, Jake cast a glance toward the coffee shop window. Sara stared at the end of the bar directly at them.

Closing his eyes, Jake breathed deeply. "Tracy, your father isn't going to like it, but this… All of this was kind of my doing, with the help of the businesses. I need to go help."

"Okay. I will text you plans for dinner," Tracy said.

Jake watched her slip away into the crowd. For a moment, he stood there, numb, wondering what had just happened. A sea of revelers flowed around him until his senses came back on line.

Determined to fix it, he headed into the coffee shop. Sara wasted no time in letting him know where things stood. Her eyes alone conveyed a strong message, Her words cut even deeper, "Thanks for the help, Jake. We've got this from here."

Bea looked across the bar at him. She started to say something but knew her granddaughter looked as though she was of no mind to hear any of it.

Jake stared for a moment before slowly walking away.

In a daze, he wandered downtown. He had never seen Wintergreen so festive. It was so much more than he could have imagined. Yet, he meandered as though his heart had been ripped out. He felt like he had conducted some traitorous act- to both the coffee shop as well as to Sara. He knew he didn't mean to, but he also knew it didn't matter.

Jake could understand how the conversation must have sounded and must have stung. Shaking his head, he absently accepted a candy cane from Mr. Fuller. With a thank you, he lumbered forward, candy cane clenched in his teeth.

Glancing at his watch, he saw it wasn't long before the tree lighting. The carriages made steady circuits bringing more and more people downtown. The voices of the high school choir started to grow above the bustle. They sounded angelic as their carols filled the air.

When it was a half-hour prior to the scheduled tree lighting Jake looped back to the coffee shop. Before Sara could dismiss him, he held his wallet, "I need to pay for Carol's drinks."

"I've got it, Sara. You run ahead. I'll catch up," Bea said.

Sara cast a steely look, clearly wanting to extricate herself from the situation. She complied, leaving without another word.

The café was quiet, just Jake and Bea. The coffee shop owner allowed the silence to take hold for a moment. Circling around the bar, she waved off Jake's wallet, "We'll deal with that later."

Jake swallowed hard as Bea stood next to him.

"You kind of let the one get away from you, huh?" Bea laughed in spite of herself. "It's not that bad. It's not good, either. But it isn't beyond repair. Why don't you tell me what's going on?"

Jake told her about his firm winning the Java Universe account. His heart wasn't in it, but he had to do his job.

Bea waved her hands, "I knew that. Your co-workers were talking about it the day I brought the samples in. I didn't give it much of a mind because it didn't matter. The work you were doing for the company didn't take away the wonderful things you were doing around here."

"You knew? I was so embarrassed, I didn't know how to tell you. I wasn't meaning to keep it a secret," Jake said.

"Meaning to or not brings us the real problem. My Sara. She will see it as keeping it a secret. Worse than that, she feels like you were leading her on. Whether you and Tracy were broken up or not, Sara feels you were keeping your options open. I know women and I have a pretty strong hunch your friend Tracy put on a show full well knowing the implications it would have for you," Bea said.

"What do I do?" Jake asked.

"First thing, give that girl some space. Trust me, Sara is best dealt with after a cool down period. Kind of a Bailey trait, I'm afraid," Bea said.

"How come you aren't mad at me?" Jake asked.

"Because I can see your heart, Jake. While your mind may not have made the best choices in how to handle things, I know your heart wants to head the right direction. You've got to get both working together or things will continue to be messy," Bea said.

Jake looked at the café owner, "You are a wonderful woman, Bea."

"Well, you break my Sara's heart and you'll see a different side of me, but thank you," Bea said. Eyeing the clock, she nudged Jake, "Turbulent evening or not, we have a tree lighting to attend."

"Thank you, Bea," Jake said as they walked.

"You're welcome, but I'd encourage you to walk on the other side of the street when we get close to Sara," Bea said.

"Sound advice!" Jake laughed.

Twenty Six

Jake retreated to the other side of the street giving Sara her space. Passing by the chestnuts, he felt even more terrible. Sara was so excited about the evening and his run in with Tracy ruined it all. Jake kicked at the sidewalk knowing it was his lack of backbone to be more upfront and share how he truly felt that ruined the event for Sara. For him.

Finding a spot near the back of the crowd, Jake watched as the mayor and his contingent took the stage with half of the choir on either side of them. Shawn gave a nod to the crowd and warm smile toward Sara.

The mayor stood in front of the microphone, "Wow. Would you look at this fine crowd? Wintergreen at its best, ladies and gentlemen! You know, there was some debate about whether the downtown tree lighting would take place this year. Some fine constituents were kind enough to remind us about tradition. And we said, heck yeah, it's on!"

The crowd cheered.

"Now, for me, this is a special honor to be here with you. To light up this tree in just a few moments. But first, I need to recognize a few folks that worked really hard to put this together and quite frankly, help their mayor see the passion that Main Street has for the community and the community has for Main Street. Jake. Jake Myers, you out there? There he is!" the mayor craned his neck looking around the crowd. "Looking for his right hand or maybe he's hers, Sara Bailey! While I know there were plenty of others with their hand in it, those two worked together to light a fire under all of us in Downtown Wintergreen."

Across the crowd, Jake and Sara exchanged glances with each other but Sara quickly snapped her head away.

Turning to a large, candy cane shaped switch, the mayor readied himself. Eyeing the aid standing at the ready by the circuit breaker attached to town hall, he called out, "Ready? Help me count this down…ten, nine, eight…"

When they hit one, the large tree behind him lit up in a dramatic fashion to the cheers of the crowd. With a wave in the air, the mayor called out "Merry Christmas!"

Escorted off the stage and back toward Town Hall, Shawn separated from the group. Finding Sara, he stopped. Whispering something to her, she laughed. Jake melted into the crowd on the other side of the street.

He didn't get far before he was corralled by Carol and her family. Seeing the pain in her friend's eyes, Carol adopted him into their family fun. Greeting Eric who had joined his wife and children, Jake reluctantly went along, sensing Carol's insistence was going to win anyway.

"So, Tanner and Bethany. I'll bet you are snowman experts," Jake said.

Tanner flayed his arms out, "Well, not experts… but we're pretty good."

"Daddy's an expert," Bethany said, hugging her father's leg.

"Don't let them steer you wrong. We can use all the help we can get," Eric said. "Carol says you are a whiz at telling stories that people want. Let's make this snowman display a story."

Carol gave Jake a wink.

"All right," Jake scratched his chin as they gathered into their defined area, demarcated for their snowman scene. Unable to help but glance toward Sara as she selected a space with Bea and Shawn, Jake blinked. Squeezing his eyes tight, he exorcised any thought other than the kids in their square. Opening his eyes, he suggested, "How about, we make snow people around a snow tree?"

"Like tonight!" Bethany squealed.

"Like tonight," Jake nodded.

"Let's do it!" Tanner pumped his fist in the air.

Eric smiled, his hands on his children's shoulders, "Sounds like a plan."

Carol looked at Jake, her arms crossed, "A snow tree? You're building that Mr. 'Creative'."

Jake laughed, "Wow, now I feel like I'm back at the office. I will take the challenge and make the best- probably the only- snow tree this competition has ever seen!"

Despite wearing a suit, Jake dropped to his knees and began making a large pyramid of snow in the dead center of their space while Eric orchestrated his family into making the requisite number and proportion balls for their snow people.

Unable to resist a sideways glance at Sara's station, he caught her eye. For a moment, they looked at one another. Sara swallowed and returned her attention to the snow people they were building.

With a deep breath, which did not go unnoticed by Carol, he resumed working on his snow tree. Once he had a skinny pyramid built, he began giving it shape. Carving large, flowing limbs cascading down the compacted pile of snow, it began to resemble a tree. At its base, Jake had to exercise great care. He wanted the bottom limbs to hang over the base snow with a defined, albeit larger than typical, trunk.

By packing the snow tight and smoothing it with his bare human body-warm hands, he created a mortar like structure holding the tree in place. He winced knowing that if his tree failed, he would be letting down Carol's entire family.

Stepping back, he saw four distinct snow people of varying sizes taking shape around the tree. "Nice work, guys!"

Tanner and Bethany stopped their work and eyed Jake's creation, "That looks like a tree!"

"I hope so," Jake said. "Problem is, I need it to look like a Christmas tree."

Carol, who had been making quick work of her Mama snowwoman, nodded to Jake, "Let's find some props."

Jake nodded, "Sounds good. Your snow person looks great."

"She could use some embellishments," Carol smiled.

According to contest rules, contestants could use anything they brought to the contest or forage items from the park that were no longer attached to a living organism. Jake and Carol strolled, eyeing pinecones, branches and boughs.

When they were out of earshot of anyone else, Carol leaned in, "Jake Myers, you are in love."

"What are you talking about?" Jake gasped.

"Sara Bailey. I can feel your heart beating from our station every time she looks your way, which I can tell you is pretty frequent when you aren't looking. She does look a touch irritated though," Carol said.

"Yeah, I got that," Jake admitted.

"The dust up at the coffee shop?" Carol asked.

Jake nodded.

"You've been helping them while running the Java Universe campaign. And you didn't tell them."

"Nope."

Carol shook her head, "Probably not wise."

"Thanks. I figured as much," Jake said.

"You and Tracy?"

Jake shook his head, "There is no Tracy and me. We are friends and her father is my boss' boss. I think that's how it should be."

"Does she know that?"

"I'm not so sure. I do understand that Henry does not know that," Jake admitted.

"Well, *that*, isn't great for you," Carol said.

"No. No it's not," Jake said.

"The truth, Jake. You are one of the most altruistic men outside of my husband that I know. Don't hide the truth. The truth is your friend. Well, maybe not for your career, but otherwise…" Carol teased.

Jake scowled.

"You do love her, don't you?" Carol pressed.

"I think I do," Jake said softly.

Carol spun Jake to look him straight in the eye, "Then let this squall clear. The sun will shine brightly on it when the clouds go away. Be you and be open. Seriously, the truth, whether people like it or not, is your friend. Always."

"Thanks, Carol," Jake said.

"Okay. Mushy stuff aside, I want to win this competition! Let's go!" Carol said, tugging Jake along the path.

Returning to their station, they dropped their bounty and began using it to add some detail to their creations. Jake took bows and draped them around the tree like garland. With a few sticks, he fashioned a star at the sacrifice of his shoelaces to use as bindings.

Carol's family used pinecones for noses and stones for eyes and smiling faces. For arms, they used branches. As an added touch, they fashioned the tips of the branches laced together to simulate their snow family holding hands around the tree.

Jake had to duck under the arms to escape his work around the tree. Eyeing the scene, he nodded, "I like it. What do you think?"

"It's awesome," Tanner said.

"I think it looks sweet," Bethany said in her tiny little voice.

"I agree, but its missing something…" Jake said scratching his chin. Removing his own scarf, he slung it around Eric's snowman.

Carol removed her beaded necklace and while her snowwoman was too large to clasp, she poked the beads in enough that they would stay.

Tanner took off his hat and had his dad place it atop his snowman. Bethany unclasped the clip on a stuffed animal from her backpack and affixed it to her snowgirl.

"That did it!" Jake applauded. "Here, let me take a picture of you guys."

Jake held out his phone and snapped several shots to send to Carol.

"Come on, your turn to get in on a photo," Carol waved her hand.

"Selfie time!" Jake grinned and holding his hand stretched out, he snapped a shot with his face just in frame with Carol's family and their snow creations in the background.

Jake looked around at the other contestant's squares, pausing at Sara's. She, Bea and Shawn made snow baristas handing a coffee cup to a customer. Jake nodded in appreciation.

Turning to Tanner and Bethany, Jake said, "You know what? Regardless of the results I say we all won. Did we have fun?"

The kids cheered as they hopped up and down.

"I think so, too," Jake said. In a low whisper, he bent over and shielded his mouth, "Just the same, I think ours is best, but I like all of them."

Bethany giggled.

"Well, thank you for your help, Jake," Carol said.

"When you get your big promotion, I hope you'll visit us smalltown folk in Wintergreen." Seeing the almost startled look on Jake's face, Eric frantically said, "Carol's been telling me about the corporate office looking to call your number. Just sad to see you go. She really enjoys working with you."

Jake nodded, "Yeah. She's been a great partner. I've always said I wasn't sure I wanted to do it without her. She deserves a promotion more than me."

"Stop it, guys. You're making me blush!" Carol teased. "With these rugrats in school, we aren't going anywhere anytime soon. I'm happy for you, Jake. You deserve it. You deserve whatever it is you want to chase after."

Jake's eyes flitted on Sara as she posed for a photo with her teammates and their snow creations.

The volunteer leading the snowman contest blew an airhorn. Using the stage microphone, she said, "All right! How fun was that? I would swear I was walking through a greeting card store looking through snow globes with all of your excellent snow people. So, here is how it works, you each have a bow. At each station, there is a fishbowl, but you can call it a snow globe dome if you like, it's more festive. Your job is easy, or should I say your task is simple, I think your job is tough. You put your bow in the upside-down snow globe dome at the station of your favorite snowman scene."

The crowd scurried. They had watched all of the teams throughout the contest, but they viewed the judging through a more scrutinizing lens. The families began moving around the snowman stations, each receiving a number of votes. When the timer went off, the event leader retook the stage.

"Who is ready to crown the family with the best presentation at this year's snowman contest? It was a close one. Every station had a lot of votes, but the bows have determined a winner… the Bateman family. I think what swayed the voters was the handholding, truly precious. Congratulations!" the contest leader reported.

Carol's family jumped up and down and clapped their hands. Jake eased himself out of the limelight and clapped for his friends. The crowd cheered.

As ribbons were handed out, Jake tried to allow the family to enjoy the credit, but Eric and Carol wheeled him in for a final winning photo with their ribbons in the air.

"Thank you again for allowing me to crash your snow party," Jake said.

"You're never crashing, Jake you are welcome any time," Carol said.

Jake nodded a thank you, high-fived the kids and clapped Eric on the shoulder before slipping away.

When the crowds cleared, Jake appeared from his long, slow walk through the park. The view of the town's celebration through tree branches and the light falling snow was almost surreal. It was most definitely beautiful. After making his rounds to thank the vendors, the volunteers and the shop owners who kept open extra hours, he slunk away from all of it.

He was content to watch the families having fun. To hear the choir provide a soundtrack for the Christmas event, and to catch the aroma of roasted chestnuts and pine. Competing with the choir was the chorus of laughter as children played, making memories with their families just as he had with his growing up.

When the event had wound down, Jake pitched in to help vendors break down their makeshift shops and thanked the choir director. He gave a hearty thank you to the carriage drivers and took a moment with their blessing to give each horse a treat for their hard work that evening.

Returning to Main Street, all of the revelry had died down. Vendors had carted off their supplies. Shops had closed. Jake peered into the Coffee Corner, hoping to catch up with Sara and have an honest conversation with her. She and Bea were gone. As he stood on the sidewalk at the entrance of downtown quickly becoming covered in snow, it was silent.

Not ready to go home, Jake slowly wandered down Main Street. He gave a thoughtful glance at all of the businesses whose owners and employees stepped up to make the event happen, to strengthen the fabric of what Downtown Wintergreen was and meant to their neighbors.

He took a deep breath. The day wasn't everything he had hoped it would be, but for the businesses of Downtown Wintergreen, it was everything he had set out for it to be and more.

Twenty Seven

"Thanks for lunch," Carol said, looking across the table at Jake.

"Thank you for inviting me to join your family last night," Jake said.

Carol smiled, "We had fun."

"It was a great event," Jake nodded.

They set their menus down and quietly studied the other for conversation.

Carol broke the silence, "What are you going to do?"

Jake frowned feigning as though he didn't understand Carol's question, "About… Java Universe? Oh, there are a few revisions. Otherwise, we are really close to final."

"No one cares about Java Universe, Jake. Tracy, Sara, Henry, the firm… all of it?" Carol asked, looking over her coffee cup, signifying she was relinquishing the podium and ready for answers.

"I don't know," Jake shrugged. "It's all a bit complicated."

"Love usually is," Carol offered a slight smile from across the table.

With a scowl, Jake huffed, "Who said anything about love?"

Carol shot a stern look back, "Jake, it's written all over your face like you were kicked by a mule with the letters L-O-V-E stamped on its hooves."

Shifting in his seat, Jake bristled, "It's different. I don't know what is going on. Tracy and I, we went on a date. We kept going on dates. I just kind of figured that's how it works. With Sara… we just were."

"It's organic. Those are the best kind," Carol said.

"No one said we were. I don't even know how she feels. I'm not even sure how *I* feel. It's all so…" Jake paused as the waiter came to take their order.

"Complicated?" Carol smiled, finishing Jake's sentence.

"Yeah," Jake said softly. He absently nodded as he glanced out the window of the restaurant.

"It's all about the truth, Jake. Be honest with yourself. Forget about what path you were on. You need to look at the paths before you. Take the one that your heart says is right. Your brain will lead you down whichever is easiest… less complicated. It's not always the right one," Carol said.

Jake looked through furrowed brows, "You ever think about being a therapist?"

"I have two kids and a husband, Jake. I *am* a therapist," Carol said.

Jake laughed.

Carol smiled, "That's the Jake smile that conquers the world. The one that sees romance in a winter tire."

Jake took a deep breath.

Leaning forward, Carol said, "Honest conversations are sometimes the most difficult to start, but they always lead to the right place even if it stings a bit at the time. Even if it doesn't go the way you had hoped. Sometimes, it takes you somewhere beautiful."

Jake shook his head and laughed, "You really need to start writing ad copy."

Carol's eyes turned cross, "I'm serious, Jake!"

"I know," Jake smiled. "And I hear you. Thank you, Carol."

With a huff, Carol said, "I've never worked so hard for a lunch in my life, Jake Myers."

"What about you and Eric? What are your plans?" Jake asked.

"Plans? We're raising kids," Carol scoffed. "Right now it is PTA meetings, soccer practices and ballet recitals. Creating family traditions with Tanner and Bethany and with Eric and I."

"What about after that? Does Eric want to expand his practice?" Jake asked.

Carol looked at Jake as their food arrived. With a shrug she said, "Wintergreen is our home. We want to build a place that even as the kids go off on their own adventures many, many years from now, it will feel like returning home any time that they need a taste of it."

Jake nodded. "Yep. It's clear. I should be your assistant. I'm switching desks with you when we get back to the office."

Carol laughed, "I don't want your desk. I told you, I like our work. I enjoy working with you, *most* of the time… I don't do politics. I see your face every time Frank or Henry knock on your door. I think your problem with Java Universe is you like to make the customer happy, but don't really care as much what Frank and Henry think. That is why you win awards. The customers see it and in the end, so do Frank and Henry. With Java Universe, your heart isn't in it."

Looking across the restaurant, Carol twitched slightly as she watched the hostess seat a new set of customers. "Your heart *really* isn't into it."

Jake followed Carol's eyes. His stomach tightened into a ball as he watched Shawn pull out a chair for Sara. He fumbled trying to help Bea who quickly scooted herself into the table. With an awkward nod, Shawn took his seat. As he did, he glanced up and saw Jake and Carol watching them.

With a smile, Shawn excused himself and walked over to Jake and Carol. "Jake! I should have invited you, too. The mayor was just so pleased with how last night went he just kept raving about the crowd and how the community came together. He's thinking about making it an annual event," Shawn said.

Jake scowled, "It *is* an annual event, or was."

Shawn laughed awkwardly, "Right. But what you and Sara put together? Wow. I bumped into her and thought lunch was the least I could do. And you, next time, lunch is on me."

"Right. Thanks, Shawn," Jake said. His eyes flitted momentarily across the room as Sara shifted her gaze away.

"Well, I'll let you guys get back to it. Nice seeing you. Great job, Jake," Shawn said with two thumbs up.

Jake nodded as he watched Shawn retake his seat at the table.

"And that concludes our deep and meaningful lunch conversation," Carol breathed.

"What?" Jake shook his head.

"Exactly," Carol said.

Jake looked at Carol as he regained his senses.

"Talk to her," Carol hissed. "Well, clearly not now. But you know what I mean. And don't let it linger, Jake."

Jake nodded.

With a sigh, Carol took her last bite and gave a soft wave toward the waiter, "All right, let's get you of here."

When the check came, Jake seemed to struggle to decipher it. Carol slapped her hand out, "Here. Sign it and give me a pen. I've seen you do math when you're stressed. I'll fill this out. You are going to have to pass by, so you might as well say hello. I'll be there in a moment to tow you to safety."

Jake did as he was told. Standing up, he nearly toppled the chair but caught it. As he pulled his overcoat off the back of the chair, it hooked, dragging the chair with a loud screech across the floor until he realized it. His cheeks flushed, and he gingerly placed the chair back in its spot. Casting a glance at an utterly unimpressed Carol, he straightened himself and did his best to walk confidently over to the table.

"Ladies," Jake's voice came out hoarse. Sara's steely, blank acknowledgment was in steep contrast to Bea popping out of her seat to give Jake a hug.

"I have something I would like you to take a look at down at the café if you have time today," Bea said.

"I'll try," Jake nodded. With a flat smile, he said, "Enjoy your lunch."

"Hi guys," Carol sang with a hand placed on Jake's back to steer him away from the table and out of the restaurant. "Back to the office. Lots of work left before the holidays."

"We heard," Sara said, quickly receiving a kick from her grandmother under the table.

"Do try to come by," Bea said.

"I'll make sure he has time this afternoon," Carol promised, giving Jake a slight shove toward the door.

Jake felt as if a hundred pairs of eyes were burrowed in the back of his neck. As he reached the hostess stand, nearly out of view of the dining room, a voice squealed, "Jake!"

Tracy rushed in and gave Jake a hug and kiss on his cheek. He felt his cheeks grow red and his head returned to the wild spin. Side stepping Tracy, he held out his hand, "Henry. You're back in town."

Henry grasped Jake's hand and pulled him close. Leaning in the marketing firm president said as he looked directly into Jake's eyes, "We have much to discuss. Keep your calendar free, Jake. I am going to take you and Tracy to that dinner we missed on my last trip. There is much to discuss."

Jake nodded, even as his heart sank. He said, "Sounds great, sir."

"Good to see you, Henry," Carol said, her hand still nudging Jake forward.

Out in the parking lot, Carol swung to Jake, "Truth, Jake. With yourself. With *all* of the people around you. And I don't mean truth from your head. Everyone knows you're an honest man, minus an obvious omission about competing clients or two. I mean, truth with your heart, Jake. There are a lot of people in that restaurant that need to hear it. And at least one in this parking lot."

Twenty Eight

Jake had never been so happy to dive into work. Even performing clean-up work on the Java Universe spread was a welcome distraction. Closing out the files one by one, he began to work on the last piece– the national campaign.

A rap at his door pulled him from his work.

"Jake, you got a minute?" Henry asked from Jake's office doorway.

"Yeah, sure," Jake said.

Henry stepped in and closed the door.

With confident strides, he stood in front of Jake's desk before plopping down in one of the chairs opposite Jake. Elbows propped on the arm rests, Henry tented his fingers together and eyed Jake for what felt to the marketing executive a bit too long.

"Jake, you have a bright future with this company. You know, we all think highly of you. You think outside the box. You make us consider possibilities that we and our clients never would have thought of. We chide you about that sometimes, but we really appreciate you," Henry said. Briefly bringing his tented finger to his lips as he considered his next words, he continued, "Frank says you've been… a bit distracted. He thinks you are all tied up with some side project for the community. I think I really know what's going on."

Jake looked at Henry, unsure where the firm's president was going to take the conversation.

"Taking the next step in your life is a big one. I get it. I was there with Tracy's mother so many years ago. You are driven, like I was. I guess I still am. Burying myself in my work, it fuels me. It's where I get my energy from. The next big account. The next acquisition. Growing the Banks Marketing award trophy case. It can be hard on a relationship. I know, I have some well-paid divorce lawyers who like to remind me," Henry said.

Shifting in his seat, Jake was surprised and uncomfortable with the course the talk had taken.

"Thing is, you're at the next step. I understand why you might be a little distracted. And with the holidays upon us, I have a hunch where things are going," Henry said.

"Sir?" Jake questioned.

"It's all right. I'm not old-fashioned. No need for that awkward talk. But I will say, you need to start to get your affairs in order in Wintergreen. *Lots* of big changes are coming your way, Jake," Henry said.

Standing, Henry held out his hand. With trepidation, Jake rose from his chair and shook.

"Big changes," Henry smiled. "All right. I'll leave you to it. Good talk, Jake!"

Henry swung the door open to find Carol standing in front of it, a stack of papers in her hands. With a nod, Henry walked past and Carol stepped in.

With a curious glance, she asked, "What was *that* about?"

Jake buried his face in hands as he slumped back to his desk and sighed, "I have no idea."

As the afternoon wore on and the grey skies darkened with the early setting sun of winter, Jake had turned in the last of the Java Universe updates.

Frank and Henry were embroiled in discussions in the conference room.

"Jake, I believe you have somewhere to be," Carol said.

Jake looked up from his desk. Having sent the files on the campaign, he didn't know what to do next.

"Bea Bailey, among other things," Carol pressed.

Jake nodded, "All right."

As he gathered his things and was heading out of the office, Frank and Henry stepped out of the conference room.

"Jake, where are you off to?" Frank asked.

Carol stepped in, "You know, we ordered proofs for the Java Universe spread. Jake and his quality control. Wanted to see the ads the way they'll look to the consumers. I was going to get them, but I need to pick up my kids. Jake was kind enough to volunteer."

Frank grunted, looking at Carol and Jake as though he was processing.

With a nod, he and Henry walked down to Jeff's office.

"Proofs, huh?" Jake asked.

Carol shrugged, "There will be. I'll send some now."

Jake chuckled and shook his head.

"Now, go!" Carol shooed Jake toward the office lobby.

Jake arrived on Main Street with great apprehension. Even giving a wave to Jennifer, he suddenly felt sheepish. Taking a breath before he stepped into the coffee shop, he was hit with the warmth, the aroma of fresh brewed coffee, crooning carols being played over the speakers and friendly greetings from neighbors and visitors enjoying a warming beverage on a cold day.

Normally all of those feelings would envelope him, adding to his support for his friend Bea and her business. And recently, there was a tinge of excitement that he was only beginning to understand when he saw Sara smile from behind the coffee bar. It was there when she would dance excitedly and nervously when talking about her paintings or the shared passion to help her grandmother and rally the businesses of Main Street and the town.

Today, the feeling of excitement was replaced by tension and anxiety, making his stomach do flips. He cast a hopeful glance behind the bar, where he saw a focused and business-like Sara alongside a perturbed Bea.

Seeing Jake walk in, Bea's eyes narrowed with determination. "Hello, Jake. Thank you for coming," she said.

"Of course," Jake said. "What can I help you with?"

"Have a seat, I'll be right with you," Bea said. Grabbing two mugs, she looked at a reticent Sara and growled, "Go!"

Like a child reluctantly obeying their parent, Sara sighed and followed her grandmother's lead. Stopping at the table where Jake was sitting, Bea placed the cups down with just enough force to make a slight thud. Looking at Jake and then at Sara, she demanded, "Now, *talk!*"

Bea walked away, retreating to the coffee bar.

Sara's eyes followed her briefly before complying and taking the seat across from Jake. Cupping the mug in her hands, she studied the heart swirl Bea had made in her cup. It didn't pass her that Jake's had the same.

Slowly, her eyes lifted to Jake's, "I guess Grandma wants us to talk."

Jake laughed, "Yeah. She tends to get her message across in very firm, yet loving ways."

"How do you think she conned me into spending my first few weeks back working in the café?" Sara let out a soft laugh. "Nah, she didn't con me. I like spending time with her. She takes such joy in a simple task like handing over a cup of coffee."

"She knows that in some way, that cup means something. A start to a new day when someone really needs it," Jake said. "Or a couple on a first or one-hundredth date."

"A much-needed moment in the day where someone can re-center themselves," Sara added.

"Or spurring a conversation that two people really need to have," Jake said, looking up at Sara.

"Yeah," Sara said. "Subtle that one. 'Oh, Jake could you stop by today? I need your help with something.'"

Jake gave a sheepish half-smile, "I guess she knows how to pull my strings."

"And here you are," Sara said, her head cocking just slightly on the other side of mug.

"Here we are," Jake said.

For a moment, they peered past their coffee cups. The warm, ceramic mugs were shields giving them protection from whatever thoughts and feelings were harbored on the other side of the table.

"I'm sorry. I should have told you I was working on the Java Universe account. I don't get to pick my assignments and I think I was sort of embarrassed. I felt like a traitor somehow," Jake said.

"You should have told us," Sara said, her voice matter-of-fact. "If you had, we probably would have had a good laugh about it. You helping us while getting handed the competitor's marketing campaign that could shut this café down forever… On second thought, maybe we wouldn't have laughed. But just the same, we wouldn't have been blindsided by your girlfriend blurting it out in the middle of our shop."

"I…" Jake started to defend himself. With a sigh, he was contrite, "You're right. Someone recently told me that I was hiding from difficult conversations. I don't want to do that with people that I care about."

"I know you care about Grandma. It's sweet. I appreciate everything you have done for her. For this café. For downtown," Sara said.

Jake's face was serious, "About Tracy…"

"I'm sorry, Jake. Maybe I misread your intentions or maybe I believed what I wanted to believe. Whatever it is. Whatever this is that you and I are doing… You have things you need to work through. And it doesn't even matter. Once you get your promotion, you are out of here. And I… I'll be working at my parent's accounting firm. Life will settle back to the course it was intended," Sara said. Her voice fell towards the end of her exasperated narrative.

Jake studied Sara for a moment. He tried to read Sara's eyes to see if there was the glimmer of light that made his heart flutter left in them, "Sara, I have really enjoyed spending time with you."

"We make a great team," Sara interjected.

Seeing she was deflecting every time he tried to speak, he blurted, "It's more than that, Sara. My heart races when I see you smile. You make me want to take on the world when you are with me."

Sara's despondent face told him that she was not ready to accept the course of the conversation.

With a deep breath, Jake said, "Tracy and I broke up. A couple of weeks ago."

"Are you sure? Because, she doesn't seem to know that," Sara frowned.

Jake bobbed his head back and forth, "She has a way of acting and pushing forward as though the world has given her way, even if it hasn't. That, and she hasn't told her father yet."

Sara laughed, "So when Henry is around, the happy couple returns. That must be fun for you."

Shaking his head, he said, "No. No, it's not. In particular, if that hurts you, confuses us."

"Us?" Sara opened her eyes wide.

Jake's eyes froze on Sara, "I would like there to be."

Sara stared back for a long moment. Her eyes sparkled just briefly before her shoulders slumped and she shook her head, "Broken up or not. You still have things to settle."

"Yeah, you're right," Jake nodded.

"And even if then, what? Your job will take you to the city. Mine will be taking on clients at my parents' firm," Sara said.

"The city is not that far away. And I hear the coffee there is lousy," Jake said.

"Isn't there a Java Universe on any corner?" Sara teased.

"Exactly," Jake grinned. With a slight squint of his eyes, he turned the conversation, "What about you? I hear Debbie wants you to be the headliner of her gallery event."

Sara paled, and let out a nervous laugh, "It's one thing to have paintings on my grandmother's wall. I can barely fathom a painting anywhere in the gallery, but headlining, I don't even know what that means."

"I think you know what that means," Jake said. "It means you are amazing, I mean, your work. Your work is amazing. It is."

Sara blushed with a shrug, "What's it all for? Accountant by day, artist by night? It's a hobby. I never even intended to display it anywhere for anyone outside of the silly presents I give to my family. But they have to say they like it."

"I don't have to say it. Debbie doesn't have to say it. The mysterious anonymous buyer didn't have to say it. You are wonderful. Your art is, well, pretty good too," Jake grinned.

Sara rolled her eyes, "No flirting with me until you figure your life out. And then, maybe we'll see. Besides, I may not even be available by then. According to Grandma, I'm quite the catch."

Jake knew Sara was teasing, but he didn't laugh. Instead, he locked his eyes with hers, and said softly, "You are."

Sara took a deep breath, averting her eyes from his.

"Friends… for now?" Jake asked, reaching his hand across the table.

Sara studied his hand and with a smile extended hers to slip inside his. She nodded, "Friends."

Looking into each other's eyes, they seemed to search for clues to the future, but any gleam of insight was dashed as the café front door pushed open.

"There you are," Shawn's voice rang through the café. "Hello, Bea."

"Hello, Shawn," Bea called.

Walking past the pre-sold painting, he gushed, "Boy, I do love that painting."

Reaching the table, Shawn cast a quick glance and a hello toward Jake before spinning directly to Sara, his chest proudly crested in front of him, "I have spectacular news. The accounting firm that was contracted with the city lost the renewal. I convinced the mayor and the council to use your family's firm. I already spoke to your folks. They said you could be a part of the team!"

"Shawn, that's great news," Sara said. "Thank you for looking out for my family."

Shawn shot a brief look at Jake and grinned, "That's what we do around here, eh, Jake?"

"Yep, we sure do," Jake said.

"At least it will make those brutally boring budget meetings more fun if we get to go together, Sara," Shawn said.

"That does… sound like fun," Sara tried to smile.

"What do you think? Celebratory drinks after work?" Shawn asked. "You're all invited."

"I'll see. It's been a long day," Sara said.

Shawn gave a slight slap to the table, "Come on. Your parents are coming."

"All right," Sara conceded.

"Great! I'll see you there! This is exciting!" Shawn smiled. Giving a quick wave to Bea, he left.

"Exciting," Sara mumbled under her breath.

Twenty Nine

Jake pulled into his driveway, where a familiar car was parked in the spot next to him.

Getting out, he tapped on the window.

Tracy opened her door stepped out. "Hi, Jake."

"Hi, Tracy," Jake said.

"It's cold out. Do you mind if we go inside? I want to talk." Tracy said.

With a nod, Jake locked his truck and escorted Tracy inside.

Shaking off the cold, he hung their jackets. With a glance toward the thermostat, Jake pursed his lips, "Why don't I start a fire? We can talk in there."

Tracy nodded, "Something to drink?"

"Sure, help yourself," Jake said as he knelt by the fireplace and set out logs on top of a small pile of kindling.

By the time the fire had begun to catch, Tracy had returned with two glasses of wine. Jake rubbed his hands together, "I was thinking tea or something, but this is fine."

Instead of having Jake move to the couch, Tracy took a seat on the hearth and handed Jake a glass.

"Daddy wants to have dinner, the three of us," Tracy said.

"Have you told your father?" Jake asked.

Tracy bowed her head and let out a soft, "No."

"Tracy…"

"It's… There is so much going on. For him, for you, for us…and I was hoping there was nothing to tell," Tracy said. "Look, I'm sorry I left. I was just feeling frustrated. I wanted to get you out of this town. Away from these smalltown… distractions."

Jake shot Tracy a look.

"It's not that I am eager to pull you away, I want you *back*, Jake. I want us to be able to be us. Not us and this town," Tracy said.

"But this town is a part of me, Tracy," Jake said.

"It's a place. People move, people grow. They make themselves better. Surround themselves in a better place," Tracy said.

"I love *this* place and the people here," Jake said.

"Jake, you need to look at the big picture. The future. This decaying little town, I'm sorry, it is not the future. It's the past. And this place has a hold on your ankle, tugging at you. Limiting your success. Limiting your happiness," Tracy said.

Jake looked at Tracy. Setting his glass down, he said, "This town doesn't limit me. It fuels me. It fuels me with good people who know each other, care about each other, help each other. There's nothing wrong with that."

"Well, it may not matter. You can't work under Frank's wing forever, Jake," Tracy said. "The rest of the world is calling and you need to pick up."

Jake sighed, looking away.

Scooting closer, Tracy put a hand on his shoulder, "Jake, at least please give it time. Give us through Christmas. I think you'll see it is time to change. Time to grow. And there is a future for... us."

"Tracy, I have enjoyed our time together..." Jake started.

Cutting him, Tracy said, "Give it time, Jake. That is all I ask."

Jake took a swallow of wine as Tracy inched closer.

"It's getting late," Jake stood up from the hearth.

Tracy looked up, her eyes almost pleading. Finally, her shoulders slumped, "Okay."

Finishing the last swallow of wine, Tracy set her glass down. Thinking she was heading for the door, Jake was surprised when she grabbed his shirt and kissed him.

"Tracy…" Jake pulled away.

"I know, just something for you to think about, Jake," Tracy sang as though the conversation had gone an entirely different way.

Helping her with her coat, she spun. Instinctively, Jake took a quick step backward.

"Touchy," Tracy laughed. "Dinner. With Daddy."

Jake looked at her wishing he had any other answer he could give than to agree to dinner with the president of his firm. "Dinner," he affirmed. "Goodnight, Tracy."

"Goodnight, Jake," Tracy said.

Jake quickly closed the door as the winter breeze was bitingly cold.

Rubbing his face he decided he wanted that cup of tea after all. Heading to the kitchen, he put a kettle on. Rummaging for the right tea bag, he was surprised to hear a knock at the door.

With a sigh and roll of his eyes, he cursed whatever Tracy was up to under his breath.

Swinging the door wide, he was surprised to see Sara standing on his front porch. A leather folder in her hands.

"Come in. It's freezing out," Jake beckoned, holding the door for Sara and promptly shutting the cold air out.

"Grandma found this at the café and thought you might need it," Sara said, lofting the folder in the air.

"My notes," Jake nodded.

"She conveniently waited until after dinner to tell me and demanded I run it over on my way home. She thought 'it looked important'. If I didn't know better, I'd say Grandma swiped it from you just to set this little meeting up," Sara said.

"Thank you. I was wondering where it disappeared, but it could have waited. I'm glad to see you anyway," Jake said. "I was just putting tea on. Would you like a cup?"

Sara bit her lip as though she were considering the invitation. Her eyes glanced at the fireplace with its inviting warmth. With a sudden change of mood, she sharply declined, "No. No, thank you. I should go."

Jake was taken aback by the abruptness but didn't fight the response.

"Okay," he nodded. "See you tomorrow?"

"Sure, Jake," Sara said. Her voice was flat as she stepped quickly out of the house.

With a frown and a slight shake of his head, Jake closed the door. Turning, he saw what made Sara exit with such haste. Next to the hearth were two empty wine glasses.

With a sigh, he backed into the door and rubbed his head.

"Great job, Jake!"

Thirty

Jake had largely spent the day in his office. Finalizing projects for the year and tidying up while Frank and Henry made several spot visits regarding the Java Universe account. Mostly, he buried himself in work, even if much of it was menial.

"Knock, knock," Carol's voice called as she cracked the door.

"Hmm?" Jake looked up.

"Can I come in?" Carol asked.

Jake looked surprised, "Yes, of course. Come in."

Carol walked up to the desk and looked directly down at Jake. With pursed lips, she studied him as he looked up at her with a raised brows. "What's going on with you today?" Carol asked.

"What do you mean?" Jake shrugged.

"You haven't spent this much time glued to your desk without strict orders from Frank the entire holiday season. And here you are… spring cleaning?" Carol asked.

"Just trying to get things in order for the holiday break," Jake said.

"Isn't there an event today downtown?" Carol asked.

"Cookies and Carols," Jake muttered.

Carol crossed her arms, her tone taking on a mother trying to extract the truth from a child, "And what is that?"

"Each business makes its favorite holiday cookie. People sing carols from business to business and sample cookies," Jake said.

"And who is the marketed sponsor of this event?" Carol pressed.

"The Corner Café," Jake said.

"And you aren't helping… because?" Carol asked. Her expression became more dour, "What did you do?"

"I didn't do anything," Jake looked up at Carol in the eyes. With a large sigh, he admitted, "I tried having a talk with Sara yesterday, well, Bea engineered. The talk went okay. We are friendly but, I quote, "I have to figure my life out."

"Probably true. That doesn't add up to your Grinchy attitude today," Carol said.

With a deep breath, Jake said, "Tracy came by last night…"

"Uh, oh!" Carol's eyes widened.

Jake went cross, "Not like that. I was clear that we were over, again. She asked me to hold on through the holidays. To give it time."

"In which you definitively said, *no*," Carol said.

"I said it was time for her to leave," Jake said.

"On point, but not definitive. Women need to hear the words, Jake. Good or bad," Carol said.

"Anyway, there was a knock at the door, I thought it was Tracy, being persistent," Jake said. "It was Sara. I had left something at the café, I guess Bea demanded she bring it by. She seemed happy to see me."

"Until…" Carol winced.

"Until she saw two wine glasses by the fireplace," Jake blurted.

"Jake!" Carol was cross. "You silly man. Did you explain to Sara?"

"No. I didn't have a chance," Jake said.

Carol's scowled, "Then what have you been hiding here for all day? Did you forget everything about our conversation? Honest.

Brutally honest. Express yourself. Let the chips fall where they fall but get it all out there!"

Jake nodded slowly with his eyes locked on Carol's like a scolded puppy.

"Go! What are you waiting for?" Carol urged. "And save me a snickerdoodle. I'm bringing the kids down later to meet the children's book author."

Seeing Carol was in no mood for inaction, Jake gathered his things, tossed his coat over his shoulders and marched out of the office.

Jake was thrilled to see Main Street as busy as it was. With children out of school for the holidays, families enjoyed time together. Moving from business to business in groups, they sang Christmas carols with lyrics from printed sheets.

Occasionally, business owners would present them with a cookie that meant something to them from their family. Some would join in and sing with the carolers. It was Wintergreen at its best.

Standing back from a crowd that had gathered outside of the Coffee Corner, Jake watched as they sang their carol. Bea and Sara came out with the cookies, smiling at their holiday serenade. Handing out shortbread cookies, Bea glanced up saw Jake and offered him a smile. With a tilt of her head, she invited him in.

Moving between groups of carolers, he slipped into the café. Offering a sheepish smile to Sara, he said, "Thank you for coming by last night. It was nice of you."

Sara looked at Jake for a hard moment before saying, "Of course. Neighbors helping neighbors. It's what we do."

"I wanted to explain…" Jake began.

"There's nothing to explain, Jake," Sara said. "You have things to work out. I know that. I shouldn't… I should allow you the space that you need to do that. And you need to take it."

Stepping out from behind the counter, Sara leaned in and faced Jake, "We're good. We need to understand and respect our roles."

Stepping back behind the coffee bar, Sara asked, "Can I get you anything?"

"No, thank you. I'm good," Jake said.

"Jake, you really need to try my candy cane latte," Bea called from behind the espresso maker. "Take a seat, I'll bring it out."

Jake complied as Sara rolled her eyes at her grandmother.

With a little hum in tune with the carolers outside, Bea presented Jake with her newest creation, "I used fresh crushed candy cane and just a touch of vanilla."

Jake took a sip, "Bea, as always, this is delicious."

Settling in next to him, Bea said, "I owe you… and Sara, an apology. Sometimes I get notions in my head and I push them on others. I love my granddaughter. And I adore you, Jake. When Sara came home for Christmas, I had the most marvelous idea that you two could… be something special. I understand that you were not in a place for that. I'm sorry."

Jake took a deep breath, "You have nothing to apologize for you. And you weren't exactly wrong… on all counts. Sara is very special. And so are you. You didn't do anything. Sara and I, spending time together, growing closer is real. Very real. She's right, I need to close my last chapter so that the next has the chance to be great."

Bea placed a hand on Jake's arm, "You have made our Christmas season one of hope. I want you to know that. You are family to me."

"Thank you, Bea. I feel the same," Jake raised his cup trying to shift the conversation, "And, *you* are a coffee making genius."

Bea laughed. "Ooh, we are hosting more local artists and writers. We have most of January already booked."

"That's great. I'm glad we were able to remind people how wonderful downtown is," Jake said.

"Thanks to you," Bea said. "You want to watch the carolers?"

"I would like that," Jake nodded.

Bea looked toward Sara, "Come on. It's Christmas."

Reluctantly, Sara traversed the coffee bar and joined her grandmother. Linking arms with Sara on one side and Jake on the other, Bea led them to the coffee shop door. Stepping out onto the sidewalk, they watched, listened, and joined the carolers.

After their third song, each more enthusiastically sang than the first, the trio laughed. A shared glance between Jake and Sara even garnered smiles from both.

When the group was done with their song list, they sampled Bea and Sara's family recipe cookies, and moved on. Bea drug Jake and Sara inside. "Now, that wasn't so bad, was it?"

Jake held his response in reserve as Sara admitted, "It was fun. But Grandma…"

"Fun was all I had in mind," Bea looked at Jake and Sara. "I love you both. I want you both happy and that's it. What you to do from here is up to you without an old woman's meddling."

Sara raised a brow, questioning the validity of the statement.

"Time for another cup?" Sara asked Jake.

With a smile, he said, "I would love to. I have a mission to secure snickerdoodles for Carol."

Sara laughed, "Check with Debbie at the gallery. While you're passing by, you have to try Jennifer's. Her rosettes are little bites of Christmas memories."

"Will do. Thanks," Jake said. As he started to leave, he turned and asked, "I'll see you two later?" He knew he was as much fishing for some sort of affirmation of atonement as anything else.

"We'll be here," Bea said. "Children's storybook author is visiting this evening and the chocolate demonstration is next door."

Sara offered a half-nod and equally reserved smile.

Taking what he could, he slipped out of the coffee shop and on to Main Street.

Strolling down Main Street, passing shoppers with bags strewn on their arms, cups of warm beverages and confections filled Jake with cheer. Whatever happened in the new year, they had this snapshot of Wintergreen in full Americana.

"Hello, Jake," Jennifer said.

"Hi, Jennifer! I was told I had to stop by and taste one of your rosettes," Jake said.

Placing one a napkin, Jennifer handed one to him.

Biting into the powder sugar coated confections, Jake nodded, "Sara was right. These are must-haves. They remind me of my mother's, but at the risk of ending up on her naughty list, I have to say yours are better."

"I put fine vanilla shavings into the mix for a bit of decadence," Jennifer said.

"Can I buy a box for my co-workers' family?"

"You can have a box, after all you have done for us. I mean, look at this crowd, Jake," Jennifer said, panning at the groups of carolers still making their way through downtown.

"I insist, please. The whole idea is to bring you all business, not literally eat into your profits," Jake said.

"A man of principle. You are good to have around, Jake," Jennifer said.

Both notions stuck Jake as he handed several bills to Jennifer. "It's kind of you to say. I just wanted to help any way that I could."

"Well, you did and then some. Thank you, Jake. I don't know what we would have done without you," Jennifer said.

"You're wonderful entrepreneurs. You would have found a way. I just gave you a little nudge at the top of the sledding hill, that's all," Jake shrugged.

"I should have charged you double for modesty, Jake Myers," Jennifer scolded.

"I'll see you later, Jennifer," Jake said, receiving a nod from Jennifer.

Passing by the pharmacy, Jake caught a waving arm in his peripheral vision. Mr. Fuller rushed to the door and flung it open calling, "Jake!"

Pivoting, Jake walked to greet the pharmacist. Jake smiled when he saw the man was wearing a light up Christmas tie. It was a jovial sight he never expected to see.

"Jake, I wanted you to meet someone," Mr. Fuller said. Encouraging Jake to follow, he stopped in front of a young man. "Jake Myers, this is Jonathan Fuller, my son."

"Pleased to meet you, Jonathan," Jake said, extending a hand.

"My dad says all of this commotion down here is because of you," Jonathan said.

Jake shrugged with a sideways grin, "I may have started the Main Street business rebellion, but it was the courageous businesses themselves that turned things around."

"Business has been good. Good enough that Pops is rethinking me taking over the pharmacy when he retires," Jonathan said.

Mr. Fuller stepped in, "It isn't so much the business. It is *enjoying* the business once again. I can't remember the last time Main Street was so full of life. It is wonderful to see."

"I'm glad. I've been enjoying it too," Jake said. "Well, I am off to fulfill a promise before they are all gone. Jonathan, a pleasure. Mr. Fuller, Merry Christmas, sir."

"Merry Christmas to you, Jake," Mr. Fuller smiled.

Jake shook his head as he ambled down Main Street. He felt like he had walked on to the set of a Christmas movie. For the moment, he was overwhelmed with holiday spirit.

Finding Debbie at the front of the gallery, she smiled, "Hello, Jake. What a fun event. I haven't seen so many carolers, well, in my life. I even sold a number of pieces today."

"That's great news, Debbie," Jake said.

"Speaking of news. Any word from your partner in crime about headlining the gallery event? The marketing is already done. It is just nice to showcase an artist, especially when they can be present," Debbie said.

Jake shook his head, "I don't know. I'm not sure I'm the one to convince her, either. But, you can corral her at one of the events this evening."

"That's right, the children's author with that cute little book and the chocolate event. I wasn't about to miss the chocolate!" Debbie grinned. "What can I do for you?"

"I'll admit, I accepted a mission to abscond with a snickerdoodle if you have any left," Jake said.

Debbie cast a pair of scrutinizing eyes, "They were more popular than I estimated, but I have a couple stashed away. Come on, I'll get them for you."

Leading Jake through the gallery, Debbie whispered over her shoulder, "A little secret between you and me... I didn't bake these. We have Jennifer to thank. I think I was under charged. They are out of this world delicious. You taking these is saving me from myself."

"Thank you," Jake said, accepting the small bag of cookies.

"Thank you, Jake. This has been an amazing Christmas. We have a lot of that to owe to you," Debbie said.

"Everyone keeps saying that. All I did was help those who were struggling see that the businesses they built were worth saving," Jake said.

"It's more than that. You showed them the path and gave them the courage to fight for themselves. That's more than a pat on the back and social media ad. That is believing and caring. Taking the time to care. We're grateful," Debbie said.

Jake's cheeks reddened, "Well, thank you. I hope it helped most of the businesses down here."

"It helped in more ways than making cash registers ring. It created a culture of physical neighbors becoming neighborly. It is a good Christmas, Jake," Debbie said.

"Thank you. And thank you for the cookies. They are going to someone very deserving," Jake said.

"Anytime, Jake," Debbie called as Jake made his way out of the gallery.

Thirty One

The Coffee Corner was packed. Jake had to sneak in to find a spot near Bea and Sara. Parents formed a ring to the perimeter of the shop while their children formed an inner ring around a woman dressed as Mrs. Clause. She sat in a chair talking with the children while a colorfully illustrated book sat on a table next to her.

Bea and Sara mouthed 'Hello' while they observed the crowd. Jake panned out. Seeing Carol and Eric, he gave a nod. Finding Tanner and Bethany in the inner circle, he smiled and waved.

When it seemed like everyone who was going to come was present, Bea slipped through the crowd.

"I want to thank everyone for coming. This is so exciting," Bea said. Dipping lower, she addressed the children directly, "Who is ready for Christmas!"

The room burst into a loud cheer.

"Me too. Me too. As we wait for Christmas morning to come, there is nothing like curling up near the fireplace or the Christmas tree and reading a wonderful book with your family. I used to read books like that to a young lady standing over there," Bea pointed at Sara.

Sara blushed and gave a little wave to the children.

"Mrs. Lorraine White wrote a wonderful story about Christmas. She lives only two towns up and thought, how nice it would be to share it with all of you. There is cocoa and cookies after the story and for those who aren't already planning on going, a chocolate-making event next door. With that, I give you Mrs. Lorraine," Bea said, her hands spread toward the woman in the chair.

Sneaking back to her spot between Jake and Sara, she received kudos from each for her introduction.

As Mrs. White began to speak, one of the children blurted, "Are you Mrs. Clause?"

Mrs. White smiled, "No, but I am a big fan of hers. So much so, I wanted to tell stories from her point of view. You know what I am also a fan of? This town of yours. We used to come down here many years ago. I had forgotten how magical it was. I think Wintergreen will be back on our annual Christmas event calendar."

She took the book from the table. Taking care so that each child could see the cover, she slowly opened it and began reading out loud. With each page, she would flip the book so the children could see the wonderful illustrations inside.

Jake glanced at Bea. She looked so happy. He was happy for her. His eyes drifted, catching Sara watching him smiling at Bea. Her head didn't dart away. Instead, she offered a warm smile back.

With the children's book event coming to a close, Jake stayed to help Bea and Sara clean up, knowing they both wanted to attend the chocolate event. Gathering cocoa cups, napkins and cookie plates, they made quick work of cleaning up.

As Sara went to grab the vacuum, Jake said to Bea, "I think that went well."

"That went extremely well," Bea beamed. "I sold so many gift cards, I may be giving coffee away the month of January, but we will live to see another day."

"You're doing that well?"

Bea nodded, "With the space next door rented out, all of the pressure is off. Sales have been up enough the last couple of weeks to make this the strongest December... ever."

"Bea, that's amazing!" Jake exclaimed.

Bea stood still looking at Jake. Her eyes welled, "I owe it to you, Jake. And to Sara. You two saved the Coffee Corner and probably Main Street."

"You and the rest of the businesses saved Main Street. There is no Main Street without you. The town just needed a reminder, especially with the new shiny things by the freeway which won't stay new and shiny for long," Jake said.

"Well, they were almost the only thing in town," Bea said.

Sara arrived with the vacuum. Bea shook her head, "You know what? I will do that in the morning. Let's get to next door. I want to learn my next new hobby."

Sara and Jake laughed as they could barely keep up with Bea as she hustled from the café to the space next door. The room was filled. Tables were lined out with a variety of cooking supplies and ingredients. In the front of the room, an instructional table was set up. Cameras angled down on the table projected onto large monitors behind a woman in a chef's coat for the crowd to watch every move.

As they entered, a woman guided them, "Little ones are in the back, they are enjoying a chocolate fountain. Up here, though, we are turning chocolate into decadent works of art."

"I'm sold on either," Jake said. Sara elbowed him in the ribs. Jake's heart fluttered as she did so.

Finding the stations filled, Carol and Eric waved them over. Realizing space was tight, Jake whispered, "You go on ahead."

Bea gave a brief "Are you sure?" glance before excitedly trotting over to Carol's station.

Jake found a spot along the wall where several people were happy enough to watch the demonstration. A few used the opportunity to keep an eye on their children at the same time. Jake followed their eyes as volunteers handed out candy canes for the children to dip into the chocolate. He was surprised to see Mr. Fuller and his son wearing aprons, their pockets lined with candy cane hooks.

Squeezing in next to Debbie who made space for Sara as well, Jake gave a wave to Jennifer who was in the front row, studiously following the chocolatier's instructions.

"I'm so glad you guys made it. This event filled up fast," Debbie hissed.

"There is no way Grandma was going to miss it. She loves all things chocolate," Debbie whispered.

"Speaking of events…" Debbie started.

Sara shifted uncomfortably.

"I won't pressure you, but, I would love the local artist who created those beautiful paintings to be able share their obvious love for the subjects. There was such care taken in their creation. There is a lot of heart. They are genuinely gorgeous," Debbie said.

Sara blushed and looked down. As she looked back up, Debbie's eyes were directly on hers. Sara could see the sincerity in them.

"Okay. Okay, I'll do it," Sara agreed.

With a warm smile, Debbie reached out with her hand on Sara's arms, "Wonderful. Thank you."

"You'll do great," Jake assured.

Debbie's eyes shot up and locked on Jake's, her lips pursed, "Oh, don't think you are off the hook, mister. There are plans for you, too. Can you meet us at the coffee shop tomorrow at nine a.m.?"

Jake raised a brow, wondering what the plans were and who "us" was. When he pressed, Debbie merely stood her ground and gave him an expectant look. Relenting, he shrugged, "Sure, yeah. I can be there."

"Good," Debbie said. Her job clearly done for the evening, she spun and focused her attention on the chocolate demonstration.

"For most of you, your truffles will need a little more time to set. For everyone here, you are welcome to come up to either side of the table and take a plate. Each table has a sampling of my favorite truffles for you all to try," the chocolatier said.

Debbie's brows bounced, as she wore an enormous grin, "This is my favorite part!"

Sara and Jake laughed as the elegant woman exhibited her childlike side.

"What do you think? Sample some truffles?" Jake asked.

"When at a chocolate event, you taste chocolate," Sara nodded.

As the tastings were handed out and described by the chocolatier and the follow-along stations were done with their crafting, the room broke into a shared joy of chocolate. Jake and Sara meandered to Carol and Eric's station. Bea looked absolutely giddy with her creations. Melted chocolate smeared on her wrist.

"It looks like you had fun," Sara grinned.

Bea frowned as she assessed herself, "I think maybe I should have been back with the kids at the fountain."

"The kids," Carol groaned. Looking at her husband, she said, "I bet they are a mess. Can they ride home with you?"

"You might be surprised. From what I could see, Mr. Fuller and his son seemed to have them in pretty good control. The fountain was shut down and they were handing out wipes before we came over," Jake said.

Carol looked relieved.

Holding up two small bags in the air, Jake said, "As requested, snickerdoodles, care of Debbie at the gallery. And these gems, Rosettes from Jennifer's bakery."

Carol's eyes widened as she accepted the bags, "I knew I liked working with you for some reason. You bring me cookies and coffee from the best places in town!"

"Thanks for setting the bar, Jake," Eric laughed.

"The way she talks about you, you are like a hero she gets to welcome home each night. I think you two are an amazing example of what couples strive for," Jake said. Given the company, his words made his cheeks redden.

"Well, speaking of kiddos, we are going to round ours up. Good night, all! Thanks for the cookies, Jake!" Carol said picking up a box of truffles and handing another to Bea.

Bea opened her box and beamed, "Aren't they beautiful?"

"I bet they taste great, too! Sara said.

With a scowl, Bea slammed the box closed and shifted her body to shield it.

"I guess I should have taken the class, too," Sara said, her voice sullen.

Making their way out of the event space, they pulled their coats a little tighter to ward off the wintry night air.

"See you tomorrow, Jake!" Bea said, shuffling off toward her car.

Sara began walking toward her own.

"Sara…" Jake called.

A glance in his eyes told Sara it wasn't a conversation she was ready for. With a shake of her head and even lips, she said, "Not now, Jake. We had a good day. I'll see you tomorrow."

Jake froze in place, merely offering a dejected nod, "Tomorrow."

For a moment, Jake stood on the sidewalk watching Sara walk away. He was oblivious of the others streaming by him until a voice said, "Nice girl. I don't know what is between you two, but I can tell there is a spark. Don't let it die, young man. The good ones don't come around that often."

Jake turned to see Mr. Fuller standing next to him, watching Sara disappear into the night.

With a smile, Jake nodded, "Yeah. You're right. You're right."

"See you tomorrow, Jake. These old bones aren't made for late evenings with a horde of children, but it sure was fun!"

"Good night, Mr. Fuller," Jake said.

Once more, he was the last person to walk to his car in Downtown Wintergreen. Those stolen moments had become some of his most memorable moments of the holiday.

Thirty Two

With just three days to Christmas there was an energy in the air. The coffee shop was a popular place for people to gather. Whether customers were catching up with friends or relatives who traveled in for the holidays or to fuel up before the last-minute shopping, the atmosphere was festive.

Regulars mixed with newcomers, and everyone seemed to relish the experience. Bea hummed to the Christmas carols played over the café's speakers. Sara worked the espresso machine like a musician, maintaining a rhythmic flow that Jake found almost mesmerizing.

Spying a table in the back, Jake set his things down and made his way to order. Debbie and Jennifer slipped in line behind him. "What can I get you?" he asked.

Reluctantly, the ladies gave him their order. They were soon joined by Mr. Fuller. With a shrug, the pharmacist requested a black coffee. Bea, hearing to order, shook him off. "Oh, no. You are getting a Christmas special!" the barista sang.

Flopping his hands, he followed Debbie and Jennifer to the table. Grabbing his and Debbie's drink, Bea arrived with Jennifer's and Mr. Fuller's. The pharmacist's had a candy cane hanging over the edge of his peppermint vanilla latte.

Jake nodded at the appropriateness of the gesture which was received with a chuckle from Mr. Fuller.

Seated at the table, Jake looked around the group who all seemed to know something he did not. Debbie straightened in her seat and led the meeting.

"Jake, the past few weeks have been nothing short of a miracle on Main Street. Collectively, around the table, we all have a lot to owe to you," the gallery owner began. "And it's not just the flow of traffic, it's the excitement that you have brough to downtown."

"I can attest to that… and nothing excites me anymore," Mr. Fuller laughed, receiving chuckles from around the table.

"It goes way beyond business. It goes beyond the events. You pulled all of us together in a way that I have never seen and I've been here a long time," Bea said.

"We have enjoyed you working with us," Jennifer said.

Jake was itchy in his seat, not knowing where this glowing conversation was headed.

"At the event last night, we all got to talking. This has been an amazing turnaround for many of us," Jennifer said with a knowing nod to Bea. "But we began to wonder what happens after the holidays?"

All eyes panned to Jake.

"And that is where you come in. We would like to form a downtown business alliance, and we would like you to run it," Debbie said.

"We have no idea what that looks like. Clearly, you can do a lot part-time. Who knows, it could turn into a fulltime thing," Jennifer said.

"None of us have a marketing budget to speak of," Mr. Fuller said, his eyes flitting on Debbie as the one notable exception.

Bea sat forward, "But we decided if we all pitched in and got other businesses to do so, too, then maybe we could afford you."

Jake looked around the table, his cheeks glowing. "I appreciate everything you have said and I am glad that things have turned around. You are right to think about the future. January could be a momentum killer. But the firm doesn't really do that sort of thing. It's a good idea…"

"We don't want to hire the firm," Bea said, her voice pointed.

"We want to hire you, Jake," Mr. Fuller said. "I would feel so much better having my son take over the pharmacy if I knew you were at the helm steering Main Street into the future."

"I can provide a template and someone can pick up the mantle. Mr. Fuller, it could be your son. Sara might be able to do it depending on her workload at the accounting firm. Debbie, you have some amazing staff that can tackle it when the gallery is slow," Jake offered.

Debbie shook her head, "No one has the marketing mindset that you do, Jake. Even then, it's more than marketing. You have affected the people of Wintergreen and the towns surrounding us. Main Street has become a destination for shoppers and consumers. But it has become so much more than that. Look at us around the table. We waved. We would visit. But you rallied us."

"My pharmacy has been on Main Street for longer than when your parents were born, Jake. Those of us that have been around, we've seen a lot. We've been through a lot. I have never seen anything like this season," Mr. Fuller said.

Jake shifted in his seat.

Debbie could sense his discomfort and put a hand out, "This is all pretty overwhelming. Why don't we let you think about it. We can get back together after the holidays."

"Yeah, that's fair," Jennifer said.

Bea and Mr. Fuller looked at Jake for a moment before nodding in agreement.

"Okay," Jake said. "I'll think about it. I sincerely appreciate that you all think so much of me and my abilities. I will think about it. Come up with options and report back to you after the holidays."

"Thank you for meeting with us and considering it, Jake," Debbie said.

One by one, the group disbanded. Jake sat at the table by himself for a few moments. His heart wanted to scream, "Of course!" But his head knew he couldn't do it. The demands of the marketing firm and the likelihood that he wouldn't be in Wintergreen forever, took the decision out of his hands. He appreciated the holidays as a respite before he had to declare his decision to the group.

Playing with his coffee cup, he couldn't help but to sketch out some ideas in his head. Suddenly filled with inspiration, Jake darted out of the coffee shop after a chorus of good bye and Merry Christmas to Bea, Sara and their guests.

Jake arrived at the marketing firm to find a nearly empty office. He could see that Frank's light was on. Few employees seemed to be whiling away their last day of work before vacation officially began for the company.

Dropping off a coffee at Carol's desk, he received a hearty thank you for the cookies from the night before.

"I hope you shared," Jake said.

"I shared the rosettes. The snickerdoodles were mine! I had no idea Debbie could bake like that," Carol said.

"Yeah, neither can Debbie," Jake laughed leaving Carol somewhat bewildered as she inspected her coffee.

Plopping his things down, he cleared space on his desk and jotted down as many notes as he could remember from the coffee shop to the office. Looking out at Carol, he suddenly had an idea. Excitedly scrambling out of his chair, he called out, "Do you have a second?"

Carol shrugged and got up from her seat to follow.

"Grab your coffee," Jake said.

With a nod, Carol snatched her cup from her desk and entered Jake's office.

"Shut the door, if you would," Jake pointed.

Carol closed the door and slid into one of the seats facing the front of his desk. "What's up?"

"The owners of some of the downtown businesses want to start a downtown business alliance. They asked me to run it, but with things here and eventually going to corporate, I'm just not the right fit," Jake said. "You, however, would be brilliant!"

Carol frowned, "Jake, I have the occasional idea or two, but I am not you. I couldn't have pulled off what you did downtown. Not in a million years. I appreciate your faith in me, but I couldn't do it. Not without someone like you by my side."

Jake considered her argument. Scratching his chin, he said, "You won't be alone. You'll have Sara. The other business owners…"

"You think Frank will let me sneak away like you do? He would have had your head if he didn't *need* you and if Henry didn't already have plans for you at corporate. There is no way he gives me even a bit of that latitude," Carol protested.

Jake frowned as he considered the options.

Carol interrupted his thoughts, "I'm sorry Jake, I'm not your gal."

Jake didn't relent, "You would be amazing in that role."

"I'm the quiet, from-the-sideline idea person. You're the battle cry and the big idea marketing guru. I latch on to your already great ideas, fuel up with your excitement and toss in a little woman's touch, a little flair to your campaigns," Carol said.

"You do more than that," Jake said. With a sigh, he relented, "But, I won't batter you. It was just an idea."

"You could do it. At least until you get promoted. Give them a head start. Get them through the January doldrums. Kick the New Year off as successfully as the last one ended," Carol suggested.

"Yeah, maybe I could do that. See, great ideas!" Jake pointed his pen at Carol.

Carol scoffed, "My biggest idea of the day is sneaking out of here around lunch time. Can you send me on some errand that will conveniently run into my official time off?"

Jake laughed, "Absolutely. I *really* need you to capture the Java Universe app experience so that I can incorporate that into the campaign. Report back to me by end of the day."

"Really?"

Jake's head fell, "Do you want a mission to go be with your family or what?"

"Right," Carol nodded. "I'm on it. I will have a full report in a three-sentence text by end of day."

"Perfect," Jake grinned. Standing up he said, "If I don't see you, Merry Christmas."

"Oh, come on!" Carol reached across the desk and pulled him in for a shoulder hug. "Merry Christmas, Jake."

She paused as she reached the door. Slowly turning, she said, "I don't know what I'm going to do when you go to corporate."

Jake shrugged, "They'll assign you whoever takes my place."

"It took me this long to get you into shape. I don't know if I have it in me for another run with someone new," Carol said.

"You are amazing. You'll be fine," Jake smiled.

Carol nodded and left the office.

Jake stared at the door, thinking about their conversation. With new ideas bubbling to the surface, Jake pulled out his notes and began scribbling furiously.

Thirty Three

"Ahem!"

Jake was so absorbed in his work that he didn't even hear the knocks on his office door. It took Henry standing directly in front of his desk, clearing his throat to get his attention.

"I'm pretty sure everyone has gone home for the holidays. Even Frank. And here you are, still working away," Henry said.

Jake cast a sheepish look up at the marketing firm president. Grateful his hastily written notes were nearly indecipherable to anyone other than himself or maybe Carol and that his computer screen was facing away from Henry.

"Just tinkering with some ideas," Jake shrugged.

"You remind me of a younger me. Well, I guess I haven't changed much. I guess empires aren't built by nine-to-fivers. But by people like us," Henry said.

"I suppose, sir," Jake nodded, straightening up his papers and shoving them under his Java Universe mockups.

"Speaking of empires, we have a lot to talk about. I owe you a dinner," Henry said. "I am hoping you are free tonight?"

"Uh…" Jake had planned on going downtown to hang an ornament on the tree. A last second push to get families to visit and make their mark on the Wintergreen Christmas, placing an ornament with their family names on it on the tree. "Yeah, sure. Yes. Of course."

"Good. I know you like the tavern along the river downtown, but I guess that whole area has been a madhouse this season," Henry said. "The hotel I am staying at has a steak house. It's a high-end chain that we have had as a client for years."

"Take care of those who take care of us," Jake said.

Henry nodded, "Right. If you're free now, we can go."

"Let me get my things cleaned up and I'll be right behind you," Jake said.

"See you there," Henry said.

As Henry left, Jake pulled out his stack of notes and placed them in his bag. Glancing at the computer screen, he studied his work. Carol was right. If he could just get the Wintergreen Downtown Business Alliance started on the right foot, especially helping them through the notorious slow January season, they might just be okay.

Scrolling through his plan for January he hit the print button. Clicking the page, he scanned the year-long timeline that he built so that the group could maintain momentum without him if needed. Jake leaned back, proud of his work. He knew they had built a following for the holidays, but those new consumer habits would be completely abandoned if they succumbed to the January doldrums.

With a satisfied smile, he finished packing. Stopping by the printer, he grabbed his final items and panned the silent marketing firm. The sea of cubicles was ringed by offices and the conference room. There was something about the still of Christmas, even in an abandoned office building that stirred a sense of excitement. Lives were put on hold to celebrate the birth of Christ. To spend time with family and friends. To focus on giving and sharing as opposed to work.

Jake took a deep breath and smiled, only to realize, his own Christmas vacation hadn't started yet. He had at least one work meeting left to attend. It was a meeting he had anticipated with enormous excitement for some time. Now that it had arrived, he wasn't excited. He stepped out of the office and hit the elevator call button with immense reservation and a pit welling in his stomach.

As the elevator doors opened, Jake tried to place this feeling. Was it just butterflies? Was it concern over his ending the relationship with Tracy, Henry's daughter? Either way, the future would be laid out at this dinner, whether he was ready for it or not.

Jake froze as he entered the restaurant and the host held his arm out to help Jake find where Henry was seated. Tracy was sitting right next to Henry. She wore an elegant dress. Cascading ringlets framed her face while sparkling gems dangled from her ears. It was Tracy at her finest. While he was sure it was supposed to have the opposite effect, it made his heart burrow into his stomach even further.

With a breath, he marched forward.

"Jake!" Tracy called out happily. Getting up from her chair, she dashed to give Jake a hug.

"You still haven't told him?" Jake whispered into her ear.

"I haven't decided we were done," Tracy hissed happily.

Letting go of their embrace, Jake helped Tracy back into her chair.

"I hope you don't mind. I figured Tracy has as much at stake in the conversation as anyone," Henry said.

"No, why would I mind?" Jake forced a flat smile and took his seat beside Tracy.

"I took the liberty of ordering some wine. Tonight is a celebration as much as it is a dinner among employees, friends… family," Henry stated.

On cue, the waiter displayed a bottle and offered to pour. Jake eagerly accepted. As his glass was filled, Jake took a large gulp, nodding as to indicate how good it was.

"I visited this winery on the way to a pitch in Silicon Valley. They have this underground cellar where I was able to taste from some of the exclusive barrels. This pales but is a wonderful example of the same varietal," Henry said.

"It is excellent. Thank you," Jake said.

Henry took a long sip. Raising a brow, he noticed a distance between Tracy and Jake. He smiled to himself, he presumed Jake was anxious anticipating the evening's discussion. Setting his glass down, he addressed Jake directly.

"It's a shame you can't join us for Christmas. We book the finest restaurant in town. It is delightful," Henry said.

"I imagine it creates some special Christmas memories, sir," Jake said.

"Tracy tells me your family has rather intimate celebrations," Henry said.

Jake nodded, "In the morning, it's usually just family. By the afternoon we either have neighbors over or we head over to them. It is nice. Typically it breaks out into games or carols or something like that."

"It sounds like one of the Christmas movies," Henry laughed. "I couldn't imagine our neighbors doing that. I guess when you live in gated estates, they are gated for a reason."

"We had Christmas catered one year. I liked staying at home," Tracy said. "Though I enjoy finding a new Christmas dress each year too. I mean, spending all day in pajamas is a bit silly."

"We've had a few Christmases like that growing up, too," Jake admitted.

They peeled their arms back as the first course was delivered.

While the conversations weren't unpleasant, they weren't terribly substantive, either. Jake glanced at his watch, hoping he had been discrete. Seeing Tracy raise a brow, he realized he hadn't been.

"Daddy, I think it is time," Tracy said, reaching out to grab Jake's hand.

The action surprised him. Under Henry's wary eye and Tracy's surprisingly strong grip, Jake didn't immediately pull away.

"Jake, you have been a star at our firm for some time, long before you and Tracy became an item. Even as an apprentice, you were delivering solid ideas. I noticed even when the marketing executive took credit for your work. You work tirelessly. Frankly, you typically deliver more work than you need to. I have grown to appreciate your Goldilocks approach when it comes to offering the sales team options. Most of our marketing team only produces a pitch to spec," Henry began.

Tracy looked impatient, "Skip the shop talk, Daddy. We all know Jake is great at his job."

"Right," Henry nodded. "Jake, it is time you take the next step with our firm, and as you and Tracy consider next steps in your lives. I think you know a promotion has been coming. What you don't know is that it is a leapfrog promotion. The V.P. of Marketing position has opened up. I think, and the board agrees, there is no one better to take that role."

Jake nearly choked. "V.P., sir?"

"Only if you start calling me Henry."

Tracy squeezed Jake's hand.

"I- I don't know what to say. This is…unexpected," Jake said.

"And don't think for a moment that you don't deserve it. It is rare that someone goes from Marketing Executive straight into the V.P. role, but you have everything it takes and can lead us into the future. Maybe even assume my position when I am ready to retire,"

Henry said casting a look toward Tracy. "Perhaps even keeping the company in the family."

Jake's throat tightened. He could feel his skin pale.

"This," he choked. "This is exciting. Do you mind if I get some air?"

Henry nodded, "Take a moment. Collect yourself. This is a big change, uprooting and moving to the city permanently. But, with your new salary, you will be able to do so in style."

Jake excused himself and nearly drifted out of the restaurant. The blast of cold air as he burst through the restaurant doors was welcome.

Letting out a deep breath which turned into a funnel of vapor as it mixed with the wintry atmosphere.

The sound of heels on the concrete turned Jake's attention. Tracy wore a sly smile as she approached. Pulling her coat over her dress, she stepped like a model over to him. "I told you something big was coming, Jake," she said.

"Yeah, it's big," Jake admitted.

Tracy cocked her head, "Are you okay? I would have thought you would have been more excited. You *should* be more excited."

"It's just all… a lot to take in," Jake said.

"It's been a turbulent season. But that's what it is, Jake. It is a season. Seasons end. A new one begins. I am hoping we can begin a new one for us. Away from Wintergreen. Away from distractions," Tracy said.

Jake looked at her. Tracy's deep blue eyes looked hopeful.

Jake's shoulders slumped.

Tracy shrugged, "We'll give it some time. Have your holiday. We can revisit this when you are moved into the city."

Noticing Jake begin to shiver, Tracy steered him back toward the restaurant, "Come on. We shouldn't keep Daddy waiting."

Walking back into the restaurant, Jake was numb. He didn't even fight Tracy slipping her arm into his.

Retaking their seats, Henry leaned back in his, "Welcome to the future, Jake. Right here, at this table is your future and boy, is it bright."

"Thank you, sir… Henry," Jake nodded.

"Can you be in the city by the second of January? Don't worry about your things. We'll have a moving company take care of that for you. Tracy already has a place picked out for you. The company will pick up the dime for the first six months, get you settled. That way you can focus on the job. I'm excited for you, Jake. I'm excited for all of us," Henry said.

"Move…" Jake considered the request. His mind reeled. "Uh, yeah. Sure."

"All right. It's settled then!" Henry beamed.

With a nod from Henry, the waiter popped the cork on a bottle of Champagne and poured a glass for each of them.

Henry leaned into the center of the table as he raised his glass, "To the future!"

"To the future," Tracy and Jake repeated. Jake's voice was nearly a whisper.

Thirty Four

Jake was drawn downtown. He had carried a glass ornament in his pocket all night with the hopes of joining the town in placing them on the tree.

As he made his way to the park, the streets were largely quiet. A few stragglers from a late dinner at the tavern restaurant ambled toward their cars.

The Christmas lights strung along Main Street leading to the tree-lined entrance to the park were magnificent. Ending at the large tree in the park with its vibrant display was dramatic. The light dusting of snow only made the brilliance of the lights glimmer with a greater sense of magic.

Hands in his pockets, Jake fumbled with the ornament. Taking a slow stroll around the tree, he admired the ones that were placed throughout the evening. From gift shop favorites to homemade ornaments to photos of families, friends and couples, the already beautiful tree was made only the more special with the personal connections each ornament carried with it.

As he circled the tree, he was almost alarmed when he saw another figure bathed in the radiance of Christmas lights. Once his eyes identified the person behind the silhouette, Jake found the image stunning.

Sara quietly looked at each ornament. Gently turning them to see the family that hung it and gingerly put it back in the position that she found it.

"Beautiful, aren't they?" Jake asked.

Sara jumped as she looked toward the voice.

With her hand clamped to her chest, she gasped, "Jake Myers! You nearly gave me a heart attack."

"Sorry. I didn't realize anyone else was out here at first," Jake said.

"What are you doing here?" Sara asked.

"Admiring the town's ornaments, like you. I didn't have a chance to get down here and place one myself yet. Have you?" Jake asked.

Sara nodded, "I did earlier. I wanted to come back and see the ones that were added. It's like each one tells a story."

"Yeah, they do. What story did yours tell?" Jake asked.

"I painted a star. It is supposed to be the Christmas star, I guess," Sara looked thoughtful as her eyes moved from Jake to other ornaments on the tree. "The stars are a symbol of hope. In an uncertain future, you can look up and see an infinite number of stars."

"One for each possible path for the future," Jake said.

"Something like that," Sara nodded.

They continued their circumference around the tree until they were face to face. For a moment they paused in the glow of the tree. The lights and the ornaments made the sparkle in their eyes dance.

The twinkle in Jake's eyes almost too much for Sara. She squeezed hers shut before she again moved her gaze to the tree.

"What about yours? What story does it tell?" Sara asked.

Jake reached into his pocket. To Sara's surprise, he pulled out a glass star. "Hopeful light in an uncertain future," he said.

Sara's cheeks reddened. With a soft nod, she said, "I guess we are both at a crossroads in our lives."

"You have no idea," Jake breathed. Seeing Sara's curious eyes, Jake asked, "You ever find yourself on a path that you have been working so long for but don't know if it's the path you really want to be on? That you belong on?"

Sara put her hands on her hips and glared at Jake, "Are you serious?"

"Right," Jake acknowledged. "What are you going to do?"

"My head says one thing… my heart says another," Sara sighed.

Jake's heart skipped a beat, "Yeah, me too."

Cocking her head, Sara looked up at Jake. As he formulated his words to speak, a voice that had become all too familiar to Jake broke the otherwise silent night.

"Jake Myers and my favorite accountant!"

"Hello, Shawn," Jake said without even turning to look at him. Shoulders slumping, he looked in Sara's eyes, longing for a few more moments alone with her.

"It sounds like congratulations are in order!" Shawn said walking up to the pair.

Sara looked at him with curiosity.

Shawn slapped Jake on the shoulder, "Jake here, is the new Vice President of Marketing at Banks Marketing."

Sara's eyes went wide. Offering a hesitant smile, she said, "That's wonderful news, Jake. I'm happy for you."

Jake looked surprised.

"Frank and the mayor are tight. Your name came up in conversation. The town's going to miss you being around, buddy," Shawn said.

Jake stammered as he looked at Sara, "I'm not sure… I…"

"Taking off right after the new year. Boy, that must get your head spinning," Shawn said. "But, hey, when opportunity like that knocks, you gotta take it."

Sara and Jake just stared at each other.

"It's going to be quite the year. Sara on the city accounting team and 'ol Jake… a V.P. position at your age. Man, you are set for life," Shawn said.

Jake looked at Shawn. He heard the words, but cast in the light of the tree with Sara's disposition clouding with each word spoken, Jake fought to regain a semblance of present consciousness. "Uh, Shawn, what are you doing here? You weren't searching the town to congratulate me."

"Naw, the mayor wanted me to put an ornament on the tree for him. I forgot all about it," Shawn pulled a picture frame ornament from his pocket and held it up in the Christmas tree light. "It's the mayor giving his speech at the tree lighting. Nice, right?"

"Yeah, nice," Jake nodded, his voice exasperated. He turned his attention to Sara who blinked at him.

"I, uh, I should go," Sara said, her voice soft and hollow. "Congratulations, Jake. Really. I'm happy for you."

"Sara…" Jake called.

Sara kept walking, her pace quickening.

"Man, can you believe how things turn out? Not so bad for you. though, eh, Jake?" Shawn slapped him on the chest with the back of his gloved hand.

"Yeah," Jake's words came out as a whisper as he watched Sara disappear out of the park.

"Well, gotta go. Congrats, man!" Shawn said and hustled out of the park himself.

Jake stood for several minutes looking in the direction that Sara went. Sighing, he realized he still hadn't placed his ornament. Dangling from his finger, he slowly made his way around the tree as he searched for the right spot.

Suddenly, he froze. Raising his arms, he carefully slid the string that carried his star onto a branch. It swung slowly, each angle of the glass creating a warm prism of light as it pulled in the colorful bulbs of the tree. It seemed to dance on the branch in rhythm to the ornament next to it.

Jake studied his star's dance partner. It was an ornament with a hand-painted star. The star was so vivid, it almost seemed to generate its own light. In the glow of the tree, it was stunningly luminescent.

Pushed by the slight evening breeze, the ornament slowly rotated. On the back was a painted signature– *Sara Bailey.*

Thirty Five

Jake arrived at breakfast in much the same fashion as he had spent the evening– in a trance. Instead of coherent thoughts, his mind played images like an old film strip running through his head.

The images were filled with the events of the past few weeks, from Bea sharing her struggles to seeing Sara behind the coffee bar. The adventure of rallying downtown to take over the town's decorating of Main Street and forcing the continuation of the tree lighting were highlights. Images of families smiling together as they explored and the shop owners coming out of their shells and working together.

They all came together in a confusing collage that Jake didn't know what he was supposed to do with. He thought of Carol and her family. Carol's genuine unhappiness to have Jake leave the Wintergreen office ran through his head.

Jake thought of Mr. Fuller cracking the first smile that he had ever recalled witnessing and the old pharmacist supervising the chocolate fountain with his son for a bunch of children. He enjoyed watching Jennifer eagerly band together with Bea to help save the coffee shop along with her bakery. Debbie seeing the possibilities of downtown and the promise of Sara's artwork warmed his heart beyond measure.

No series of images stung Jake as deeply as the ones of Sara. From her smile across the coffee bar to her laugh as they decorated Main Street, the pictures in his mind made his heart flutter. Like falling embers burning through the smiles and laughter, images of Sara's disappointment time and time again with him. They rode a roller coaster of hopes and growing closer together to Jake leaving Sara feeling betrayed, led on, and abandoned.

"Jake… Jake, are you with us?" Tracy's voice cut through the cinema in Jake's head.

"Yeah," Jake nodded. "A long night, that's all."

"Well, this should wake you up if the Java Universe espresso isn't enough," Henry said. Smacking a stack of papers down on the table with an elegant pen placed on top.

Jake watched the pen roll onto its clip and stop.

"You are a few signatures away from being the Banks Marketing's youngest vice president ever," Henry said.

Jake stared at the papers. His eyes glanced at Henry and then at Tracy. Tracy shifted in her seat as she waited for Jake to pick up the pen. It was if she knew the moment the ink dried on the paper, Jake's life would change. He would be pulled away from Wintergreen, his friends, his family… and Sara.

"Java Universe is just the start. With you at the helm, we are already getting inquiries from other large national companies. This decision isn't just about you, Jake. It truly is about the company's growth. You make…" Henry stirred his coffee, staring at it with a bit of a shrug. "You make some pretty average coffee into a story. Your marketing makes this coffee taste better to millions of people around the country. Those millions of cups of coffee turn into very nice houses and early retirements for you and me, Jake."

Jake held the pen in his hand. He looked at the people in line as they placed their orders and stepped forward. Not once had he heard the words Merry Christmas uttered by patron or employees. He scarcely saw a smile. A simple roll back of their eyes as the customers took the first hit. The first sip of the coffee that their palates had become used to was the closest thing to an emotion that he could see.

Tracy must have sensed Jake's hesitation and became antsy in her seat. Flopping down a glossy sheet of paper, she said, "I brought the flyer for the place I picked out for you. You are going to love it!"

Jake glanced over at the luxuriously appointed condominium.

"It has a large balcony with an amazing view of the city," Tracy said.

"Heh," Henry looked at his watch becoming agitated himself. "Let's go, Jake! I've got a plane to catch and need to drop those off at corporate."

"I, uh, I don't think I can do this," Jake said. Gently, but firmly placing the pen down, Jake looked at Henry and then at Tracy.

Henry's face turned bright red, "What are you doing, Jake? I went to bat for you."

"I appreciate it. I really do," Jake said.

"This isn't a joke, Jake. Your future is right here on this table. Sign the papers, Jake. That is not a request," Henry fumed.

"I'm sorry, Henry. My future is somewhere else," sliding away from the table, Jake held out his hand for an unrequited handshake. "I am grateful for the opportunity to have worked at Banks Marketing. I really am. Excuse me."

Jake began walking away. He could hear Henry's irate voice growl, "Talk some sense into your boyfriend, Tracy!"

As Jake stepped outside, Tracy called, "Jake, wait up!"

Jake turned.

"Jake, don't do this. Don't throw everything away that you have worked so hard for. Even if you and I aren't a thing- if we never work out- you are great at your job," Tracy said, grabbing his arm.

Jake spoke with the most clarity he had felt in weeks, "I'm not throwing anything away. I have finally found my own path and I'm taking it. You should too, Tracy. You need to find what makes you truly happy."

"*You* make me happy, Jake," Tracy said, the words almost a pout.

"No, I don't," Jake shook his head. "I fit into your world. I fit into your father's world. That isn't passion, Tracy. Seeing the person you love shouldn't just feel good. It should make your heart race. When they smile across the room, your heart should melt. When their eyes light up at something they're passionate about, you should encourage them, share if just a tiny bit of that passion- for them. When their heart breaks, yours should too."

Tracy's eyes searched Jake's for a window.

"I check your father's boxes, Tracy. I need to check *all* of your boxes. I don't," Jake said.

"I…" Tracy started to argue but no words came out. Her eyes welled with tears, but her posture was of resigned acknowledgment, not of sadness.

Jake pulled her in for a hug, "I loved spending time with you and getting to know you. I see the sparks of passion in you. I hope you find them for yourself and chase after them with everything you've got. Whether it's what Henry thinks is the right path for you or not."

He could feel her nod as she burrowed her teary eyes into his shoulder.

"You're going to be okay," Jake said, pulling away so that he could look into her eyes. "I am sorry all of this happened right at Christmas. I would have loved to have shown you a different version from what you're used to."

"In pajamas… with games?" Tracy asked.

Jake laughed, "Yeah. In pajamas… with games."

Tracy wiped her cheeks and straightened herself up, "I may have to try that sometime. But I think I am more the Christmas dress type."

"I know," Jake smiled softly. "Merry Christmas, Tracy."

"Merry Christmas, Jake," Tracy's voice rattled as she let go of Jake's hand. Clearing her throat, she spun on her heel. Collecting herself, she strode back into the coffee shop as dignified and together as she did the first time.

Jake watched her go. He could see Henry looking at his watch while his lips moved rapidly and angrily near the mouthpiece of his phone.

Heading toward his truck, Jake almost looked at the world through one wary open eye, expecting him to instantly regret the six-figure decision he just made. To his surprise, he practically floated across the parking lot. He felt light and free.

Climbing into his truck, he gave it a start. With a smile, he shifted into gear and headed toward town. He had news and he couldn't wait to tell the world.

Jake had tried all day to sneak time to pull Sara aside and speak to her. With his personal house in order, he was ready to dive all in on Carol's advice to tell Sara, tell the world how he feels.

The café was busy early in the day. Aside from a simple wave and hello, the only stolen moments would have had to come out in a hurry. Jake didn't feel what he had to say was the blurt-out type of conversation. His hopeful eyes fell on Sara who did everything she could to avoid locking eyes with him. Bea offered a warm smile and was quickly pulled into a customer conversation.

Working his way down Main Street, he found more of the same. The business owners were busy with last-minute shoppers,

Jake didn't want to interrupt their flow or disrupt business. Even the gallery was in full swing, preparing for the event that evening. Debbie walked around with a feverish pace, clutching a clipboard tight to her chest.

Debbie paused for just a moment, "Your posts on the gallery event and our headliner were fabulous. We sold out our VIPs!"

She could see that Jake wanted to talk but offered an apologetic smile, "I gotta run. See you at the event!"

Jake nodded and Debbie disappeared into the gallery, chasing after a florist with holiday arrangements.

Turning to look at Main Street, it was flourishing with activity. A far cry from how the holiday season started. He loved the fact that the people swarming the sidewalks and the shops weren't lured in by sales and discounts, but the intrinsic value that the hometown shops offered. They were there because it was their community and they wanted to be a part of it.

Thirty Six

It seemed like the entire town had turned out for the gallery event. Dressed to the nines, people from Wintergreen and all over the state strolled down the tree-lit streets. The gallery, just offset of the tree-lined park and the grand tree with its jeweled lights and heartfelt ornaments, was lit in its own grandeur.

The building was radiant with amber light and festive, elegant decorations. Valets parked cars and scurried back into position to receive another.

Jake stopped by the Coffee Corner. Adjusting his tie in the reflection, he found a hearty smile and wave from inside. Straightening himself, Jake stood tall, his arm at the ready to receive his escort for the evening.

The café door swung open and an arm interlaced with his. "Madam," Jake said in his most distinguished voice.

"Sir," his escort replied with a slight giggle in her voice.

"You look lovely this evening," Jake observed.

"You turned out rather dapper yourself."

"Shall we?" Jake asked, taking a small step forward.

With a nod, they were off.

"I hear you have news."

Jake paused for just a moment and looked at the woman to his right. "You have no idea. I just, I just think Sara needs to hear it first," Jake said.

Bea looked up. Her eyes danced with wonder.

"This has been an exceptional, life-changing Christmas season. But tonight, it is all about your granddaughter and the gallery," Jake said.

"Gallantry and waiting for the right moment has led to many a battle being lost," Bea warned.

"And won. Besides, I would rather lose doing things the right way than win the battle at the expense of someone else's moment," Jake said.

Bea patted him on the arm, "I think someone has waited long enough."

"You know, I'm just happy to celebrate tonight. Celebrate Main Street. Celebrate Debbie and the gallery as a wonderful anchor for the town. And celebrate your granddaughter, whose art is genuinely exceptional," Jake said.

"Then let's celebrate!" Bea beamed as they crossed the street toward the gallery.

Jake's eyes swept over the entrance to the gallery. In typical Debbie fashion, it was impeccably decorated. Grand, yet tasteful. An entourage of servers waited on either side of the entrance. Champagne and mulled wine were offered as attendees entered.

"The mulled wine mix is from the coffee shop," Bea beamed.

"Then I should try some," Jake said, lifting a cup. Taking a sip, he was hit with notes of citrus before a collection of spices warmed his throat. Hints of red wine and brandy danced delicately in the background. "It's delicious. You should sell the mix at the coffee shop next year."

"Maybe I will," Bea said.

Programs for the evening had a photo of Sara next to one of her winter scenes on the cover. Both Bea and Jake flipped through the guide to land on Sara's page.

"She looks so beautiful," Bea said. "And her art… She certainly looks like she belongs here."

"She is… I mean, she deserves it. Her art is beautiful. Her bio reads like someone who really puts heart into what they do," Jake said.

On the back page, all of the Main Street vendors that pitched in for the catering and flowers were listed. "Looks like both you and your granddaughter are immortalized in this program," Jake said.

"That was nice of Debbie, but like you said, this whole evening is about Sara and the artwork," Bea said.

Throughout the gallery, up-levelled beverages from the Coffee Corner, elegant desserts from Jenn's Bakery, mature beverages from the Tavern Restaurant and even handmade truffles from the holiday vendor made their way around the crowd. A squadron of deft-handed servers danced around the busy gallery offering their delectable treats.

Jake's eyes darted around until they landed on the jewel he was searching for. His heart quickened as he took in her vision as though he were drawing in her image in the form of a breath. Sara, in an elegant, long, flowing dress stood next to one of her paintings.

The lighting was set so that both Sara and the painting were perfectly in focus. Debbie stood next to her, giving a quick smile to calm her nerves. Checking the time, Debbie placed a steadying hand on Sara's arm before raising her champagne glass high in the air.

"Welcome to Wintergreen Gallery's Annual Christmas Gala! Thank you all for coming. I look forward to this event all year long and seeing so many of you, more than I can ever remember, filling these halls warms my heart," Debbie took a long pause as she scanned the crowd. Even the servers froze in place as Debbie spoke.

"I have the pleasure of introducing an artist, a truly remarkable talent, who hails from right here in Wintergreen. One of the great joys I have as a curator is to find true gems that the world has not discovered yet and shine a light on that extraordinary talent. Tonight, I get to do that very thing with our own Sara Bailey. Sara has several of her paintings on display throughout the gallery tonight. Through the holiday season, she has had a few exhibited on the walls of the Coffee Corner café, whatever they could keep from being sold right away and ripped off the wall," Debbie announced.

Turning to Sara, Debbie held her arms in front of her. "I give you our Christmas Gala headliner, the very talented Sara Bailey. Come say hello. Enjoy her art. Enjoy each other's company and Merry Christmas! Salut!"

Debbie raised her glass high in a toast and brought the crystal flute to her lips to take a sip. A jittery Sara followed suit, her shaking hands barely containing the bubbly liquid in her glass until it reached her lips and she took a delicate sip.

"You might as well bottoms-up that, honey. Calm your nerves," Debbie smiled. Placing her hand on Sara's arm, she leaned in, "You'll be fine. They want to know about you, what inspires you and things like that. Speak from the heart and you'll do great."

Giving way to the circulating crowd wanting to get a peek at the painting Debbie had selected from Sara's collection. Sara was engulfed with questions about art, technique, her subjects and as Debbie had said, her inspirations.

Sara beamed, using her champagne glass hand to gesture around the gallery crowd, she said, "This. This is my inspiration. The people of Wintergreen. The beautiful setting where we live. And in some cases, reflecting on simpler times when we could relax. Have genuine conversations with each other. We could breathe. I think the paintings are my way of escaping into a calmer world. They take me to a place where my thoughts and my heart are pure. The challenges of the world melt away with each brush stroke."

"And it shows," a dapper man in the front of the crowd commented as he studied the scene next to Sara.

The painting showed the rolling hills just outside of Wintergreen, covered in snow. The river that ran along the tavern snaked its way through with ice building just alongside its banks. The heart of the painting was Wintergreen itself. While it didn't look like Wintergreen in the same lens that most had experienced it in recent years, it was remarkably similar to the Main Street that she had worked on with Jake and Bea and all of the others.

"Beautiful," the man nodded, his hand cupping his chin as he explored the world Sara had depicted.

Debbie leaned over and whispered to Sara, "Carlos is a friend of mine. He owns a gallery in Los Angeles."

"I could drink one of these hot toddies I was given at the front door and stare at this painting all evening. Escape into a different era. Well done, Ms. Bailey. Very well done," the man said, lifting his mug in the air.

Sara beamed, "Thank you."

"Wonderful eye, Debbie. Wonderful eye," Carlos said as he moved on.

Bea and Jake slowly made their way in front of Sara. Bea stood back, a broad smile crossing her face, teary eyes sparkling in the lights.

"Oh, no. Don't you do that. I don't normally wear this much make up and I have no idea what crying will do to it," Sara said reaching her arms out to give her grandmother a hug.

"You… Your painting," Jake swallowed hard. "It's all beautiful."

Sara looked at Jake for a moment and released a soft smile, "None of this would have happened without you. Thank you, Jake."

Standing awkwardly, unsure of whether to hug her, kiss her or run, Jake's decision was made for him as the entourage nudged him out of the way. Even as Sara cast a parting glance at Jake, she was quickly overwhelmed with praise.

Her parents led the group with Shawn on their heels. Sara traded smiles and hugs as they surrounded her, gushing about how proud they were. Seeing her receive a warm hug from Shawn, Jake retreated following the flow of the crowd perusing the gallery.

Bea watched from the edge of the group. Her eyes trailed him as he weaved through the crowd. Pausing at the next exhibit, he glanced out of the corner of his eye before studying the piece in front of him. Leaving Jake to his thoughts, Bea slipped in with her family in support of Sara.

As the crowd slowly dwindled through the festive evening, conversations became easier and most of those who remained were local. Jake migrated to each of Sara's works. Debbie had been circulating through the crowd and paused, "What do you think?"

"I think it tells a story. Family and friends gathered, it's like you sense there is an energy in the air. Christmas is coming. And yet, there is a calmness to it as well. Peace and hope," Jake said.

Debbie laughed, "I meant the event. But, yes. The painting weaves in love and hope and peace. That is what drew me to Sara's work. It isn't just painting a picture. It is a snapshot of an emotion. I have to say, however, that I may need to hire you to write copy for my works as they go on display or in the catalog."

"The event is… amazing. Elegant joy, if I were to give it a phrase," Jake said.

"You are definitely hired," Debbie said. "Though I hear bigger things are in store for you. I'm happy for you."

"Yeah, about that…" Jake began but was cut off by a caterer requesting Debbie's attention.

"Excuse, me. Say goodbye before you leave town," Debbie said as she turned to follow the caterer.

"You and Sara see through the same lens," a voice from behind Jake said.

"Hmm?" Jake turned to see Bea standing by him.

"The way you described the painting. She didn't use the same words, but that is how she spoke of it, too," Bea said.

A figure with a crab Rangoon in one hand and a glass of wine in the other paused next to them. "Isn't it great? I mean, it so… Christmassy. People shopping, the snow, the decorations. An old-fashioned Wintergreen," Shawn said.

"Yep, it's pretty… great," Jake agreed.

Bea looked at both men. Shooting a glance toward her granddaughter, she swung her gaze back to the gentleman. Seeing the mayor with a small group meandering the gallery with him, Shawn spun to join them.

Seeing Sara had a moment of respite, Bea nodded in her direction. "Some battles are won by taking advantage of the first opportunistic moment," Bea said.

Taking the cue, Jake walked up to Sara. Taking a breath, he calmed his voice and said, "This has been a tremendous evening. You have really been able to speak to people through your art."

"Thank you, Jake. I will admit, it hasn't been as bad as I thought it would be. Though, I still cringe every time someone leans in to really study my paintings," Sara admitted.

"You have absolutely no reason to cringe. Your work is amazing. Emotional," Jake said.

"Emotional?" Sara looked surprised.

Jake nodded, "The settings are beautiful. The people… that is where your art really comes to life. They aren't just people walking or holding packages or singing in half-circle. They are sharing a smile, stealing a moment out of life to be together. They love one another."

"You get all that? From my paintings?" Sara asked.

Jake frowned, "Of course…"

"There she is. The woman of the hour!" Wintergreen's mayor bellowed as he walked up.

A small crowd enveloped around the mayor as he addressed Sara, Shawn and her parents included.

"What lovely depictions of our small town, especially taking such a snapshot of how it used to be," the mayor said.

Sara shrugged, "I kind of see it that way outside… right now."

"Yes, yes," the mayor nodded. "The snow, the decorations, lovely, really."

"She might need to get busy painting more. All of the works we had catalogued for tonight have been sold," Debbie said. "That doesn't happen for every artist. Sara has something special."

"And I hear that talent will be working for us starting next year, albeit in a different capacity," the mayor said. "We'll have to buy a painting for my office."

"We'll certainly do that, sir," Shawn said.

Sara's father and mother stepped forward. Her mother said, "We're really proud of you, honey. To take your hobby and make it work for you and to share it is a tremendous thing. Not everyone can do that."

"And rest assured, Mr. Mayor, she'll be top notch in her official role, guaranteed," her father said.

The conversation made Jake's heart sting. He knew Sara's parents meant well with their words, but he also knew it was not what Sara wanted to hear. Certainly not at that moment.

"We can shop talk after the new year," Shawn interjected. "For now, it is all about Sara and her art."

Jake nodded in appreciation of Shawn's statement.

"Right. We will save accounting for another day, I'm sorry. Bring a numbers person to a swanky event…" Sara's father said as his wife elbowed him. "I'm just saying, make a living that sets a solid foundation and then use that to dabble with your other interests. It is smart and I'm proud of you."

With encouragement from Sara's mother, her father let Sara have her moment.

Jake and Shawn remained in front of Sara. "Thank you. Both of you," she said.

"I have been in support of your art from the beginning," Shawn said.

"I know you have," Sara nodded. "And Jake, you encouraged me, getting me to agree to do this with Debbie. Thank you."

Shawn shot a look at Jake and then grabbed Sara's hand, "We have been through a lot over the years. To see where we have ended up. It's amazing. You, you are a gem in this town. All this time, Sara Bailey, you mean the world to me."

Sara looked startled. She didn't pull her hand away but with a slight frown stammered, "You… mean a lot to me, Shawn."

Jake nodded, turned and walked away.

"Sara, I…" Shawn attempted to continue.

Sara's eyes lifted over Shawn's and landed on Jake as he walked away.

"Shawn," Sara interjected. "Would you please give me a moment?"

Looking bewildered, Shawn spun as Sara dashed by, "Sure…"

Sara ran as fast as she could in her heels but by the time she reached the gallery entrance, Jake was gone.

"Ms. Bailey," a voice called her. "I am Stan Baskin, with the American Art magazine. I would love a photo with you and perhaps set up a feature for one of our upcoming issues."

Sara spun, "What? Oh, yes. Yes, of course."

Returning to the gallery, she cast one final glance over her shoulder.

Thirty Seven

Sara would focus and smile when the camera was ready. When the lens wasn't panned on her, her eyes were drawn to the door where Jake had left. She didn't think anyone had noticed since she would quickly engage in conversation.

Her grandmother noticed.

"Looking for someone?" Bea asked.

"No. This has been a wonderful, but long evening. I suppose I'm ready to relax and not be 'on' for a moment," Sara said.

"I see. You followed Jake when he left," Bea said.

Sara scrunched her eyes, "You don't miss anything, do you?"

"Not when it comes to my granddaughter," Bea said.

"It's… nothing. I just feel like there may be some things left unsaid. It doesn't matter anyway. He's leaving. I'm here in Wintergreen, working for my parents and enjoying riveting town hall budget meetings. I just want the best for him. I want him to know that. We are friends after all, Grandmother," Sara said.

"Mm, hmm," Bea nodded.

Sara raised a brow.

Bea smiled a thin, knowing smile.

Sara's parents joined them. Her father looked uncomfortable. "Honey, I'm sorry if I didn't express myself properly. I'm all numbers, a bit fumbly with words. I am very proud of you. Your artwork is amazing. We have counseled many creative people in our firm that, having that solid, traditional foundation gives them the ability to do the work that they enjoy."

"Your father's right, dear. We think it is exciting to launch both chapters of your life," her mother said.

"The mayor's team is excited to have you on board," Shawn added. "If you like, we can get together next week and I can get you spun up so that January second, you are ready to go."

"That's really kind of you, Shawn," Sara forced a smile.

Sara's father clapped Shawn on the shoulder, "How about you come over for dinner the day after Christmas?"

"That would be great," Shawn said. "It will be like old times. Right, Sara?"

"Hmm?" Sara was watching a couple admire one of her paintings. They waved Debbie over and quickly elicited nods from the gallery owner.

"Dinner. At your parent's house. Just like old times," Shawn repeated.

"Right. Old times…" Sara broke away from the group as Debbie approached.

Debbie wore a broad smile, "That's it. All four pieces have been sold. You sold out of your first showing. And I posted them on the high end for a debut artist."

"And with the ones in the café sold, you have had quite the start," Bea followed Sara. With a snap of her fingers, she said, "The painting from the café. Did the anonymous buyer pick it up? They said in their note that they wanted it available for the gallery event and they would pick it up at the event's closing."

"That's now," Debbie said, looking at her watch.

They scanned the room.

Sara sighed, "Shawn. I mean, it was Shawn, right?"

"He walked out with the mayor when we saw Debbie," Bea said.

"He can get it tomorrow, I suppose," Sara shrugged.

"Why don't you take it back to the café with you? I don't want it to get mixed up with the breakdown of the event," Debbie said. Her face fell slightly, "It does bring us to a bit of a problem. Your remarkable success has left the gallery without any of your work."

Sara chewed her lip. Her words came out soft, "I brought one more that day that I left in my car. It's sitting in the café storeroom. I wasn't sure I wanted to… share it."

Debbie cocked her head and proposed, "Would you mind me displaying it as a non-sale item? It needs to be of similar quality of your others, of course. I want to show your work at its best."

Sara nodded, "I think so. I'll run and get it."

"Okay. I'll get this extravaganza shut down," Debbie said. As Sara started to leave to retrieve the painting, Debbie sang, "You did wonderful tonight. Beyond my wildest dreams. You are a star, darling Sara."

The valets had turned over the last set of keys and the service staff was making quick work of cleaning up the gallery. Debbie wandered, running through notes on her clipboard as the controlled chaos of putting the event together reversed itself.

Sara's face was nervous as she carried the craft-paper wrapped parcel into the gallery. Finding Debbie at her desk scribbling out a check, Sara stopped in front of her.

Debbie's eyes went wide, and she clapped her hands excitedly, "Let's see it!"

The expectation only made Sara's anxiety worse, so she tore at the corner of the paper as though she were removing a band-aid. Revealing the painting, she held her breath as Debbie stood up and stepped forward to examine it.

Gently tilting the canvas toward the light, Debbie's eyes swept over the scene. Her mouth opened, letting out a little gasp, "Sara, this is incredible. It is your best painting yet. I can't believe it wasn't part of the show. Please, can I put this in the front window of the gallery? I have apparently sold the one I have in there now."

"I mean, if you think it is really good enough," Sara smirked.

"Sara, if you do wish to sell it… I will buy it. After I have had the opportunity to display it to the world, of course. It is lovely. It makes me feel like I can be pulled into it. Like living a Christmas movie," Debbie said.

"Uhm, can I think about it? The selling?" Sara asked.

"Of course. For now, it will be display only," Debbie said. "You are going to be very busy this year. We are going to need more paintings, Sara, my dear."

Sara was taken aback. She hadn't even thought of next steps. Suddenly, her mind was awash in possibilities. The word "busy" struck her. As she thought about their consequence, her heart sank. She would be busy, apparently beginning the day after Christmas with the accounting firm. She wasn't sure when she would have time to paint.

Debbie could see Sara lost in her head. Placing a soft hand on her forearm, Debbie said, "We can worry about that later. For now, enjoy the holiday. I am going to immediately put this in the front window. But before that…"

Reaching over her desk, Debbie ripped a check from its pad. "This is for you."

Sara accepted the check in her hand. Glancing at the numbers written on it, her eyes grew wide, "Uhm, this can't be right…"

Debbie smiled, "Oh, it is correct."

Sara shook herself, her eyes squinting as she absorbed the reality in her own mind. "Thank you," her words came out in a hoarse whisper.

"You are quite welcome. I look forward to many successful showings. Your work is truly heartfelt and it shows. Way more important than brush strokes and technique. You can have classic technique without the heart and you get an emotionless splash of paint. The passion from within, is what makes a painting great. That is what makes *your* paintings wonderful," Debbie said. "If you'll excuse me, I need to place the gallery's newest display in the window."

Sara nodded. She didn't know what she was supposed to do. She stood frozen in the gallery. The check was still in her hand. The service staff had nearly completed the cleanup and the last guest had left.

As Debbie walked by, she whispered into Sara's ear, "Go home. Enjoy the win. You had a fabulous evening."

Sara nodded, numbly walking toward the door. Putting the check in her pocket, she picked up Shawn's painting.

Reaching the wintry night air, brought Sara closer to consciousness. Main Street had become still. Snow, heavier than it had all week started to fall, coating everything in a blanket of white. The world always seemed to fall even more silent when covered in snow.

After the stress, excitement and attention, walking down the sidewalks enveloped in the still night brought Sara peace. All at once, the emotions of the evening, of the season, cascaded down on her. She was happy. She was excited. She was confused.

She was alone. She wasn't lonely, but she knew something was missing.

Thirty Eight

Leaving the gallery, Jake was happy for Sara. Seeing people fall in love with her art as he had, filled him with warmth. He hoped the evening erased any doubts that she carried as to her own abilities.

Safely in the shadows, Jake turned to look back toward the gallery. In the entrance, he could see Sara look out only to be pulled back. With a nod, Jake knew she was embarking on the journey of her life. He was happy to slip into the shadows and let her flourish without distraction.

Thinking he could slink off into the night, his plan was detoured.

"Jake?" a voice called.

"Hey, Jake. What an event, right?" another echoed.

Jake watched as Carol and Eric emerged along the tree lit path that led to the grand Christmas tree in the park.

"It was. I mean, it is. It's still going," Jake said.

Carol cocked her head, "I'm surprised you left."

Jake wrinkled his lips, "It is a moment for Sara and her closest circle."

Sensing his mood, Carol suggested, "Why don't you join us? We were just heading to the tavern for a nightcap, closing out the dwindling hourglass sands of date night."

"Date night?" Jake put his hands in his pockets and rocked back and forth. "I can't intrude on date night."

"Give us a chance to speak to another adult for a while? Trust me. It would be as much for us," Eric laughed. "Besides, I hear you have some big news to celebrate. I'd love to buy you a toast."

Carol's expression showed her heart fall at the notion. Kicking at the snow, she said, "Yeah, I would rather not think about that until after the new year."

Jake looked at Carol. Suddenly, his eyes grew, "You know, I *would* like to have that drink with you. But my treat, for crashing date night."

It seemed most of the town had turned out for the gallery event. While many migrated to the Tavern Restaurant, the dining room was nearly empty at the late hour. The hostess had been accommodating dessert and coffee service in the main room to free up space in the bar. Sitting at a candlelit table by the window, Jake watched as Eric pulled out Carol's chair for her. The chivalry made him smile.

"So, it's finally happened. The big move to corporate," Carol wasted no time sulking.

Jake shifted in his seat, "Yeah, about that. I was offered the role, but I… kind of quit."

Carol's eyes were round as saucers, "You what?"

"I turned the offer down, which didn't go terribly well, but I realized I don't want to do ads for Java Universe or any other giant company. I want to help small businesses get their brand out there. Help them compete against the big companies threatening to squeeze them out," Jake said.

Carol looked blankly across the table. Finally, she said, "I don't see Henry… or Frank… or even Jeff going for that."

"Neither do I," Jake said. "*That* is why I am going to open my own firm."

Carol and Eric looked at Jake.

Jake frowned, "It may start out of my garage, but I think I can build it into something. It may never be big like Banks Marketing, but in truth, I never want it to be."

Eric smiled, "Jake, that's a great idea. Is there a market for that? I mean, it would take more than the Coffee Corner and Jenn's Bakery to make a business."

"It will take some time to get up to speed, but yeah. There is a market for it. I have an in, as well. The businesses along Main Street are looking to start a business association specific to downtown. They asked me to run it. I'll start there. I had to turn it down because of my work at the firm, but, well, now I can," Jake said. Looking at Carol he said with a sheepish tone in his voice, "I'll need some help."

Carol glanced at Eric and said, "I'd rather be your assistant at a start-up than work for a new marketing executive at Banks Marekting."

Jake shook his head, "I don't need an assistant. I need a partner."

Carol's face fell, "Jake, I..."

"Carol, working with you is like, well, it's like having a conversation with my conscience. You allow me to blurt out big ideas but smooth them into shape where they are actually viable. Besides, you have amazing ideas of your own. You are way bigger than the assistant role at Banks Marketing," Jake said. "I have everything, well, most things worked. I have the capital needed to get us off the ground. You just need to bring yourself. Do what you do. Help keep me steered on track and not be afraid to tackle ideas yourself."

Carol blushed. The smile on her face told Jake what he needed to know.

"I think it's a terrific idea. Carol was really concerned about what the office would be like without you," Eric said.

"I was going to work on my resume after Christmas," Carol admitted. With a deep breath, she said, "I'm in. There's just one thing…"

Jake raised an eyebrow, "What's that?"

"I'm not working out of a garage," Carol scowled.

Jake laughed, "Deal. We will come up with alternate arrangements. I may already have a few ideas on that."

"Of course you do, Jake," Carol said. Her head cocked to the side. "If you aren't running off to the city, then…"

Jake's face fell. With a shake of his head, he said, "I think that ship has sailed. You were right. I waited too long to tell her how I feel. Sara's life is about to take off. She has everything. A great career ahead of her, a budding fanbase of art fans, her family and she has Shawn."

"Shawn?" Carol frowned.

"They were high school sweethearts. He's tight with her family. She is joining the family business. She has her life. It makes sense," Jake said.

"If love on paper made sense, you'd still be with Tracy," Carol snapped.

Eric nodded, "She's right. I've seen the way Sara looks at you and, frankly, how she looks at Shawn. She's into you, brother."

"Ah, there *was* a spark there, I think. But I messed it all up. I'll be happy if she still sees me as a friend," Jake said.

"Eric, close your ears," Carol said. Her husband feigned covering his ears with his hands and avoided eye contact as he panned his head around the room. "When a woman gets mad at little things, it isn't because they are actually angry about the *thing*. They are upset because they are disappointed- because their heart was hurt. I watch Sara and Shawn and I don't see him being able to hurt her heart. When I see you and Sara, I see a woman terrified to have her heart broken."

Nudging her husband, Carol let Eric know he could drop his hands.

"She's right, not that I could hear *anything* she just said," Eric said.

"Where did you two leave things?" Carol asked.

"The last time we had a chance to actually talk was last night by the Christmas tree in the park. I was ready to tell her everything. That I was staying in Wintergreen. That I… That I had feelings for her," Jake said.

"And?" Carol pressed.

"And before I could get *any* of that out, Shawn walked up. He congratulated me on my promotion and she walked off," Jake said.

Carol and Eric looked dumbfounded at Jake.

"And then you went after her, right?" Carol asked.

Jake shook his head, "I started to… I wanted to…"

"But then you pulled her aside today," Eric said.

Again, Jake shook his head. "This was her day. Her gallery event. I didn't want to take any of that away."

Carol looked at Jake for a long moment. Her eyes were cross, "Don't you think she would have enjoyed her day *even* more if her heart was whole? If she knew how you felt about her?"

"If she really carries those feelings," Jake shrugged.

"Everyone in town knows she carries those feelings, except for you, Jake!" Carol's words nearly came out as a scream.

Eric nodded, "It's true. Even Shawn. He watches how Sara interacts with you. It's probably no accident he pops up at just the right time."

Jake looked shocked.

"Maybe she is still wrapping up at the gallery," Carol suggested.

Nodding, Jake was awash in an avalanche of thoughts.

"Go! Go!" Carol swished him away. Pulling Eric close, Carol added with a grin, "Besides, you're cramping date night. Get out of here… partner."

Jake nodded and pushed away from the table. Pausing, he turned to put a few bills on the table, "I promised it would be my treat," he said.

Neither Carol nor Eric were amused by Jake's delay.

With a nod, he dashed off.

Carol squeezed her husband as Jake ran out of the restaurant.

Away from the tavern, the town was still. No one was on the sidewalks. The streets were empty though under a growing layer of snow.

Running, Jake passed Coffee Corner, passed the bakery, and the pharmacy.

Reaching the gallery, he pulled up short. The exterior lights were on in their full Christmas event augmented glory, but the interior lights were off, save for the displays. Jake tried the handle anyway with the expected result- no avail.

With a deep, disappointed breath, he looked into the gallery. His mind replayed images of Sara in her elegant dress. Her smile melted the crowd as much as her art did. His mind keyed on her eyes locking with his. From shared smiles to moments of disappointment. He did not want to disappoint her — ever again.

Sullenly, he slammed his hands into his pockets. He took a breath as his eyes swept the quiet Main Street. As he turned to head out, his eyes caught the display in the front window. It was different than the piece that had been there for the event.

Looking closer, his eyes fell on the signature at the bottom of the canvas. He didn't need to see it to know, but it confirmed it was Sara's. It was stunning. A snapshot of Main Street Wintergreen, decorated exactly as they had. At the end of Main Street, kiddy corner from the gallery, was the row of lighted trees leading to the colorful downtown Christmas tree. On the sidewalk, outside of the Coffee Corner, was a couple.

Jake's heart melted when he leaned in to look closely at the couple.

Thirty Nine

If Main Street had buzzed with Christmas spirit on days past, it was absolutely electric as Jake stepped foot on the sidewalk. The town was painted white in snow. Twinkling lights, splashes of evergreen boughs and red ribbons sprayed color throughout the lush winterscape.

Jake drew a deep breath. The crisp morning air filled his lungs like fuel for the day. With a bounce in his step, he was ready for whatever the day had for him.

Entering the coffee shop, he was instantly greeted with a chorus of "Merry Christmas!". A few congratulated him as he made his way toward the coffee bar.

Shawn held a brown leather attaché wrapped in a red bow. Jake's heart flipped as he stood in line, unable to ignore the interaction.

"I wanted to get you something as you start your new journey," Shawn said to Sara.

"Shawn, you didn't have to do that," Sara said.

With a shrug, Shawn said, "I wanted to. Besides, I'm excited to have you by my side… at the meetings, I mean. Trust me. That is your present to me."

"Yeah," Sara offered a half-hearted nod. "Looking forward to it, Shawn."

"I gotta run, but if you have time for lunch or dinner…" Shawn started as he moved toward the door.

"I'm running from here to my parents' for Christmas Eve. It sounds like I'll see you the day after Christmas," Sara said.

"Right, I'll see you then," Shawn said. Hand on the door, he called back, "Merry Christmas!"

"Merry Christmas, Shawn," Sara said.

As Shawn pushed the door open, Sara called, "Shawn, wait!"

Shawn turned, a hopeful expression sprawled across his face.

Sara ran from around the coffee bar and dashed through the café, "You forgot this. The note said you would pick it up the night of the gallery event."

Shawn looked at the painting in Sara's hands.

"It was the first painting I ever sold. It was a sweet gesture," Sara said.

Shawn's eyes fell before glancing up, "I, uh, that's not mine. I didn't buy the painting, Sara."

"I believe that's my painting you're holding," Jake said, stepping out of line.

Sara wheeled, the painting spinning with her, "Yours?"

Jake nodded, "It's mine. And it's not the only painting of yours that I'm interested in."

Sara cocked her head as she studied Jake. Her eyes danced with curiosity of what he meant.

"The painting at the gallery… the one in the window," Jake took another slow step forward.

Sara nodded with her eyes locked on Jake's, "Uh, huh."

Shawn shuffled awkwardly as he watched the Jake and Sara connect.

"I'm… I'm gonna go…" Shawn said, suddenly feeling very left out of the conversation. Without another word, he slipped out of the café.

Sara couldn't hold back a wry smile escaping her lips, "You saw that one, huh?"

"I did. It's beautiful in more ways than I can put into words," Jake said.

"You think so?"

"I do," Jake nodded.

"I guess this is yours," Sara handed him the painting. She looked up at him, "Why did you buy it?"

"Because it's beautiful. It fills me with joy and Christmas spirit," Jake said. "And I wanted to give you a jump start. Encourage you to put yourself out there. Chase a star that seemed uncatchable."

"Why didn't you tell me?"

Jake took a deep breath, "I didn't want you to think it was a pity purchase. I wanted it to be someone who simply admired your work."

"Oh, we all assumed it was an admirer, all right!" Bea called back from behind the coffee bar.

Jake and Sara were suddenly very aware that they were in the middle of a busy coffee shop with an audience keen to every word. Glancing around, their cheeks blushed.

"Merry Christmas, Jake," Bea said.

"Merry Christmas, Bea," Jake returned.

Sara swung toward her grandmother.

"Why don't you put that… Jake's… painting away before you ruin it?" Bea suggested.

"Right," Sara nodded. She looked at Jake, "I'll be right back."

Rushing to put the painting in the storeroom, Sara disappeared into the back.

Bea beckoned Jake forward. Looking through frowning eyes, Bea said, "She was like a lost puppy last night after you left. Couldn't keep her eyes off the door."

"I didn't want to be in the way of her moment, with her family," Jake said.

"You were a part of her moment, Jake," Bea said. "I know, you're moving away, but that doesn't mean feelings can't follow."

"I…" Jake started.

From across the room, Sara could see her grandmother in full meddling mode, "Grandma…"

Closing the distance, she stood between Bea and Jake, "What are you giving Jake an earful about?"

Bea bristled and shifted, her eyes in a scowl, "I was wishing him a Merry Christmas and good luck on his promotion."

"Yours was not the face of a congratulatory discussion," Sara snapped. Her eyes moved from Bea to Jake.

Jake looked at Sara. Looking at Bea, he gave her a soft smile before returning to Sara. "Can we… go for a walk?"

Sara turned to her grandmother.

"Go, I've got the shop covered. Besides, it's Christmas Eve. Cups are filled with cheer even if they come out of the coffee bar a little slower," Bea said.

With a glance toward Jake, Sara ran to get her coat.

Jake looked at Bea who slipped back behind the espresso machine, ready to greet the next customer.

"Whatever those feelings are, I intend to address them in Wintergreen," Jake assured Bea.

Seeing the woman's face light up filled his heart. Having her granddaughter run up beside him with her winter coat on made it swell.

Forty

Jake and Sara walked slowly, side by side, as they had so many times over the past few weeks.

"Last night, wow, you were… amazing," Jake said.

"It was horrifying and wonderful. A lot of fun," Sara admitted. "I wish you hadn't left."

Jake shrugged, "You had your family. I didn't want to get in the way of that."

Sara cringed, "You can't get in the way, Jake. Not after all that you have done. For Grandma, for me."

"I'm sorry if I've been a bit muddled through all of this," Jake said.

"Muddled," Sara looked up, almost amused by the word.

Jake's head bounced from side to side as he took a deep breath, "This Christmas season has had so much going on. Wonderful things, exciting things, and things that didn't happen. Things that couldn't happen."

Sara stopped and chuckled, "I think I am beginning to understand what 'muddled' meant."

Sinking his shoulders, Jake shook his head, "I guess I have had a hard time being clear. I suppose that is what happens when the path you're on collides with the one you realize you want to be on."

Scrunching her eyes, Sara motioned her hands like a wheel, "Keeping going. I sense you are getting closer, but I don't have a clue what you are saying."

Jake looked past the bakery and the pharmacy. Waving at people as they passed, Jake led Sara to the park. Finding a spot under the limbs and among the lights, he turned, "I turned the promotion down. I'm not moving to the city."

Sara looked surprised, "How? I thought you had been wanting that for a while."

"I thought I did. Until I started helping your grandmother… and the other businesses. Helping the small, independent shops made me feel excited. Fulfilled. I enjoyed my work at the firm, but it never gave me that," Jake said. "I want to help business owners like Bea chase after and capture their dreams. I know it's tough, but I think I can help them."

"You *have* helped them. Just look at what happened on Main Street. Look at this park," Sara said, twirling with her arms wide as her eyes swept their transformation.

"And then there's you," Jake said, swallowing hard.

"Jake," Sara protested, though her words did not match her eyes. "Tracy…"

"Tracy and I, we broke up a couple of weeks ago. I've been trying to tell you. I mean, I suppose it took *her* all that time to grasp it herself. And her keeping it from her dad and making me play along. I suppose it was all a bit…"

"Muddled?" Sara offered.

Jake laughed, "Yeah. Muddled. And I'm sorry."

"So, this whole time…" Sara began.

"This whole time, I was no longer in a relationship," Jake said.

"The wine glasses?" Sara asked.

Jake kicked at the ground, "She came by. She asked for us to have another chance. But I said no."

"I see," Sara said. Looking at Jake, Sara gave a stern glance, "You can be rather soft and unclear, *especially* in matters of the heart. With your clients, with the town, you paint these amazing thirty-second stories or images on a flyer that are so clear, and have so much depth of emotion. But when it involves you and the real world around you, you're a little hard to read."

Jake nodded, "I needed to be more direct with her. More definitive. I needed to be more direct… with you."

"What happened between you two? I thought you were this power couple?" Sara asked.

"We were, on paper. But, she just… She isn't you," Jake said, squaring in front of her.

"Isn't her father your boss?"

"Well, he would have been if I accepted the promotion. Let's just say, my time working at the firm has come to an end," Jake said. "I tried to tell you all of this, but I just never found the right moment. I tried to tell you how I felt. I didn't want to spoil the fun. I didn't want to spoil the mood. Get in the way of your big night. I didn't want to interfere with you and Shawn."

"Jake, you never have to hide what's really going on from me. I need you to be clear with me. Understand?" Sara said. Her tone was firm.

Jake nodded. Looking into her eyes, he said, "I am one hundred percent falling for you, Sara Bailey. Check that, I am one hundred percent in love with you."

Sara's eyes widened, "Now *that* was clear."

Pressing up, Sara brought her lips close to his.

"What about you and…Shawn?"

"Shawn and I could never work," Sara grinned. In a breathy whisper, she said, "He just…isn't you."

The moment the words escaped her lips, Sara pressed into Jake. Arms draped around his neck, she held their lips together. His arms wrapped around her waist, pulling her in tight.

The world spun around them in a blur of white snow, twinkling lights and green boughs. For a moment, they were the only people in Wintergreen and they didn't mind.

As their senses returned, they separated.

Sara kept her arms around Jake's neck and looked up into his eyes, "I love you, too, Jake Myers."

Walking back, their fingers interlaced, they walked as though they were floating. Passing by the gallery, Jake paused. With a look toward the painting in the window, Jake looked at the couple. Standing in front of the coffee shop, a young woman pressed up on her toes while embraced in a kiss with her Christmas love. The man held her tight, his scarf blowing gently in the breeze.

Jake absently pulled on his scarf, a dead match for the one in the painting.

"That couple…"

Sara just grinned and shrugged, pulling Jake back into stride on their walk.

"So, what are you going to do, now that you are unemployed?" Sara asked.

"I'm going to kick off the downtown business alliance like Debbie and your grandmother asked. Along with it, I'm going to start my own marketing firm, dedicated to helping small businesses, like the Coffee Corner. I even have a partner," Jake said.

"You do?" Sara cocked her head at Jake.

With a nod, he said, "Carol. She and Eric ran into me after I left the gallery. In fact, I think it was the run-in that pushed me forward."

"Well, I'm glad something good came from you running out on me," Sara teased.

"I didn't run out on you," Jake said as they stood out in front of the coffee shop.

"I don't *want* space," Sara said. Pressing up on her toes, she pressed her lips into his.

With a glance in the coffee shop window, Jake caught their reflection.

"You know, I think I have seen this exact image somewhere…" he said.

Sara smiled wide, "I saw it first. Right here."

Pointing to her heart, Sara grinned. "That picture has been in there longer than you know, Jake."

Forty One

Christmas Eve on Main Street was a different feeling entirely. The bustle and excitement of leading up to Christmas had largely given way to a sense of peace. Shoppers and shopkeepers transformed into friends and neighbors. Instead of rushing from place to place, the visitors were there to visit.

For Jake, walking downtown was like a Christmas event where the whole family was invited. There were more hugs and welcome conversations than there were cash registers, but nobody minded.

Walking into the coffee shop, Jake was quickly greeted by a crowd. Chairs were pulled out and largely facing inward, like a giant circle, instead of accommodating individual tables. Some people casually leaned against counters and poles as they sipped their beverages.

Saying hello and liberal offerings of season's greetings, he made his way into the café. With a chuckle, he found Bea, who gave him a big hug.

"This is more like a Christmas party than a coffee shop," Jake said.

"It is. I hope it is like this every Christmas Eve from now on," Bea nodded.

Seeing Sara wheel around the coffee bar, they shared precocious smiles with their eyes locked in knowing glances. Arms wide, Sara collapsed around him for a long hug. As their chests came together, their hearts pounded wildly. The longer they hugged, the more in rhythm their beats became.

"Merry Christmas," Jake said softly into Sara's ear.

"Merry Christmas *Eve*, good sir," Sara leaned away from their hug. "Grandma had a wildly, wonderful idea. She would like to invite your family to visit mine on Christmas day."

Jake pulled back and studied Sara for a moment, "That would be great. My parents have missed large family Christmases since my grandparents passed. I think they would love that."

Spinning, the pair, still linked with one arm around the other were suddenly acutely aware that they had once more become lost in each other while in the center of the coffee shop. All eyes landed on them as they finished their exchange.

Bea's smile declared how over the moon she was.

Glancing around the room, Jake realized most of Main Street was represented. While Bea slipped a cup of Christmas coffee in his hand, he made his rounds, saying hello to the regulars and visiting Mr. Fuller and his son, Jonathan. Debbie and Jennifer giggled in the corner, leaning next to one another as they watched the smiles and rosy cheeks of Jake and Sara when they came together.

As he approached, they each sipped from their cups as though they hadn't been whispering about the new couple at all.

Jake offered a sheepish grin as their ruse was not well veiled, "Good morning, ladies."

"Good morning, Jake," they chorused.

Debbie looked over her cup, "I hear you have new news to share, Jake?"

"Yes, Jake. Any new news?" Jennifer urged.

Jake could feel his cheeks redden, knowing the ladies' inference.

"I have declined the promotion at Banks Marketing and decided to step away entirely. I want to stay here, in Wintergreen and build a business exclusive to helping independent, small businesses find success," Jake said.

Both ladies frowned, "No… other news, Jake?"

Volleying a scowl in return, Jake asked, "Other news?"

Debbie and Jennifer's eyes slipped past Jake and landed on Sara.

"She has been floating on air all day," Jennifer said.

"Absolutely glowing," Debbie added.

Jake couldn't resist a glance toward Sara as she flitted amongst the guests, ensuring their cups were full. Even in that simple task, Jake found her stunning. She did seem to float, almost dancing from customer to customer, her smile radiant. Forgetting for a split second that he was in the midst of conversation, he drew a deep breath.

"She's not the only one," Jennifer said.

"Hmm?" Jake turned his attention back.

Debbie smiled, "It's about time. We were wondering when that would happen."

"It was pretty obvious," Jennifer chimed in.

Jake wasn't sure if his cheeks could turn a darker shade of crimson.

"She is a special woman," Jake admitted softly.

"You both are," Debbie said, her tone firm as she looked directly into Jake's eyes.

"So… you're going to be sticking around," Jennifer's said, her tone almost a question.

Debbie looked expectantly at Jake.

"Yes," he smiled. "I will launch the Wintergreen Downtown Business Alliance. I'll bring with me a business partner who will have some brilliant ideas of her own. And of course, we'll have an art director for amazing images."

Jennifer wrinkled her nose, "I think she was pegged as the treasurer."

"Then that, would be a waste of her true talent," Jake said.

Debbie smiled, "I couldn't agree more."

"What are you all jawing about?" Sara flitted over, eyeing the group.

"We are talking about the happy news that Jake is staying in Wintergreen," Debbie said.

Sara's eyes twinkled, "That *is* happy news. You all seemed a bit more engrossed than that."

Debbie looked down, "We may have talked a little business, since we have him here."

Sara looked cross, "On Christmas Eve? Oh, no, this is a party! No shop talk."

The ladies laughed.

"Jake, dear, would you help me with something in the backroom? I have something on the high shelf I can't seem to get," Bea asked.

"I can get it Grandma," Sara offered.

"You stay on the floor. Make sure everyone has what they need," Bea said.

Jake shrugged and said to Debbie and Jennifer, "We'll catch up after the holiday."

As he left, Debbie and Jennifer swung their eyes to Sara.

"What?" Sara feigned through her glowing expression.

Jake followed Bea into the storeroom.

Looking at the shelves, he asked, "What can I get for you?"

"I don't know. How about those lids up there?" Bea shrugged.

Jake cocked his head at Bea.

"I just wanted a moment with you. You have been a treasure. To me. To this shop. To this town. …To my granddaughter," Bea said, looking at Jake with as serious an expression as she had ever given him. "When I teased you about Sara, I don't even know why I did it. I think you remind me a bit of Sara's grandfather. He was kind, hardworking. He put the family before himself. He put the town before himself. And… he was a handsome man, I'll tell you that. Right up until the day he passed."

Bea's eyes drifted into a memory for a moment.

"A grandmother dreams about her grandbabies. We want to watch them be happy. We don't have the same practical concerns their parents have. No, we are blessed to watch them from a different level. The one that encourages astronauts over businessmen. Novelists over reporters…" Bea began.

"Artists over accountants?" Jake added.

Bea nodded, "That is one of the things I adore about you, Jake. You see with the same lens. Everyone around Sara was pushing her to stay on her path. You didn't. You encouraged her to let her heart take the lead."

"To her painting," Jake said.

"To you," Bea said.

Jake's heart skipped at the words.

"Profession or love, I want what is going to excite my granddaughter, not make her happy, not just content, but fulfilled and *joyful*. That young lady has been skipping around here today like I have never seen her, Jake," Bea said, her eyes looking at Jake.

Jake blushed, "She told you?"

"She didn't have to, but yes, she told me," Bea nodded.

Jake shifted uncomfortably.

Placing a hand on Jake's shoulder, she smiled, "I am happy for you two. Almost as over the moon as my granddaughter is."

Jake smiled back. Leaning in, he gave his friend a big hug.

"We are so thankful for everything you have done for us this season, Jake," Bea said.

"I'm the grateful one, Bea. You all called me home before I made the mistake of leaving," Jake said. Pulling back, he looked at Bea, "Falling in love with your granddaughter, isn't something I planned."

"The best loves happen organically," Bea said.

Jake laughed, "And with a little friendly push."

"I just planted the seed. You decided on your own to nurture it. Takes more than soil and rain."

The two studied each other for a moment before Bea pointed to the shelves, "Now, about those lids, I don't really need…"

Jake laughed, reaching up to retrieve the package of lids for Bea.

When Jake and Bea emerged from the backroom, Sara cast a wary glance in their direction. Her glance was only more suspicious when Bea emerged with a set of lids that she tried to find a place to stow.

Sara met Jake, "So, she just *had* to have those extra lids?"

"Christmas Eve is a big to-go day of the year," Jake said.

Sara scanned the room of patrons who were content to stay and sip out of the ceramic mugs.

"Maybe everywhere but here," Jake shrugged.

Glancing around and seeing Bea behind the bar, Sara grabbed her coat, "Come on, I want to tell you something."

Tugging Jake by his coat, Sara led him outside. Stepping to the corner of the building a step from Main Street, Sara curled her fingers around either side of the front of Jake's coat to hold him close. Looking up at him, she smiled.

"I wanted to personally thank you for saving Grandma's business," Sara said.

Jake's lips started to quiver as they assembled a response, but Sara cut him off in the best way possible. Pushing up on her toes, she met him with a kiss. Their mouths met with a passion neither of them knew they possessed and with the tenderness that made their moment gentle- thoughtful.

Even before their lips parted, Sara smiled, "I can get used to this."

With a playful swat to his chest, Sara separated enough that she could look up at Jake.

"You have inspired me, Jake," Sara began. "I am not going to work at my parent's accounting firm. I am not going to endure budget meetings at the town hall. For which, I am grateful on so many levels."

"What are you going to do?" Jake asked.

"I am going to paint. I'll help Grandma at the café to make ends meet. Debbie already has three other galleries wanting my work and that is in addition to the gentleman I met at the event," Sara said. "Debbie wants to showcase me at the gallery and on her online digital gallery."

"Sara, that's great!" Jake said.

With a nod, Sara smiled, "I think so, too. I'm nervous, but a very handsome man has encouraged me to follow my heart."

Sara reached up and gave Jake a kiss.

"So far, I like following my heart!"

Forty Two

Jake stood by his parents, his arms laden as his mother rang the doorbell.

In moments, the door was flung open by a half-dozen peering eyes singing out, "Merry Christmas!". In the front of the crowd were Bea and Sara.

Bea wore a gingerbread apron, and her hands were still clad in oven mitts.

Sara smiled as she reached out to hug Jake's parents and invite them in. She was a picture of Christmas joy to Jake. Her bright smile was painted on her delicately beautiful face. The light freckles on the bridge of her nose danced in the twinkling Christmas lights.

His heart fluttered like butterfly wings when she reached up to kiss him on the cheek before leading him to where he could set his armful of items down.

When his arms were finally free, she spun him. Wrapping him up in a hug, she grinned looking into his eyes, "Merry Christmas, Jake."

"Merry Christmas, Sara," Jake said.

Lost in the moment, they slowly moved in for a kiss. Their lips had barely touched when a pair of nieces and nephews cut in with a chorus of "Ewws!"

Sara put her hands on her hips and looked up at the ceiling, drawing their eyes up with hers.

Seeing the mistletoe strategically placed, the children relented, "All right…"

With a broad smile, Sara pressed her lips into Jake's.

Leaning back from the dinner table, Jake smiled to himself. The families merged surprisingly well. Swapping Christmas traditions and stories of Jake and Sara when they were younger and the snapshots of life when their lives had crossed over the years.

Everyone at the table shared the sentiment that they loved how the town of Wintergreen had come together over the holiday season and it was the strongest sense of community any of them could recall, including Bea.

When dinner was over, Jake and Sara offered to clear the table while Bea lorded over them.

As stacks grew on the counter and the sink was filled with hot water and soap bubbles, Jake and Sara rolled up their sleeves to dive in.

Jake leaned next to Bea, "Thank you for having us."

Bea shrugged, "You're like family… You *are* family, Jake. You are always welcome."

"Well, thank you just the same," Jake gave Bea a kiss on her cheek that turned it a deep shade of scarlet.

"We've got this, Grandma," Sara said, her voice in a chipper tune.

Bea raised a brow, staggering after the kiss on the cheek. Through pursed lips, she said, "All right. But don't be long. We have games and carols!"

"I love games and carols," Sara nodded. "But, don't hesitate to start without us."

Sara delivered a grin that turned Bea's raised eyebrow to a sharp look of mock disdain. With a smile, Bea left the kitchen.

"Your family is wonderful," Jake said as he dried a dish that Sara handed to him.

"They are," Sara nodded. "Especially when you can get them out of work mode. Holidays were always great because Grandma instituted a no shop talk rule. A rule people quickly learned they should follow at all costs."

"At the risk of violating that rule… how did your parents take the news?" Jake asked.

"You? They *love* you," Sara hip checked Jake playfully.

Jake smiled, "I meant you and your goals?"

Sara sighed, "Yeah, telling them I wasn't joining the family accounting business was a tough one. They weren't happy, at first. After a solid hour lecture about sound economic decision making and establishing a solid foundation before chasing fanciful notions, Grandma stepped in and told my dad to can it. She told him I had a right to find my own way and more importantly, be happy. Even if he wanted to argue, the look on Grandma's face was pretty clear that she wasn't having it. After my dad backed down, my mother didn't even try."

"I think it still took them a bit to get over the fact that I didn't want to follow in their steps and take over the family business. But, when I gave them their presents, I think they started to understand it a bit," Sara said.

She nodded toward the dining nook where her eyes landed on a pair of canvasses. Jake walked over, still drying a plate with a towel as he wandered.

Leaning against dining chairs was a painting of a family playing on a beach. As Jake looked closer, the family almost looked familiar.

"One of my favorite memories. We used to go to the beach every year. Other than holidays, one of the few times my parents stopped thinking in numbers and just played. We would have so much fun. That painting is from a memory etched so clearly. It's the first thing I think of when I'm asked about my childhood. Funny how of all the days in between, it's the moment that sticks," Sara said.

Jake swapped plates and studied the second painting. It was a shot of Main Street Wintergreen, but not as Jake had seen Sara depict it before. The general structures of the buildings were similar, but the era was more modern. Not recent, but not too far in the past.

A man and woman stood in front of one of the buildings, a young girl at their side. A man in a suit stood in front of them with a large pair of scissors.

"Mom and Dad's ribbon cutting when they opened up the accounting firm downtown. If you look, the Coffee Corner is there," Sara said.

Jake leaned in, "I remember that sign."

"Grandpa painted it for Grandma. She'd probably still have it up, even if it isn't the most modern or professional," Sara said.

"What happened to it?" Jake asked.

"Remember that storm? We would have been in Elementary School. It was so windy and we had so much rain the river ran over the banks?"

"I remember that. The town was a mess," Jake said.

"Somewhere in that mess, was Grandpa's sign," Sara said.

"And now, it's in the painting forever," Jake noted.

Sara nodded, "Yeah. I think that changed my parents' perspective. They realized they weren't just drawings in paint on a canvas. They were stories. They're memories we get to keep no matter how much things change."

"They're beautiful," Jake said, returning to retrieve another dish.

Sara's eyes welled up, "I only saw my dad cry one other time, at Grandpa's funeral. He cried when they opened their paintings."

"I can understand why," Jake said, his voice soft.

Sara's eyes widened, "Oh, and get this. They decided they aren't going to move the office to the new Commerce Center. They are staying downtown, where they started. They talked about a remodel and maybe even expanding with the empty office next door.

They said, 'Besides, that is where all the action is in Wintergreen, now'!"

Jake laughed, "That is great news."

"I don't think they even thought through it that much. They were just following the trend of the other businesses," Sara said. "It was only in that moment, that they considered they would be moving away from Grandma's café and all of the relationships they had made downtown over the years."

Handing Jake the last plate, Sara sighed. "Everything was in motion and I feel like we were all just being carried along with it. I mean, I went to school for four years for something I didn't even really want to do."

Jake nodded, "I worked day and night for a boss and a company that I did not share a vision with. I get it."

Sara looked at Jake, "I think understanding the story. What is behind what we are doing? Where we are heading? Is it the story we want? You look at the story. You looked at Grandma's story. The town's story. They were just being carried along. *I* was just being carried along."

"I'm excited for your *real* story. The Sara Bailey story," Jake said.

Sara squinted, "I can tell you one chapter that I am very excited about."

"Oh?" Jake asked.

With a soapy finger, Sara booped Jake on the nose, "The one where I fell in love with you one Christmas."

"I hope there are many of those chapters in your story," Jake said.

Sara looked up at Jake with a hopeful smile, "Me too."

Drying her hands, Sara glanced out the kitchen window. Yanking Jake by the collar, she grinned, "It's snowing. Come on, let's go outside!"

Leading Jake outside, Sara pulled him close. Huddling, they looked up at the sky. Snowflakes softly drifted down toward them.

A flake landed on Sara's nose. Jake's fingers lighted on her chin. With his thumb, he gently wiped it away. Sara let out a light gasp in response. Their eyes locked and their lips quivered. They leaned in together, their lips meeting in a sweet, deep kiss.

They stayed in that moment, enjoying the still of the world on that snowy Christmas night. Allowing it to spin around them while they were content to just be, together.

A chill from Sara woke Jake from his blissful stupor, "We should get you inside. You're cold."

"Not yet," Sara smiled. Dashing to the couch on the back porch, she presented a package wrapped in craft paper. "Your present."

Jake looked suspicious, "I think you had this moment all planned."

"I had the moment all… hoped," Sara squinted. "Come on, open it!"

Jake smiled and walked over. Taking a big sigh, he looked at Sara. She and the joy on her face was all the present that he needed. Relenting, he took a corner of the paper and pulled. As he slowly began to reveal a scene painted on canvas, his heart jumped. Suddenly, the rest of the paper was whisked away left to fall onto the floor of the porch.

Holding the painting to capture the light, he shook his head, "The painting from the gallery."

Sara looked up at Jake with a hopeful nod.

"It's stunning. I thought…" he started.

"Debbie wanted it, but I knew it had to be with its rightful owner. He is, after all, one of the subjects in it," Sara said.

Jake flashed a smile and pulled her tight. "I love it. Almost as much as I love the *other* subject in it. That *is* you… right?"

Sara scowled at Jake and smacked him on the chest.

He looked closer, "I see. I would recognize the other end of that kiss anywhere."

"Like this?" Sara asked, drawing him in for a kiss.

Jake nodded, "That's the one. Exactly like that."

Digging into his pocket, he fished out a small package. "It's not as magical as the gift you gave me, but I have something for you."

Sara took the package in both of her hands and brought it to eye level. Tearing through the wrapping, she freed a tiny box. Lifting the lid, she revealed gems that sparkled in the Christmas lights.

Pulling one from the box, she held it up to her ear and smiled, "The earrings the movie star wore!"

"You *are* a star, Sara Bailey," While Jake meant the words with every fiber of his being, hearing them out loud, he cringed. With an apologetic laugh, he said, "I'm sorry. That was pretty corny."

"No," Sara breathed. Pushing up on her tiptoes, she said, "Not corny at all."

Finishing her sentence with a kiss firmly pressed against Jake's lips, she wrapped her arms around his neck and she pulled him.

"I love you, Jake Myers," Sara's voice was barely more than a whisper.

"I love you, Sara Bailey. I am so glad you came back to town this Christmas," Jake said.

"I am so glad you decided to stay," Sara said.

Jake laughed and held Sara tight, "There is no place I would rather be than right here, right now, with you."

"You can tell me that over and over, Christmas after Christmas," Sara whispered.

"I said we should follow our hearts," Jake said.

"And look where it led us. Smart little hearts," Sara said. With a deep kiss, she gripped him with all her might.

"Merry Christmas, Sara."

"Merry Christmas, Jake."

About the Author

Seth Sjostrom is a serial entrepreneur, adventurer and author. His novels include the thrillers *Blood in the Snow, Blood in the Water, Blood in the Sand, Penance, Penance: Unredeemable, Penance: Absolution, Patriot X, Patriot X: Insurrection, Dark Chase* and *Dark Chase: Dead Run* as well as the romances *Back to Carolina, Finding Christmas, The Tree Farm, Letters from Santa, The Nativity* and *The Toy Store*. He recently released the first of his Beach House Mysteries series *Trouble on Treasure Island*. Seth partners with Hire Heroes USA with proceeds and volunteer hours dedicated with sales of his Patriot X series. Sales of *The Christmas Café* help to support Jen Lilley and Ale Boggiano's "Christmas is Not Cancelled" charity fundraising for foster children. Seth also shares a portion of author proceeds of his Penance series with the Mel Greene Institute to Stop Human Trafficking.

More Books by Seth

Christmas Titles
Finding Christmas
The Tree Farm
The Nativity
The Toy Store

Beach House Mysteries
Trouble on Treasure Island
A Caper on Carolina Beach (2024)
Peril on Palm Beach (2025)

Children's Books
Letters from Santa
The Heart of a Reindeer
The Hollow
A Puppy Whisperer Christmas (2024)

Other Titles
Back to Carolina
Penance
Penance: Unredeemable
Penance: Absolution
Dark Chase
Dark Chase: Dead Run
Patriot X
Patriot X: Insurrection
Blood in the Snow
Blood in the Water
Blood in the Sand